A BLANCO COUNTY MYSTERY

To Kirby –
All my best –

Ben

For my good friend Jim Lindeman,
with best wishes on his retirement.

HOG HEAVEN

BEN REHDER

ACKNOWLEDGMENTS

I am very grateful to all of the people who helped with this novel. Their impact has been enormous. Special thanks to Jay Juba for answering dozens of questions. Much appreciation to Tommy Blackwell, Jim Lindeman, Becky Rehder, Helen Haught Fanick, Mary Summerall, Stacia Hernstrom, Marsha Moyer, Greg Rosen, John Grace, Martin Grantham, Leo Bricker, and Tony Turpin. All errors are my own, although I usually blame them on Red O'Brien.

CHAPTER 1

On a muggy, moonless night in July, just before ten o'clock in the evening, one of the best running backs ever produced by the Texas high school football system plowed his recently acquired Kawasaki Ninja into the side of a four-hundred-pound feral hog. Sammy Beech was taken by surprise. The Ecstasy he'd swallowed several hours earlier, chased with vodka and Red Bull, surely couldn't have helped. Besides, Sammy Beech had been more worried about the danger *behind* him, emphasized by the occasional crack of a gunshot, rather than any potential danger in front of him.

It all happened so quickly.

One moment, Beech was zooming around a curve on a winding county road at just under eighty miles per hour. The next, a massive, dark, hairy, tusked behemoth loomed mere yards in front of the motorcycle, as suddenly and unexpectedly as a cop from behind a billboard.

Beech had no time to hit the brakes. He did have time, albeit less than a fifth of a second, as he hurtled through the air headfirst, to wish that he were wearing a helmet. And to wonder whether he would ever carry a football again.

Turned out the answer was no.

His obituary described him as a "fine young man" who had "overcome some hurdles" to "become one of the nation's brightest college football prospects." Understandably, it did not mention the unflattering toxicology report.

And because Sammy's father was even better known, the

hastily written headline in the *Blanco County Record* read
SON OF BEECH KILLED IN HOG MISHAP.

There was no obituary for the pig.

What Game Warden John Marlin wanted to know was,
how could anyone mistake a mockingbird for a white-
winged dove? Yet here he was, standing on the edge of a
sunflower field, speaking to a hunter who had done
precisely that.

It had been a busy dove season so far. Abundant rain
throughout the summer meant a healthy bird population.
That, in turn, brought the hunters out in droves. Some of the
more popular leases had sounded like a war zone for the
past three weeks, shotguns booming from dawn till dusk,
with only a slight let-up at mid-day. Not all of that birdshot
hit the right target.

This particular hunter—a crisply dressed software
engineer in his thirties—had pulled the dead mockingbird
from his game bag and laid it out on the tailgate of his King
Ranch edition Ford F-150. Marlin would bet that the man
couldn't find the King Ranch on a map.

"You ever hunted dove before?" Marlin asked, checking
the man's license. It had been purchased the previous day in
Austin.

"First time."

Surprise, surprise.

"This is the only bird you've gotten?"

The hunter grinned. "Only one I've been able to hit."

"What kind of gun you using?"

"Remington twelve gauge."

"Be honest. Did you practice with it at all before coming
out today?"

The hunter looked nervous. Marlin sometimes forgot that his height—six foot four—could be intimidating. Other times, of course, he used that to his advantage.

"Uh…" the hunter said.

"That's what I thought. You lease this place for the weekend?"

"No, for the year. I'll be hunting deer out here in a couple of months."

Great.

"Let me show you something." Marlin waited—it didn't take long—until a dove flew past. "See that there? Notice how it doesn't fly like a mockingbird at all?"

"Well, in my defense, the mockingbird does have some white on its wings. Besides, it wasn't flying."

"What was it doing?"

The hunter pointed. "Sitting in that cedar tree."

Marlin had to bite his lip to prevent himself from laughing in disgust. Shooting a bird on a limb was one of the most unsportsmanlike things you could do in the field. Besides, it wasn't a cedar tree, it was an oak. The difference was, oh, night and day.

Marlin felt the cell phone vibrate in his pocket and it gave him a start. He still hadn't gotten used to it. He'd resisted owning a cell phone for the longest time, but once he'd broken down and made the leap, he had to admit that it was a handy and practical tool. But he ignored the alert for now.

"You understand that the mockingbird is the state bird and it's a protected species?"

"You gonna write me a ticket?"

"What do *you* think?"

Red O'Brien had just exited the Johnson City Quik-Pak with a case of Keystone Light and a king-sized package of jalapeño-flavored Corn Nuts when he saw something that caught his eye—a small poster tacked to the bulletin board just outside the store. The headline at the top?

REWARD! $50,000

Beneath that, a photo of a pig.

Whoa, hold on. That looks interesting.

Before he read further, Red had to wonder: What kind of idiot would pay fifty grand to find a lost pig? That had to be one hell of a swine, probably trained to perform some sort of special trick or marketable skill. Maybe it was like that swimming pig they'd had at Aquarena Springs way back when. Or it could be an actor-pig, like the one that had herded sheep in that movie.

But none of that really mattered, did it? The important thing was that somebody's pig was missing and they were offering a huge-ass reward to anyone who brought it back. Then Red studied the rest of the poster and saw that the situation wasn't quite what he thought. Still good—very good—but different. The text said:

My fellow citizens

Central Texas is being overrun by feral hogs. The population is reaching catastrophic levels. Herds of pigs damage the environment, destroy crops, harm native wildlife, and worst of all, create a deadly traffic hazard. The state isn't doing enough to address this issue, so I'm doing it myself. Recently, a wild pig was released here in the county with a fifteen-digit number tattooed inside one ear. The person to bring that pig to me—dead, not alive—will be presented with a certified cashier's check for $50,000, no questions asked. There is no time limit on this offer. The pig in the photo is not the actual pig in question. The tattooed pig might be black, white, brown, or any combination thereof. It might be large or it might be small. Happy hunting. Please obey all applicable laws.

Grady Beech
Double Eagle Ranch
Blanco County, Texas

Red could feel his heart rate picking up. Fifty thousand damn dollars. For a wild pig!

He read the poster again. Then a third time, just to make absolutely sure he understood correctly. Then he pulled the poster off the board, folded it up, and stuck it in his pocket. Why leave it up and let even more people know about this amazing opportunity? He looked around to make sure nobody was watching him. As was usual in his day-to-day existence, nobody was paying any attention to him whatsoever.

The call had come from Phil Colby, Marlin's closest friend since childhood. Marlin dialed him back from his truck.

"You never answer the damn phone," Colby said. "I'm starting to think you're taking a nap or something."

"Every chance I get."

"You got a minute or are you conducting extremely

important state bidness?"

"What's up?"

"You heard this crazy stuff that Grady Beech is up to?"

Beech was a well-off real estate developer, originally from Wichita Falls, who had bought a two-thousand-acre ranch in Blanco County in the mid-nineties. At first it was simply a place for hunting excursions that generally devolved into wild parties, but Beech had eventually retired and moved in full-time with a lovely new bride named Leigh Anne. Much younger. Some would have called her a trophy wife if she'd been flashier, with lots of makeup and various enhanced body parts, but Leigh Anne's was a wholesome girl-next-door type of beauty, and there was some substance to her. Just four years earlier, she had earned an MBA from a small private college in San Antonio. She was smart and friendly, but she also had a tendency to overdo that whole southern sorority girl persona, like she was always in the running for a Miss Congeniality Award, which could be annoying. Plus, there was the age gap, which sometimes made Marlin wonder what she and Grady talked about around the dinner table.

Not long after earning her master's degree, Leigh Anne announced that she wanted to open a vineyard—apparently a pet project to put her education to use. And she believed her idea had a lot of potential. So Beech had dedicated about a hundred acres, and hundreds of thousands of dollars, to getting the project off the ground. In the years since, the Double Eagle Vineyards, like a handful of other vineyards in central Texas, had become a modest success.

Marlin told Colby he hadn't heard anything about Grady Beech recently.

Colby said, "You're not gonna like this. Imagine how your average toothless banjo strummer would react to a wild pig with a fifty-thousand-dollar bounty on its head."

"What are you babbling about?"

"Just what I said. We all know how Grady Beech feels about pigs, especially with Sammy and everything."

Beech had always been very vocal about the need to control feral hogs, chiefly because of the damage they inflicted to grape crops. Even with an eight-foot-tall fence around the perimeter of the vineyard, the powerful pigs found ways through or under it. Beech allowed locals to hunt pigs at night with a spotlight on his ranch—including the vineyard, as needed—which was completely legal. In fact, since wild pigs were a non-game, non-indigenous species, you could hunt them around the clock, any time of year, with any type of weapon. In cases of depredation, you didn't even need a hunting license. Still, the pig population was booming, on the vineyard, in Blanco County, and across the state. As the saying goes, a sow can have a litter of eight piglets and ten will survive. For a guy like Beech, trying to run a vineyard, pigs were a nightmare. And Beech's disdain for hogs had grown even more intense after his son had died in a motorcycle collision with a huge boar two months earlier.

"What's this about a bounty?" Marlin asked.

"Okay, I'm not positive this is true, but I heard it from Trey, and you know he's not some old gossip. He said Grady had this idea about a way to get rid of all the pigs in the county. What Grady did was, he had his ranch foreman tranquilize a pig and tattoo a number on the inside of its ear. Then he turned it loose. That pig could be anywhere by now. The deal is whoever shoots that pig gets fifty thousand bucks. Beech's way of making sure a whole bunch of pigs get annihilated."

Marlin had to think for a second: *Does Phil have any reason to pull my leg?* He actually hoped the answer was "yes," because if what Colby was saying was true, Marlin's life was about to get a lot more complicated.

CHAPTER 2

The Big Buck Inn on the western outskirts of Fredericksburg, Texas, catered to hunters, as the name implied. It had previously been called the Fredericksburg Motel, but Vijay Sharma, the owner for three years now, had changed it immediately upon purchase, and had commissioned a new logo that featured a sweeping set of antlers. Vijay knew a thing or two about marketing to Americans, and "Fredericksburg Motel" had had very little going for it. Generic. Bland. Predictable. No personality.

But "Big Buck Inn" captured the essence of small-town Texas culture, such as it was. Everybody loved big bucks. Big bucks were frequently the topic of enthusiastic conversations, with unshaven truck-driving men earnestly discussing "points," "scrapes," "drop tines," "G2s," "the rut," and many other terms and phrases that Vijay did not fully understand, or care to. In the fall, the Fredericksburg newspaper often printed photos of the week's biggest buck—dead, of course, its tongue lolling, after a local hunter had assassinated the deer with a high-powered rifle from the safe and comfortable vantage point of an enclosed blind.

"Big Buck Inn" wasn't just a name, it was a brand, and its effectiveness was evident in the number of outdoorsmen who booked rooms there. Of course, the customer base wasn't made up solely of hunters. There were traveling salesmen, vacationers, retirees here for the winter, and so on.

And, though it was not all that common, Vijay was aware that his rooms were used occasionally for illicit purposes.

Romantic purposes, to be blunt. Trysts. Couples—one or both of them married, though not to one another—would rendezvous for an hour or two, or maybe for an afternoon, without staying the night. They typically slunk in and out of the room with sunglasses on, heads kept low. None were repeat customers.

Except for one.

A woman, surprisingly. Well, it was a couple, Vijay assumed, but he only saw the woman. She was the one who came into the office to book the room. She showed up once or twice a month, as she had earlier today. As usual, she had asked for a room on the far side of the building, away from the street, away from the eyes of passing motorists. She did not have to make this request; Vijay knew what she wanted. And not long after she booked the room, Vijay would see a truck pull into the parking lot, avoid the office, and drive straight past the pool to the back of the motel complex. Same truck every time.

Of course, the behavior of these two people was none of Vijay's business, and as a rule, he kept a cordial but distant relationship with his customers. But in this case, with this woman, he was tempted to speak, to ask questions. After all, she wore a large diamond ring and fine designer clothing. She drove an expensive imported car. She had no visible bruises or marks. Vijay wanted to say, "It appears your husband takes good care of you. Why are you here? Does he deserve this sort of dishonor?"

In fact, Vijay had struggled with the idea that perhaps it was his duty to inform the husband. Vijay knew that if his own wife was conducting herself in the manner of this woman, he would want to know. It *was* an option—telling the husband. The woman always paid cash, but Vijay insisted that all customers show a photo I.D. So he knew her name.

He had even gone so far as to do a Google search for her on the Internet. What he found had made it even more tempting to alert her husband.

"Betty Jean gets off at five," Billy Don Craddock said, handing Red a cold beer. Not one of Red's Keystones, of course. Red had left them out in the truck. Why drink his own beer when he could mooch Billy Don's? "Which means she'll be home at ten after," Billy Don added as he eased his three-hundred-pound physique into a recliner that must have had a steel-reinforced frame.

Billy Don was Red's longtime best friend, poaching partner, and former trailermate, so the men knew each other well. Almost like brothers. Red could read between the lines.

"So you want me outta here before she gets home?"

"Wouldn't hurt."

"And you're not even gonna be subtle about it. Not gonna pretend everything is cool?"

"Would you stop? I ain't got the patience anymore. Not my fault y'all don't get along."

"Hey, I get along with *her* just fine. It's the little problem of her thinking I'm a idiot."

Billy Don grinned. "Woman is a good judge of character."

"Ha, ha. Funny. Funny as the time she asked if I'd suffered oxygen deprivation as a child. Or when she asked if I had a bit part in *Deliverance*."

"You gotta admit, that's pretty clev—"

"It's insulting, is what it is. She could at least make an effort." Red wanted to add that it would be real easy for him to turn the tables and make fun of Betty Jean, especially in regards to her weight, but that would be walking on dangerous ground. Billy Don had a temper.

"Now you got fifty-five minutes," he said.

"Sheesh. Relax. I just want you to look at something." Red pulled the flyer from his pocket, unfolded it, and handed it to Billy Don. The big man could usually read to at least a middle-school level, if you didn't pressure him.

So Red waited patiently, figuring it wouldn't take long for Billy Don to get as excited as Red was about the four-legged gold mine roaming the hills.

Sure, Red would be the first to admit that he'd had his fair share of wacky schemes and get-rich-quick ideas over the years. And, yes, Billy Don had grown weary of hearing the ideas, much less taking part in them. Couldn't blame him, because none of the ideas had actually turned out so good, and some, to be honest, were disasters.

But this was different. Easier. It wasn't shooting fish in a barrel, but it *was* shooting pigs in a field. Or in a cedar break. Or off the side of the road.

Billy Don looked at Red, then looked at the flyer again. "Wait. This is for real?"

"Sure looks that way."

"Fifty thousand dollars for a pig?"

"Well, not just any pig. Gotta be the right pig. But I figure the odds are pretty good. I mean, how many pigs could there be in Blanco County?"

"There's something like two million in the entire state, so if you divide by—"

"No reason to get bogged down in the details. Regardless of how many there are, does it matter? I mean, come on. This is right up our alley. We're talking about big money for *shooting a dadgum pig.*"

"Which is something we do on a reg'lar basis anyway."

"Exactly!" Red said. "It's like when they give away prizes when you buy a bottle of sody pop. Heck, you're gonna drink it anyway, so you might as well check under the cap and see if you won anything. Same deal here. We already shoot pigs, so we might as well check the ears for a tattoo."

Billy Don didn't say anything.

Red said, "Well?"

Billy Don took a massive gulp of beer. "I don't know."

"What's there to know?"

"My time is tight right now."

Red let out a sigh. "Really? You're gonna use that lame excuse again?"

Billy Don said, "Planning a wedding ain't easy."

Red shook his head. He still couldn't get used to it. It was like some big practical joke that just wouldn't end. "I can tell you one thing. I sure never expected to hear *those* words come out of your mouth."

"Well, it's only fair."

A couple of months earlier, after a lot of soul-searching and a case of Keystone, Billy Don had proposed to Betty Jean—and she had shown extremely poor judgment by saying yes. And then, a few weeks later, Billy Don mentioned to Red that Betty Jean had asked if he'd mind making the wedding arrangements.

"You got to be kiddin' me," Red had said. "Plan a dadgum wedding? That's woman's work."

"Not if a man does it."

"What does that even mean?"

Billy Don shrugged. "I ain't got a problem with it, because she's working steady right now, whereas my work is a little more, uh…"

"Imaginary?" Red asked.

"Hit and miss," Billy Don said. "And you're one to talk. When's the last time you had a full day's work?"

Red didn't have a snappy comeback, because it was true. Red was a jack of all trades—he was skilled at masonry, construction, plumbing, electrical, brush clearing, general ranch work, and just about anything that didn't require a college diploma—but work had been slow lately, for both of them.

So he said, "You're actually gonna do it? Plan the wedding?"

"Yep."

"Even so, how much time could that take? You just schedule a preacher and order some little finger sandwiches and maybe ask someone to play a harp. Twenty or thirty minutes and you're done."

"What about a venue?"

"A what?"

"A place to actually have the wedding. Then you have to deal with the rings and the cakes and the license and the flowers and about a million other details."

"Like picking your best man," Red said. That was the one detail he figured was a foregone conclusion. Billy Don didn't have to make a decision, because the choice was obvious.

"Exactly," Billy Don said, and nothing more.

Red waited. Still nothing.

"Damn, Billy Don, I guess all this wedding stuff will hardly leave you any time to get your nails done, or to have brunch with your girlfriends."

"Go ahead. Tease me all you want."

"Oh, I will."

"Maybe someday you'll have a woman you love so much that you'd do the same thing."

"Do you even hear yourself? You are getting gayer by the minute. Why don't you show some balls and just tell her y'all are gonna elope to Vegas?"

Just for a moment, there was a glimmer in Billy Don's eyes, showing that he was tempted, and that he was actually considering it. But then he frowned and shook his head.

"Betty Jean wouldn't want to do it in Vegas. Too tacky."

Red had to laugh out loud. "Billy Don, the woman has eighteen different Christmas sweaters that require batteries. She eats up tacky by the truckload."

And then came the menacing glare—the unmistakable sign that Billy Don was on the verge of getting really angry. Red had edged right up to the line, but he hadn't quite crossed it. Best to let the topic drop, at least for the moment.

That was three weeks ago. And since then, not only had Billy Don failed to say anything to Red about being his best man, he still hadn't come to his senses and told Betty Jean to plan the wedding herself, like any self-respecting woman should. As far as Red was concerned, a groom had only one responsibility, and that was to show up at the wedding on time, nearly sober, without any cops looking for him or strippers in tow.

Besides, being practical, if Billy Don was tied up with wedding crap, what was Red supposed to do about the fifty-thousand-dollar pig? Hunt it by himself? That wouldn't be nearly as much fun, and besides, two hunters working together would have a greater chance of success. They'd have to split the money, sure, but that was better than no money at all. Red figured he had one last card he could play in an attempt to get Billy Don on board.

"Y'all figured out your honeymoon plans yet?" he asked, innocent as could be.

"Hell, no. Betty Jean wanted to go on a cruise, but everything's so damn 'spensive. We figure the wedding'll just about leave us broke." Billy Don was sounding downright glum.

"That's a damn shame, Billy Don. Sure is. Nobody wants to start married life like that. Creates all kinds of stress. On the other hand, now that I think about it… just imagine what kind of cruise you and Betty Jean could take with twenty-five-thousand dollars in cold, hard cash."

Billy Don guzzled the last half of his beer, then let out a deep belch.

Red said, "In fact, I imagine you could take a world-class cruise for no more'n about four or five grand. That'd leave twenty grand in your pocket. And I seem to remember Betty Jean saying something about wanting to remodel her kitchen. Twenty thousand would cover that easy, with money left over to buy yourself a new deer rifle or a year's supply of beef jerky. Think about it, Billy Don. You'd be her hero. Just for shooting one little pig. Seems like a pretty smart solution to me."

Billy Don didn't say anything for the longest time, which meant he was thinking about it, or that he'd gotten distracted by the beef jerky comment. Finally he said, "Let me talk to her tonight. See what I can do."

CHAPTER 3

John Marlin could vividly remember a time, several years earlier, when word had spread nationwide that a chupacabra was on the loose in Blanco County. Was that ridiculous or what? The chupacabra was supposed to be some sort of terrible reptile-like creature with razor-sharp claws, bulbous red eyes, and fangs. Some people said it looked like a monkey, while others said it had spikes or quills running down its back. It was supposed to hop or leap or maybe even fly. "Chupacabra," translated literally, meant "sucker of goats," because the creature allegedly preyed on goats like a vampire. All nonsense, of course, but that didn't stop hundreds of delusional chupacabra hunters from descending on Blanco County, hoping to trap or kill the beast and somehow make a fortune in the process.

Would this pig bounty scheme dreamed up by Grady Beech create an even bigger uproar? It was possible. If the rumor was even true. So Marlin was making a trip out to the vineyard to see for himself.

He drove his green state-issued truck over a cattle guard and onto the Double Eagle Ranch, past row after row of grapevine hanging from trellises, and up a long, gentle slope to the vineyard's visitors center and tasting pavilion. He knew that was what they called it, because a large sign out front said VISITORS CENTER & TASTING PAVILION. A different sign reading WINERY pointed the way to a larger, more utilitarian building in the distance. Marlin had never really pondered the difference between a winery and a vineyard, but he figured there must be a distinction. He assumed a vineyard was where they grew the grapes and the winery was where they turned the grapes into wine.

Marlin pulled in front of the tasting pavilion, which was a striking wood-and-glass structure with floor-to-ceiling windows that provided an impressive view down the slope to the vineyard, across McCall Creek, and to the rugged cedar-covered hills beyond. He parked next to a Chevy Avalanche, Grady's truck, the only vehicle in the lot. Not surprising on a weekday morning.

Marlin had been here a few times before—twice to discuss Grady's pig problem with him, and once purely on pleasure, with Nicole. She liked the occasional glass of wine, so they'd stopped by one afternoon the previous fall to do some sampling. Ended up taking a case of wine home. A Viognier. Pretty good stuff.

Marlin stepped through the front door and immediately saw Grady behind the serving counter, hanging wine glasses from an overhead rack.

"Hey, there, John Marlin!" Grady called out. He was always an affable and outgoing guy. Richer than hell, but the kind who'd fit right in around a campfire, drinking beer and telling hunting stories. Here he was, trying to keep up a cheery countenance, despite the fact that his son had died a mere two months ago.

"Hey, Grady," Marlin replied, weaving his way through the small tables where visitors would sit and try the vineyard's offerings. Or the winery's offerings. "You doing all right?"

Marlin reached the bar and the men shook hands.

Grady said, "The creek looks great, doesn't it? You know, when I bought this ranch, I had no idea it would be a damn good place to grow grapes. All the limestone-filtered water we need, and we got the eastern exposure, so the grapes can cool down from the heat. Got a dry breeze through the vineyard most of the time. Pretty nice set-up."

"You've really turned it into something."

"Hey, mostly Leigh Anne. She runs the place. I'm just the hired help. What brings you out? My guys doing too much late shooting?"

"Nothing like that," Marlin said.

"You ready for some more Viognier?"

"Nearly, but not quite yet."

"We're running a two-for-one special at the moment. Gotta make room for some new stuff."

"Actually I came out to verify a rumor. Or hopefully to dismiss one. I heard something about you placing a bounty on a wild pig." Grady was already starting to show a sheepish grin. "Please tell me I heard wrong."

"Wish I could, but…"

"Aw, Grady…"

"You don't think it's a brilliant idea? What we're talking about is mass annihilation of an invasive species. A pest. A highly destructive pest."

"Yeah, but—"

"A *dangerous* pest."

"No argument there."

"What is it up to now? The population of wild pigs in Texas? Two million?"

"Thereabouts."

"Shouldn't we be shooting every last one we see?"

"Lot of people think so."

"Well, I figured this would make a pretty good dent. Maybe some other landowners around the state will follow my lead and do the same thing. Hell, we can turn it into a contest, like a bass fishing tournament, but with pigs. We could have teams and sponsors and trophies with—"

"Grady."

Beech finally stopped talking.

Marlin said, "Look, don't get me wrong—I don't blame you at all for wanting to do something like this. But, Grady, come on. This is the wrong way to go about it. You make an offer like that, all kinds of crazies are going to show up. It's just asking for trouble."

"Am I breaking any laws?"

"That depends. Where did you release the pig?"

"On my own place, but outside the high fence. Not that the high fence stops them from going wherever they want."

"Okay, then technically, no, you aren't breaking any laws. But all the people hoping to collect fifty grand? They'll break some laws to do it. Besides, a lot of them are gonna figure out that you were required by law to release it on your own place, so it wouldn't surprise me if you end up dealing with a bunch of trespassers, or worse."

Grady had been slowly wiping down the top of the bar with a white towel. Now he stopped. Didn't say anything for a few moments. Then he let out a sigh. "Maybe I shouldn't act on ideas I have after drinking a full bottle of Syrah."

Marlin laughed. "One of the drawbacks of your profession, I guess."

"Yeah, probably so. But here's the problem: Even if I decided to put a stop to it, it's too late."

"Why's that?"

Grady reached under the bar and came out with a piece of paper showing the layout of an advertisement— something produced by a graphic artist. The ad featured a small photo of a feral pig. Above that, a headline: REWARD! $50,000.

Grady said, "That ad is running tomorrow in forty-three newspapers across Texas."

Just as Marlin started his truck, Leigh Anne Beech pulled up on his passenger side in her low-slung BMW with the top down. She gave him a quick little wave, then opened the driver's door and swung both of her long legs out of the car. Wearing shorts this afternoon, because of the warm weather.

Marlin needed to get back to the sheriff's office, but he didn't want to be rude, so he lowered his passenger-side window.

"Hey, Leigh Anne."

"Well, hey there, you. I was wondering how long it would take for you to show up."

Her hair was a little different than the last time he'd seen her. Sort of a strawberry blond, rather than just blond. And now she had bangs. She really was lovely. She'd look right at home on a parade float, waving at her adoring fans.

"You been doing all right?" Marlin asked.

"Went shopping this morning in San Antonio. I love it down there. I go a couple of times a week." Now she turned back toward her car and bent inside to retrieve a couple of Nordstrom bags from the passenger's seat. When she emerged again, she said, "So…you mad at Grady?"

"Well, I wouldn't put it that way, but I wish he'd talked to me first. Maybe I could've talked him out of it."

"Doubtful. I tried that myself. That man is on a mission. Death to the pigs!"

"You'll probably want to keep your front gate locked up tight after sundown. Starting tomorrow night."

"What for?"

"Poachers."

"Oh, God, I hadn't even thought of that. Think we'll have some around here?"

"Wouldn't surprise me. Listen, I didn't get much of a chance to talk to you at the funeral, but I wanted to say I'm really sorry about Sammy."

"You're sweet. I appreciate that."

"It was a real tragedy."

"I loved him like he was my own son. I miss him every day."

Marlin didn't mean to be cynical, but she didn't look very mournful with a shopping bag in each hand.

A few hours later, Marlin was kneading a raw egg and Worcestershire sauce into a pound of ground venison—preparing burgers for the grill—as he told Nicole about his visit with Grady Beech. She was leaning against the counter, dressed in yoga pants and a loose T-shirt, nursing a glass of the Viognier Grady had mentioned that afternoon. Geist, Marlin's white pit bull, was also lingering nearby, hoping for a dropped morsel or scrap.

"Sounds like he's still pretty angry," Nicole said.

"At who?"

"Just angry in general. Sorting through his grief. Maybe this contest will bring him some sense of closure."

That made Marlin feel a little cold-hearted. His first concern, when he'd heard about the pig bounty, was that it would bring a bunch of lawbreakers to the area. Nicole, on the other hand, immediately wondered whether the contest might help Grady get past the death of his son. Didn't surprise Marlin a bit that she responded that way.

They'd been married now for fourteen months, and Marlin had learned in that time that Nicole was perhaps the most compassionate person he'd ever known. She had worked for the Blanco County Sheriff's Office when he'd met her—a stunner with long auburn hair and curves that were hard to ignore, even though she tried to disguise them with a loose uniform. She was also an excellent deputy, and she seemed to enjoy the work. But when the victim services coordinator for Blanco County had retired, she had surprised her co-workers by applying for the position.

Since then, Nicole had positively thrived in that role. She'd fought for, and received, several federal grants to expand the victim services program, and the impact was undeniable. Victims of crime and tragedy in Blanco County now felt that they had a powerful, knowledgeable advocate who could help them cope with trauma and grief, navigate the judicial system, and provide many other types of emotional and legal support. Marlin was proud of her. She was a shining light in the life of just about everyone who came into contact with her.

Marlin told her about the brief conversation he'd had with Leigh Anne outside the tasting pavilion.

Nicole said, "I don't know how close Leigh Anne and Sammy were, but I guess it's natural that she wouldn't feel the impact as much as Grady does. You putting green peppers in those?"

"Just in mine."

"Thank you."

"You're aware that green peppers have powerful anti-aging properties?"

"Where'd you hear that?"

"Made it up."

"What I thought. Have you warned Bobby about this great pig-hunting extravaganza yet?" Bobby Garza was the sheriff of Blanco County.

"I left him a voicemail. Asked him to call me in the morning."

"Well, I think we should be optimistic. Maybe somebody

will shoot the right pig on the first day and it'll be over before it really gets started."

"That would be great. Otherwise, I might not be around much in the next few days."

She sipped her wine and gave him a wide grin. "Then you'd better eat two burgers. You're gonna need your strength tonight."

CHAPTER 4

Dexter Crabtree—54 years old and winner of the Bronko Nagurski Trophy 32 years earlier—had reached the point where he just didn't feel one hundred percent without at least two Adderall tablets tucked into his anus at all times. Gave him such an amazing boost. So much vitality. Like he was a kid again. Like he could still drive a running back into the ground and feel his ribs crack like dry sticks. Or knock a quarterback unconscious during a well-executed blitz.

Sure, there were other ways to take the powerful prescription stimulant. It could be swallowed whole, chewed, or ground up and snorted or injected. But Crabtree preferred the practice known as "stuffing"—sticking the pills into any orifice with a mucous membrane. You didn't get the hard-hitting rocket-blast effect you got with shooting or snorting, but those were the methods of junkies, which Crabtree most certainly was not. He had more self-control than that. Besides, stuffing provided a balanced and long-lasting buzz.

Crabtree had first tried Adderall a couple of years earlier, just to see what all the fuss was about. College kids were always talking about it online. Raving about it, really. So he'd gotten hold of some and—wow! He'd loved it. What a rush. Reminded him of some of the pills he and his friends used to pop, way back in his playing days. Okay, so Adderall was supposedly a little bit addictive, but so were a lot of things. Mexican food. Cuban cigars. The sweet young masseuse who visited his office once a week. Winning football games.

As far as Crabtree was concerned, there were only a few minor drawbacks to Adderall, with one of them being, obviously, that he had to stick the pills up his butt. Not exactly the most dignified method, but he'd gotten used to it. And it was well worth it for the energy it gave him.

At this moment, he was burning off some of that energy by drumming the fingers of his right hand on the steering wheel of his Mercedes CL600 coupe and waiting with all the patience he could muster, which wasn't much. Another minor drawback of Adderall.

"What time does his class get out?" Crabtree asked.

"Eleven fifteen, I think," said Ryan, Crabtree's son. There were times when Crabtree could hardly stand the sound of Ryan's voice. Meathead.

"You 'think'? You're supposed to *know*."

"Eleven fifteen."

"For sure?"

"Yeah, Dad, for sure."

Crabtree kept drumming, because it soothed him. Same old cadence—the fight song of the University of Middle Texas. You'd hear the same tune if Dexter honked his horn. And of course, the customized navy-blue paint on the exterior of the Mercedes, and the cream-colored interior, perfectly matched the official university colors.

To say that Crabtree was a bit of a UMT football fan was like saying Adolf Hitler was a bit intolerant, or that Luciano Pavarotti had a decent singing voice. But there was a good reason for Crabtree's nearly pathological loyalty. When other universities had been unwilling to take a chance on Crabtree because of his size, UMT had stepped up. They'd realized there was more to a player than his physical stature. What about heart? What about determination? What about the killer instinct, which Crabtree had in spades, both then and now?

Ultimately, UMT had gone out on a limb and offered Crabtree a full scholarship and a starting position, even as a freshman. The result? Dizzying new heights of success for the university, thanks to one of the most barbaric—and effective—defenses ever seen in college football.

Bottom line, UMT had made Crabtree what he was today: a former NFC defensive MVP with four division titles and two conference championships to his credit. A legend. A multimillionaire with an allegiance to his alma mater that was as much a part of him as his blond hair and green eyes. Unlike most alums, when Crabtree said, "I'd kill for UMT to win a national championship," friends and family members joked that he meant it literally.

Fortunately for Crabtree, cash usually got the job done. Lots of cash. A river of cash that flowed to potential recruits and their family members. Not just from Crabtree, but from a secretive consortium of like-minded alums—all of whom were willing to skirt what they saw as unreasonable laws restricting the free market for talented athletes. As a result, UMT had made tremendous additional strides over the years.

It wasn't just some piss-ant oversized regional college anymore. UMT was now a legitimate force in Division 1 ball, and many of the best players in the nation put UMT on the list of schools to consider. UMT had won all three of their games so far this season—and they'd looked damn good doing it—but next year was the season everyone was anticipating. It was no stretch to say they'd be a contender for the national title. Finally. After decades of hard work, on and off the field.

"That's the dude," Ryan said, pointing. "Just coming out the door. Blue jacket and cargo shorts."

A couple of dozen students had just emerged *en masse*

from the front door of the school in South Austin.

"You sure? You were iffy on the time."

"Yeah, that's him."

Kid's name was Adrian Lacy. He didn't look like a ball player. Not big, even as cornerbacks go. No more than five-eleven, one-eighty. Dexter Crabtree caught himself, and recognized the irony in the assessment he had just made. Lacy might be small, but that didn't mean he wasn't a total terror on the field.

One thing for sure, Adrian Lacy was terrorizing UMT's recruiting efforts. Making a major nuisance of himself. Creating problems that Crabtree didn't appreciate.

"How you wanna do this?" Ryan asked.

"Let's see where he goes."

"Want me to get out and follow him?"

"If I wanted you to do that, I would've said so."

Ryan had a story of his own. Good enough to play at UMT, thanks to a few pulled strings, but not good enough to go pro. Actually, not smart enough. Dumb as a stump, really. He had the physical attributes—big, and stronger than a goddamn bull—but nothing between the ears. Twenty-five years old now and working for Daddy. Assistant vice-president of market development, a meaningless title. That's okay. Dexter needed him for situations like this.

Adrian Lacy walked toward the parking lot, and Dexter pulled the Mercedes around after him. Just as Lacy opened the door to a tricked-out Honda, Dexter pulled alongside.

"Hey, Adrian?"

Lacy turned. "Yeah?"

"How's geometry going?" Everyone knew Lacy needed a passing grade to keep his football dreams alive.

Lacy had shades on, but now he lifted them up and said, "I know you?"

"Dexter Crabtree."

It had the effect Crabtree wanted. Lacy's eyes widened. "Oh, shit! For real?"

"That's me."

"Excuse my language, but damn! You're, like, one of my heroes."

"That's good to hear, son."

"Coach shows us footage of your old games all the time. You were the bomb!"

"I appreciate that."

"That tackle you made in the Cotton Bowl? Dude, that was legendary."

"Well, there was a little luck involved, along with some help from above. You busy right now, Adrian? You got about ten minutes to spare?"

"You bet."

"How about you hop in and we take a ride?"

When Marlin stopped in Sheriff Bobby Garza's doorway, Garza was behind his desk, cell phone in hand, dialing, but he stopped when he saw Marlin. "Damn, this thing is powerful. I was just calling you. I must've hit the button that makes you magically appear."

"What's up?"

"Why don't you come on in and close the door."

Marlin did, then he took a seat across from the sheriff.

"Lady was walking her dog yesterday afternoon on McCall Creek Road and found a cell phone in the weeds. It looked like it had been run over at least once—pretty much crushed—and it wouldn't power on. So she was just going to toss it, but then she saw a name engraved on the casing. Sammy Beech."

"Near the accident site?"

"No, actually it was about a half-mile away, which seems odd, until you hear the rest. Her teenage son pulled the memory card out of the phone and it wasn't damaged at all. So he went rooting around in the contents and found an interesting video. His mom called me, told me what they had, and, of course, I needed a search warrant to go any further. Judge Hilton signed off on one about an hour ago. Come take a look at this."

Marlin circled around the desk and stood behind Garza's chair as the sheriff opened a video clip on his computer. All Marlin saw at first was a dark screen, accompanied by the sound of what he took to be a motorcycle engine. The pitch of the engine fluctuated, faster and slower—as if the rider was negotiating a curvy road.

"Okay," Garza said, "apparently what happened was that Sammy pulled his phone out, while he was driving, and started recording. Dangerous as hell, but he had a reason. Look here—"

The video screen filled with a bright flash of light, but only for a split second. Then darkness again. Then more light, just for a very brief moment. Garza paused it. Now Marlin could tell that the bright light was actually created by two separate lights. Headlights.

"Someone was chasing him," Garza said. "He was trying to get them on video."

"Why not just call 911?"

"Best guess is, it was easier to shoot video. The model of phone he had, all he had to do was hit one button to start recording. He was probably able to do that without even looking down. A lot easier than dialing. Besides, service is pretty spotty through there, and he probably knew that, since he lived right down the road." Garza looked at the computer screen. "Honestly, when I first watched it, I was wondering if it was just him and some of his friends screwing around."

"I wish we could tell more about the vehicle."

"Yeah, and it doesn't get any better, unfortunately. I'm hoping we can at least figure out how far apart the headlights are, maybe how high they are off the ground. Might tell us if it's a car or a truck."

"I think we'll be lucky if we can get that."

Garza looked up at Marlin, grinning. "I'm glad you said 'we.' Here, check this out. We're just getting started."

Garza hit the Play button and the video continued. The next thirty seconds was a swirled, shaky mess of darkness and light, darkness and light, as Sammy Beech attempted to record the pursuer behind him. But it had obviously been very difficult to aim the phone backward accurately while driving.

Then Marlin heard a gunshot.

CHAPTER 5

"Whoa."

"Yeah," said Garza.

The sound of the shot was almost masked by the noise of the motorcycle engine, but it was faintly audible, and it was clearly a gunshot.

"Definitely not some of his friends screwing around," Marlin said.

"Nope."

Garza let the video play, and a few seconds later, Marlin heard another gunshot. Then a third. Garza paused it again.

"What do you think?" the sheriff asked. "Handgun or rifle?"

"Well, that audio isn't so great, but I'd guess handgun."

"That's what I was thinking."

"Any calls to Dispatch about shots that night?" Marlin asked.

"No. You know how isolated that road is. Middle of the night, air conditioners running, probably not much chance anyone's gonna hear it. And if they did, they'd figure it was a poacher and call you."

"Nobody did. I heard about Sammy early that next morning, and if I'd gotten a call about shots on McCall Creek the night before, that would've raised a big red flag."

Garza let the video roll again, showing more jumbled, useless footage—darkened screen, occasional flashes of light, and the rising and falling drone of the motorcycle engine.

Marlin said, "If Sammy knew who was chasing him, it

would've been simple enough for him to hold the phone near his mouth and say the name out loud. He could've told us exactly what was happening."

"Probably, but sometimes adrenaline does some weird stuff. Makes you overlook the obvious. Now watch this."

The audio changed drastically and suddenly. The whine of the engine quickly dropped, replaced by a loud crash, then a sustained rumble.

"He dropped the phone," Garza said. "Or tossed it. Pretty sure that's the sound of the phone sliding along the pavement."

The screen was dark, so it was hard to tell exactly what was happening. The rumble slowed, then came to a full stop. Just seconds later, a vehicle passed. The pursuer, roaring by. No video, just audio.

"Sounds like a decent-sized engine," Marlin said.

Garza fast-forwarded through the next five minutes of video. The screen was totally black—no stars—so Marlin figured the phone had landed with the camera lens downward. Not helpful. Garza returned the video to normal speed, and after a few seconds, Marlin again heard the sound of a passing engine. Sounded like the same vehicle, roaring by just as quickly.

Garza said, "I think the person followed Sammy until he wrecked—maybe got out of the vehicle at the accident site, checked to see if Sammy was alive, then turned around and hauled ass. The video runs for another hour and a half—nothing interesting—and then I guess the battery died or the memory ran out."

"Anything else helpful on the phone? Texts? Photos?"

"Haven't looked through it all yet, but I will. Meanwhile, I've got Bill, Ernie, and a couple of reserve deputies searching the shoulders of McCall Creek Road to see if they can come up with any casings."

That's how small the Blanco County Sheriff's Office was—that the chief deputy and his second in command were out combing the weeds in search of spent brass. It also meant that there were occasions when Garza asked Marlin to assist with larger investigations. After all, Texas game wardens were fully commissioned peace officers and could enforce any state law, not just those pertaining to hunting, fishing, and boating. Marlin, Garza, and Bill Tatum had known each other since childhood, and they worked well together. There were also times when Garza would turn Marlin loose to work on his own and see what he could find. Marlin enjoyed helping out. It was almost always an interesting change of pace, and he'd found that he was a talented investigator—so much so that there had been times when Garza had tried to persuade him to come work for the sheriff's department. Marlin had always graciously declined.

"You looking for some extra manpower on this?" Marlin asked.

"Sure wouldn't hurt. Didn't you have some kind of hunting weekend with Sammy and his friends a few years ago?"

"They came out for a youth hunt I ran at Phil Colby's place."

"A youth hunt? What's the bag limit on youths these days?"

Marlin grinned. "Never heard that one before."

"You got time to help out?"

"Sure. But first, some bad news for all of us." Marlin told him about his meeting with Grady Beech the previous afternoon and the $50,000 wild pig bounty.

"Is that even legal?" Garza asked. "Can he do that?"

"Nothing in the Wildlife Code against it," Marlin said.

"Pretty creative, I'll give him that."

"Gonna bring some idiots to town in the next few days."

"To say nothing of the local idiots," Garza added.

"Good point."

"I'll reach out to all the reserve deputies, so we can focus on Sammy Beech," Garza said.

"Whoever was chasing him—what could you charge them with?"

"Ideally, murder."

"Even though Sammy actually died in a wreck?"

"Doesn't matter. Whoever fired those shots chased Sammy to his death. At a minimum, it would be manslaughter. Depends on what we can prove regarding the pursuer's culpable mental state and other jargon. The bottom line is, was he trying to kill Sammy?"

"Maybe he wasn't actually shooting *at* him. Maybe he was just trying to scare him."

"I'm betting he'll say exactly that, if we can figure out who it was."

"So what's the next step?"

Garza let out a sigh. "Right now I need to go talk to Grady. Let him know what's going on."

"What would you like me to do?"

Adrian Lacy continued to gush—expressing appreciation for some of Crabtree's greatest on-field accomplishments—as they drove a short distance from the school and parked in the service alley behind a Home Depot. No other vehicles or people were anywhere in sight.

Lacy was a smart kid. A genius, compared to most of the other recruits, based on the clever tactics he'd been using to ensure the success of his future college career. What Lacy had been doing—and Dexter had to admire the initiative—was tweeting regularly to a select group of blue-chip ball players across the state, encouraging them to rescind the verbal commitments they'd made to various schools and choose the Texas Longhorns instead. Together, Lacy said, they would be unbeatable. Which was almost certainly true. And there was nothing illegal about the tweets, either; communication between recruits was virtually unrestricted.

Several players had recently taken Lacy's advice and switched to the 'Horns, and at least one more—a kid from central Texas who was headed for UMT—was rumored to be waffling. That kid, the waffler, was one of the top offensive linemen in the nation, and he, along with a couple of other key players, would make UMT a legitimate contender for the national title. Crabtree hadn't made any offers to that offensive lineman yet, but that might be the next step, if this meeting didn't go well. Crabtree couldn't risk losing him.

He'd already lost Sammy Beech a few months ago—although there was admittedly some consolation in the fact that nobody else could have the superstar either, not with him being dead. But there couldn't be any more defections, or UMT would once again be nothing more than an also-ran.

Crabtree twisted around to face Adrian Lacy in the backseat and said, "Listen, son, I need to ask you for a favor.

"Really? Shoot."

"It's a pretty big favor."

"No problem. Name it."

"That's very kind of you. It involves these tweets you've been sending out...very creative. But I want you to lay off of Spillar. We need him at UMT. He could really put our program over the top."

Lacy smiled. "You want me to stop tweeting?"

"Only to Spillar. No need to be greedy, right? Leave a few of the good players for the rest of us. That seems fair, doesn't it?"

"Man, I ain't doing nothin' wrong. Tweeting ain't no big

deal. I ain't breaking no rules."

Crabtree could feel his patience wearing thin. "I realize that, but—"

"Just using every advantage I can get. That's how you win."

Not only had the kid interrupted, his tone had become condescending.

"So you won't quit tweeting to Spillar, even as a personal favor to me?"

"I'd like to, but I can't do it."

Crabtree said, "Ryan."

Ryan opened the passenger door, got out, then got in the backseat with Lacy. The kid knew something odd was happening, but he wasn't sure exactly what. He was looking back and forth between the two Crabtrees, starting to get a little nervous. Ryan outweighed Lacy by about fifty pounds.

Ryan held a hand out, grinning, as if asking Lacy to shake hands, and the kid took it. Maybe not so smart after all. Ryan made a quick move, immediately twisting Lacy's entire arm downward and rotating it clockwise, putting a considerable amount of pressure on the wrist and elbow ligaments. Lacy yelped in pain. "Son of a bitch!"

"Quiet, Adrian," Dexter Crabtree said.

"What the fu—"

"Quiet! One good twist and you'll need rehab for a year."

Lacy yelped again, but not as loudly. Learning quickly. Ryan was a meathead, but he was also an expert at some kind of Korean martial art with a strange name Crabtree could never remember. Useful as hell.

After a long silence, Crabtree said, "You know, the game has changed a lot since I played. Less physical contact nowadays. You can hardly touch a guy without drawing a flag. We keep adding all these new rules, it'll wind up a sissy sport, like soccer. I've seen you play, Adrian. You never would've made it in my day. You're not tough enough. You should be out there tearing heads off, but instead I see you limping around like some kind of pussy."

Crabtree waited to see if Lacy would respond to the insult, but the kid wisely kept quiet.

"So here's the deal. New plan. No more tweeting at all. Hear me? None. Not just to Spillar, but to any other recruits at any school. Agreed?"

Ryan must've been twisting pretty hard, because Lacy immediately said, "Yeah! Agreed!"

"If you decide to change your mind later—"

"I won't!" The kid was almost crying.

"And you don't say a word to anybody about this conversation. Ever."

"I promise."

"Not only would Ryan and I deny that it ever took place, but I happen to know a young man who's ready to say he gave you a blowjob at a party last year. Not that you're a homosexual or anything like that, Adrian, but you'd both had too much to drink and things sort of got out of hand. So you let him get a little freaky on you. A one-time thing. Maybe you were even imagining your girlfriend when this guy was going down on you, but it really doesn't matter. See, something like that, whether it's true or not—it'll be all over the Internet in a matter of hours. Can you imagine how your teammates would react? Or the college coaches?"

"Fuck!"

"We cool, bro?" Now Crabtree was the one being condescending, and it felt good.

"We're cool!"

Crabtree nodded, and Ryan released Lacy's arm. "I knew I could count on you, Adrian. I appreciate it. I really do. Now you better go get some ice for that arm of yours, before it swells up."

CHAPTER 6

"Were you aware that the average wedding costs more than twenty-eight thousand dollars?" Billy Don asked. He gave a whistle of amazement. "Dadgum. Of course, that includes the reception, but still."

"I could not possibly care any less than I do right now," Red replied.

"And the average engagement ring is nearly six grand. Six thousand bucks. For a goddamn ring. I've never even paid that much for a vehicle."

Red was glad that Billy Don had managed to persuade Betty Jean that it made sense for him to hunt the $50,000 pig—which was what they were doing. But the downside was that Billy Don had done a lot of research and "number-crunching" to see how much it would actually cost for him and Betty Jean to get married. Now he felt compelled to share that information with Red.

"You know how many couples get married every year in the U.S.?" Billy Don asked. "You ain't gonna believe this."

Red didn't reply, but instead kept staring out the window of the deer blind—a box at the top of a 12-foot tower—waiting for even one pig to appear at the deer feeder one hundred yards away. True, pigs mostly came out at night, but sometimes they surprised you. You might see them in the morning, or even in mid-day if they were hungry enough. So far, however, nothing was moving. Not even a squirrel or a rabbit. Red was normally a patient hunter, but he was getting antsy, and he was starting to understand why. This wasn't much of a plan. Not much chance for success, really, now that he'd thought about it some more.

"Go ahead, Red. Take a guess."

Red took a long drink from the 16-ounce Keystone that was nestled between this thighs. "About what?"

"About how many couples get married in the U.S. every year."

"If I had free and clear title to a rat's hind end, I would not swap it for that information."

"Two point three million. More than six thousand weddings every damn *day*. Does that sound right? Where *are* all these weddings? I don't know about you, but that don't sound accurate to me. Otherwise, you'd be seeing cars draggin' tin cans all over the place."

Red had tried to be logical about it. Grady Beech had tattooed a wild pig and then turned it loose. Okay, but where? Red knew for a fact that you couldn't just trap and move a wild pig all over creation. There was a law against it, because government types were always sticking their noses into everything, making up random, senseless rules and regulations for no good reason. But in this case, it was actually helpful. Red figured that a smart guy like Grady would've been careful to keep his scheme legal, which meant he couldn't turn the pig loose on someone else's property. He had to have turned it loose on his own ranch. And not on the high-fenced part where they grew the grapes, either, because pigs loved grapes.

In fact, Red and Billy Don had once taken Grady's foreman—Emmitt Greene—up on his offer to let them hunt pigs at night on the ranch, because the pigs were always getting into the vineyard. Only problem, Emmitt hadn't made it clear that he didn't want them using Red's SKS. That didn't make sense, because if you wanted to get rid of pigs, a semi-automatic with a 65-round banana clip could get the job done in a hurry. Just after midnight, with Red manning the spotlight, Billy Don had opened up on a herd of pigs. Five minutes later, Emmitt had driven up, grouchy as hell, saying it sounded like Da Nang down there. Then he said they'd have to leave. Show's what you get when you try to do a favor for someone. Didn't matter. There were plenty of pigs around. But where was the one special pig worth fifty thousand bucks?

"On the plus side," Billy Don said, "the average wedding gift is worth about eighty bucks. Multiply that by, say, a hundred and fifty guests and that works out to…well, a lot. Think it's tacky to ask for nothing but cash? Or, hey, gift cards!"

Red further deduced that, since the vineyard was on the west side of Grady's property, fronting on McCall Creek Road, Grady had probably released the pig on the east side of his ranch, way in the back, in the hopes that the pig would be more likely to wander off his property. That was convenient for Red, because he happened to know that the landowner who shared a rear property line with Grady lived in Houston and never visited his place outside of deer season. Man named Kringelheimer. Never around. And that's why Red hadn't been worried about trespassing onto the ranch and taking up temporary residence in one of Kringelheimer's deer blinds.

But even if some pigs showed, what were the odds that the tattooed pig would be in the herd? Slim, really, and to find out, Red and Billy Don would have to shoot as many pigs as possible. But since they technically didn't have permission to hunt there, it would be wise to keep the shooting to a minimum, so they wouldn't draw attention to themselves. Sure, Red could hear shotguns from all directions—dove hunters blasting away—but any idiot could tell the difference between a shotgun and a large-caliber rifle.

Red figured he was bound to start hearing rifle shots fairly soon. Maybe tonight. Maybe tomorrow. Other hunters would be out looking for the pig, which would suck, but once the rifle shots started coming from every direction, every few minutes, Red would be free to shoot as much as he wanted. The game warden couldn't possibly keep up with it all. Until then, shooting more than once or twice would be risky, because some nosy neighbor might call it in.

If only there were some way to know what the tattooed pig looked like. Black, white, brown, or a combination thereof? Big, small, or medium? Sow or boar? Would be a lot easier if they knew which pigs *not* to shoot.

"Then there's the wedding dress," Billy Don said. "That's another two grand, easy."

Red opened his mouth, but didn't say anything. So close. He'd just come so close to disaster by saying that Betty Jean's dress would cost twice that, because it would take twice the material of an average dress. Which would've been downright suicidal.

Instead, he said, "Where did you learn all this crap, anyway?"

"Magazine."

"Which magazine?"

"Don't remember. Just some magazine."

"Not exactly the kind of thing they mention in *Texas Fish & Game*."

"How long we gonna hang out? What time is it?"

Billy Don was trying to change the subject.

"You got somewhere to be?"

"As a matter of fact I do. Meeting Armando at four."

"Armando?"

"Guy I'm working with."

"Damn, man. You got some work and didn't tell me? Does he need another hand?" Red was irritated that Billy Don had been holding out on him. Times were tight, and friends should share leads on possible projects.

Billy Don said, "It ain't that kind of work. Well, it is for him, but not for me. I'm his customer."

"Wait a sec. What does Armando do exactly?"

"Florist. For the wedding. Coming down from Marble Falls."

Red hung his head for a minute and took a deep breath. This was almost more than he could handle. "Let me get this straight. We have to stop hunting a fifty-thousand-dollar pig because you have to go talk to some guy about flowers?"

Colton Spillar sat on the weightlifting bench in his garage and used a towel to wipe the sweat from his forehead. His heart was absolutely thundering, as it usually did when he worked out.

Colton was eighteen years old, a high school senior, and he could bench-press 380 pounds. That was his personal best. He could complete 28 reps of 225 pounds. His biceps were larger than the average person's thighs. His thighs were larger than the average person's waist. He stood six-foot-three, weighed 303, and his shoulders brushed on both sides of an average doorway.

Still, he didn't know if he had the strength—in the mental sense—to do what he was about to do. Push one little button. That's all it would take. Send a tweet and change his future. He would let a few people down, yeah, and he didn't like letting people down.

He'd made a verbal commitment, but players changed their minds sometimes. Was that something to be ashamed of? Sure, it was nice of UMT to offer him a full ride, but so had the University of Texas. And the way things were shaping up, UT was the place to be.

Adrian Lacy said so.

Adrian Lacy was going to UT, and he had managed to convince some major badasses to join him. On both offense and defense. Not just stars, either, but less visible players who were nonetheless critical for a team's success. Nose guard. Blocking back. Punter.

Colton fit in that category. Not a star, because how often were offensive tackles stars? You didn't see many newspaper articles about offensive tackles, and they didn't win trophies that the average person had ever heard of. Offensive linemen didn't score heroic game-winning touchdowns, but they sure as hell *allowed* those touchdowns to be scored. So the stars—guys like Adrian Lacy—knew how important players like Colton were.

And Adrian Lacy had been reaching out to Colton on Twitter and Facebook. Flattering him. Reasoning with him. Promising big things. A shot at a national championship. A better chance at a pro career. Tempting as hell, especially now that Sammy was gone. Sammy had been a true superstar, and when he had originally committed to UMT, it had made Colton's choice all that much easier. But now...

Colton looked down at the screen of his cell phone. He tapped out a message.

Got nothing but love for UMT, but I've decided to be a Longhorn instead. Hook 'em!

His finger lingered over the button. Not yet.

CHAPTER 7

Aleksandra Babikova made her way toward the boarding gate with a handful of her fellow first-class passengers, fully aware that she was the subject of intense scrutiny by virtually every person—man or woman—in her immediate vicinity. Some of her fellow travelers were ogling, others were glaring judgmentally. Some were simply in awe. Some were discreet, others were not.

It had been this way for all of Aleksandra's adult life. She was, after all, a striking person to behold: Nearly six feet tall and ridiculously beautiful—even here in Dallas, where attractive women were as commonplace as cowboy boots. Many of these Texas women were blond, whereas Aleksandra's hair was as black and shiny as a raven's wing. Her eyes were a shade of turquoise normally only viewed from a beach in the Caribbean.

"Poarding bass, please," the young man at the gate said. "Uh, boarding pass."

She handed it to him, noticing that he was becoming flustered, as many men did in her presence. Their cheeks would flush bright red. They would become tongue-tied—even more so when she was dressed in a manner they found pleasing. Today's ensemble included a form-fitting pencil skirt that reached mid-thigh, four-inch heels, and a sleeveless silk blouse unbuttoned just far enough to catch the eye.

"Thank you for flying American, Miss, uh, Babe…"

"Babikova."

He grinned sheepishly. "I have to say that I really like your accent."

A woman behind Aleksandra released a small sigh of impatience.

"Ah, but you are the one with the accent," Aleksandra said.

"Ha. I hadn't thought of it that way. Enjoy your flight to Houston. San Antonio. I mean Austin."

She continued down the ramp, to the airplane door, past the female flight attendant who gave her a quick up-and-down appraisal and showed the smallest frown of disapproval. Aleksandra did not care in the least. She took her seat in the first row, beside the window. A man across the aisle stole a glance at her. Then, a few seconds later, he glanced again.

It was possible some of the oglers recognized her. It wasn't that long ago that she had made a career for herself as a volleyball player. It began with an Olympic silver medal and a starting position with the elite team Dinamo Moscow. Then came modeling contracts, mostly in eastern Europe, then in western Europe, and eventually here in the States, including one for a leading lingerie company. That led to a small part in an American big-budget spy thriller and appearances on various reality shows, followed by a tastefully done nude pictorial in one of the more discriminating gentlemen's magazines.

It had been a whirlwind, but it was all behind her now. She had suffered a career-ending knee injury, and then, for reasons her American agent could not fully explain, the offers and opportunities slowly came to an end, despite the fact that she was every bit as stunning as she had been at eighteen.

"Your fifteen minutes of fame are up," the agent had said with a shrug. "Remember Darva Conger? Carrie Prejean?

Rebecca Loos? Those names ring a bell? Probably not. That's how it works sometimes. Not much we can do about it. Be glad it lasted as long as it did."

So that was it. She was washed up, as they say, at the age of twenty-three. Then, to add insult to injury, she'd discovered that her pig-dog of an ex-husband had not only been sleeping with her longtime volleyball teammate, he had squandered the bulk of the modest fortune she had managed to amass. So she had decided it was time for a divorce, and a new start. She had immigrated to the U.S. two years earlier and begun a new chapter in her life.

For a brief time, she worked as a reporter and commentator for a now-defunct cable sports channel. It was during this stage of her career, while researching a story about the recruitment of college football players, that she recognized a way to carve out a unique and extremely lucrative career for herself in the world of athletics. Too bad it was a serious violation of NCAA rules.

Of course, that hadn't stopped her.

Kurt Milstead fit the bill for a Texas football coach. Ruggedly handsome, with blue eyes and some gray around his temples. Not overly talkative or loud, but charismatic nonetheless. Friendly. Likeable. Courteous. His players routinely said he was the kind of coach who made you feel good about yourself, so you didn't want to let him down. You wanted to earn his approval and respect. He had a way of bringing out the best in the people around him—players and staff.

More important than Milstead's personality was the success he'd brought to the Blanco County High School football program since he'd arrived in town four years earlier. Turned them from a mediocre team into a contender that had gone twelve and one the previous season, ending the year with a narrow loss in the state semifinals.

"Next year's team will be even better," Milstead had promised in the post-game interview at Cowboys Stadium in Arlington, unaware at the time that Sammy Beech—the core of the team—would no longer be around to carry the ball. "I hate to see my seniors go, but the rest of these kids have heart like you wouldn't believe, and I guarantee we'll be right back here next year, and this time we'll be taking the trophy home."

So far this season, that prediction did not look promising. The team had opened with two losses, followed by two narrow victories over teams they'd crushed last year. It was plain that the offense didn't have anywhere near the same potency without Sammy in the backfield.

That wasn't good news for Milstead, and Marlin was about to make his Sunday afternoon even worse. The coach was washing his white Chevrolet truck when Marlin pulled into his driveway in Rancher's Estates. Marlin didn't beat around the bush, but instead got right to it and told Milstead the reason for his visit.

The coach was visibly shaken. "You're saying someone chased Sammy to his death?"

Sometimes, during an investigation, it could prove useful to keep key details secret. But Marlin and Garza had agreed in the sheriff's office that morning that it would likely be beneficial to publicly share what they had learned from the video on Sammy's phone.

"I'm afraid so," Marlin said.

"Who would do something like that?"

"We don't know."

"And why? That's just so crazy."

"We're working to find that out."

Milstead shook his head, obviously at a loss for words. Finally, he said, "It's just...tragic."

Marlin said, "You mind if we go inside and talk for a few minutes?"

"You are a smart young man," Aleksandra said to the dumb young man across from her. His name was Colton Spillar. They were seated at a small dinette table in a kitchen that had last been updated in the early 1970s, judging from the wallpaper.

She said, "You must weigh all options carefully. I understand that. But I am obligated to be honest with you. I believe the proper choice is transparent. OTU is the right place for yourself."

An hour and a half earlier, she had landed in Austin and driven the rental car—a black Cadillac DTS—west to Blanco County, to this boy's home in the country. She knew that his father lived in California and that his mother worked on weekends at the Wal-Mart thirty minutes away. The mother had not taken time off to attend this informal meeting, which was not at all unusual. Aleksandra was no longer amazed by parents who did not participate in the recruitment process. To them, it was just football. But this boy's future—his career—was at stake. And here he was, navigating these treacherous waters by himself, which was fortunate for Aleksandra, because it meant she would not have to create an excuse to meet with him again later, alone.

Was this young man qualified to handle their upcoming conversation? Of course not. He was full of hormones that made it difficult for him to concentrate or even maintain a normal conversation. In many ways, he was still a boy, with braces and a face full of pimples, but he was in the process of becoming a man. He was as tall as Aleksandra, and he outweighed her by at least sixty kilograms. He was also sneaking looks at her cleavage at every opportunity.

She said, "Seven times OTU wins the national championship. These other schools you are considering— can any of them assert the same success? Perhaps best of all, OTU needs a lineman such as yourself. I have seen the game tapes. You are enormously strong like ox. You have quick feet and accomplished hands. Also, you are gifted with intelligence. You have…instinct."

He was smiling self-consciously, enjoying the flattery and attention.

Aleksandra said, "You will almost certainly start in your freshman season. You will be seen nationwide on the television. And what about your future, after college? The OTU staff is best in country. Surely this is acknowledged. You will learn and grow. By the time of your graduation, you will be prepared for a career in the National Football League."

Of course, she didn't mention that his scholarship could be dropped after the first season if he didn't perform, or even if the staff simply found another player to replace him. It was business. The school would feel no more allegiance to this boy than they did to the crew that cleaned the stadium after games.

"The thing is, I already made a verbal commitment to—"

"We all know that carries small meaning."

"I, uh, well, even so, I've really been thinking about Texas. They've been rebuilding the last couple of years."

She said immediately, "Have you not been aware that the Texas assistant coaches are receiving offers that cannot be resisted?"

She knew no such thing to be true.

"Which coaches?"

"Offensive coordinator," she said. "Offensive line coach." She shrugged. "Perhaps they remain, or perhaps not. Timing is key. Do you want to participate in a program that is…" She struggled to find an appropriate phrase in English. "…descending from a peak like a rollercoaster?"

"Couldn't that happen at OTU?"

"We have endless history of success. Why would any coach leave program of that caliber? Our head coach understands the value of planning for the long term. That is why he is attentive about you."

She said "we" and "our head coach" to give Colton the impression that she was an employee of some sort within the Oklahoma Tech University athletics department. She was not. She was a freelancer. A specialist. What some people might call a hired gun. But no actual universities were on her list of clients. As far as she knew, nobody at OTU even knew she existed, and they would almost certainly condemn the tactics she used.

She herself did not know who her client was in this case, because that was the way she had set up her business. The client could remain anonymous. It could be an OTU booster skirting the NCAA rules. It could be an independent recruiting scout who had recommended this young man to the OTU coaches. There were many different types of people who had a vested interest in college football recruiting. They didn't know what tactics Aleksandra Babikova used. They only knew she got results. Nothing else mattered. They also knew she could not control what happened in the weeks and months that followed one of her visits. The young man might change his mind once again. That was out of Aleksandra's control. But it was a risk her clients were willing to take.

Unfortunately, this particular young man did not yet appear convinced. He was not making eye contact. She waited. And then he said, "I need to think about this some more. Talk to my mom."

It was not acceptable to allow him to think. She would not earn her fee if she allowed the boy to think.

So she nodded, then gave him a large smile—the one that said, *It is obvious that you are a wise young man.* She said, "It is obvious that you are a wise young man. You understand how these things happen in the real world, no? I believe you do."

She briefly glanced around the kitchen—at the ancient avocado-green refrigerator that was making strange noises, and at the peeling vinyl flooring—subtly reminding him of his living conditions. Reminding him that his mother made minimum wage and they lived in a rat hole.

She lowered her voice, to give it an air of intimacy and confidentiality, and she gave him her most engaging smile. "We make special deal, okay? You make the verbal commitment today to OTU—I give you five thousand dollars. In cash, of course."

She had to hope nobody else had beaten her to it. Five thousand might seem small in comparison to other offers he might have received.

The boy said, "Whoa." He was attempting to hold back a grin, but he could not. She now knew she was the first to make this sort of offer. He obviously found it enticing, but still he shook his head. "Five thousand bucks. Man, I don't know…"

She waited again.

He said, "I appreciate it, but I don't know if I should do that. Isn't that against the rules?"

"Who will know except you and I? I will tell no one. It will be a secret we share, yes? This is the way it works with other players. You would be foolish to decline."

He took a deep breath—almost there, but he needed

something more. She stood. Now she towered over him. She said, "For you, I will add something extra to the offer."

Very slowly, and with great nonchalance, she began to unbutton her blouse.

His eyes sprung open wide.

She finished with the lowest button, removed her blouse, and laid it gently on the tabletop.

His mouth fell open.

She stood there in her bra—red lace with black trim— letting him enjoy the view for a long moment. Then she said, "My final offer. You use the Twitter—make the verbal commitment to OTU—and I will remove the bra for five minutes." That was as far as she ever took it—no touching of any kind—and it had never failed. Not once.

He gulped. His eyes were riveted. "Plus the money?" he asked.

"Yes, plus the money."

He began to nod. Slowly at first, then rapidly.

CHAPTER 8

Like many homeowners, Dexter Crabtree always kept a supply of latex gloves on hand. Not because he might decide to undertake some messy chore, such as cleaning the barbecue grill or changing the oil in his lawnmower, but because the idea of sticking Adderall tablets into his anus with his bare fingers was, quite frankly, disgusting. So he kept gloves handy in various locations throughout the house, and also in his Mercedes Benz.

Crabtree had just entered the bathroom of his eight-thousand-square-foot Highland Park home and had snapped on a glove—it was almost Pavlovian how the feel of the latex gave him a giddy rush of anticipation—when his phone alerted. An incoming text.

Crabtree followed various high-profile recruits on Twitter, and he received their tweets as texts. Most of it was useless crap, of course—to be expected from teenage boys who thought the world needed to hear their every waking thought.

This particular tweet was from a UMT recruit in Blanco. The kid named Colton Spillar, who'd prompted Crabtree's discussion with Adrian Lacy. Spillar would really make a difference on the offensive line next year. Could be *the* difference.

Crabtree opened the text.

He read it. Then he read it again, to make sure he hadn't misread it the first time.

"Son of a bitch," he mumbled.

He felt the heat rising in his face.

"Son of a bitch!" he screamed.

He had to resist the temptation to smash his phone on the Italian marble floor.

The flower guy drove a light-green Toyota Prius, which didn't surprise Red at all. The car was parked on the street, under some shade, looking about as homosexual as a vehicle could look, when Red arrived at Betty Jean's at ten till four.

"There's Armando," Billy Don said.

"I sorta pieced that together," Red said as he parked in the driveway and killed the engine. They both climbed out of the truck and walked a few paces toward the street.

Red could see a young Mexican guy inside the car, having an animated conversation on his cell phone, gesturing with his free hand. Red didn't want to be here, but Billy Don had said that Red needed to meet Armando. He wouldn't say why.

They waited some more. Armando made the gesture again, a short backward flip of his wrist, like he was waving away a bug.

"Think there's a mosquito in there with him?" Red asked.

Billy Don didn't say anything. They waited some more. At one point, Armando made eye contact through the windshield and held up one finger, meaning "give me just one more minute." Several minutes passed. Red was getting fidgety.

Then, finally, Armando put his cell phone away and stepped out of the Prius. "Oh. My. God! That woman! Don't even get me started!" Apparently, he was one of those people who launched right into a conversation instead of saying hello. He walked up the driveway toward them, saying, "That client—remember the one I told you about, Billy Donald?—now she's saying she ordered daffodils, but I have my original notes and it was clearly orchids from the beginning. Not that we can't change the order, because we can, but hello? Can't she just be honest and admit that she screwed up instead of blaming me?"

Red was thinking: *"Billy Donald"? Did this guy just refer to Billy Don as "Billy Donald"?*

As Armando approached, it was fortunate that Red had a few seconds to adjust to what he was seeing. The florist was wearing very tight slacks featuring a snakeskin print, and his shirt wasn't really a shirt, but appeared to be more of a blouse. A woman's blouse. A bright-red silk blouse. That kind of get-up would never fly in Johnson City, but Armando was from Marble Falls—population six thousand—and Red knew that big cities were more accepting of Armando's type.

"Orchids?" Billy Don said.

"Yes!"

"Those are so last year."

Now Red was thinking: *Did Billy Don just refer to orchids as "so last year"?* This all had to be a practical joke, right? Or maybe Red had inhaled too many gas fumes when he'd filled up the truck on the way over here.

Armando said, "Oh, I know! But at this point, I just have to give her what she wants, right? It's that or have an aneurysm." Suddenly Armando turned and focused his attention on Red. "You must be Red. I have to say, I think you and Billy Donald will make a wonderful couple, and I support your relationship one hundred percent."

Red's face instantly became warm, but before he could reply, Armando let out a sharp little bark of a laugh.

"I'm just *playing* with you, honey," he said. "Don't get so freaked out."

"Yeah, Red," Billy Don said. "Don't get so freaked out."

"The look on your face was priceless!" Armando said. "You'd think I suggested a threesome."

"Red can't even count that high," Billy Don said.

Red didn't like the way this was going. Not even a little bit. Billy Don wasn't usually a smart-aleck like this. Armando was clearly a bad influence. And it wasn't over yet.

Armando said, "Well, anyway, Billy Donald has told me a lot about you…and I'm surprised you're not in prison."

Red said, "I will be if you both keep teasing me."

"Oh, he speaks!" Armando said, sounding positively gleeful. "And quite the charmer, too!" Red had had enough. He was balling one hand into a fist when Armando added, "No wonder Billy Donald wants you to be his best man!"

Red stopped. Relaxed his hand. Took a deep breath. *Best man?* Okay. About damn time.

"Oops!" Armando said, looking back and forth between Red and Billy Don. "Did I let the cat out of the bag?"

"Naw, that's okay," Billy Don said. "That's why we're here. Red, Armando has volunteered to give us some advice on picking out tuxedoes. He said he needed to get a feel for your body type."

"And don't worry," Armando said. "'Get a feel' is just a figure of speech. I promise not to touch. Somehow I'll restrain myself."

"So what do you say?" Billy Don said. Now he was getting down on one knee, hamming it up, pretending like it was a proposal. "Will you be my best man?"

Billy Don and Armando burst out laughing.

Red's face was flushing again. He didn't like being made fun of, especially by a total flamer and a halfway illiterate cedar chopper. "Y'all are hilarious," he said. "A real comedy team."

That only made them laugh harder. When they recovered, Billy Don stood up again and Armando said, "So...I understand you've been out hunting pigs. Did you catch anything?"

Red gave a derisive snort, trying to make it obvious that he thought Armando was an idiot. "You don't *catch* pigs, you shoot 'em."

"Unless you're hunting with Red," Billy Don said. "Then you wonder if there's a living animal within fifty miles."

Red glared at Billy Don, but the big man didn't notice.

"*Au contraire*, I caught a pig once," Armando said. "Caught him with my boyfriend! They were both pigs, to be honest."

Red was not at all comfortable with this line of conversation.

And then, without any warning at all, Armando switched gears and said, "In all seriousness, Red, I know that Billy Donald thinks very highly of you, and that's why he wants you to play a special role in the most important day of his life. I'm certain you understand what an honor that is."

Now they were both looking at him. Waiting for him to say something, but Red was at a loss. He wasn't good at this stuff.

Armando ended the awkward moment by saying, "Well, I have no doubt you will do a fantastic job. If you have any questions, just ask me. Now about the tuxes. I'd say you're about a 40 regular, am I right?"

CHAPTER 9

"I wish I knew," Coach Milstead said. "This whole situation really blows my mind."

Marlin had asked if the coach had any idea who might be firing shots at Sammy Beech during a high-speed chase. They were seated in a pair of matching upholstered chairs around a coffee table in Milstead's living room. Milstead's wife, a quiet woman named Jessica, was attending a function at church.

Marlin said, "Did Sammy have any kind of disagreement or argument with any of his teammates? Anyone he didn't get along with? Even kids on other teams? Fans? Anybody?"

"Nothing that I know about. Sammy was really easygoing and friendly. Everybody liked him."

"What about the Ecstasy in his system when he died? Any idea who he might've gotten that from?"

"No. I had no idea he was into that sort of stuff or I would've put a stop to it. I mean, I understand that most boys his age are going to sneak a few beers now and then, but drugs? I have a zero-tolerance policy about that, and so do college coaches. A positive test for drugs at the college level and his career would've been over."

"Who were his best friends? Who did he hang out with?"

Milstead mentioned some names and Marlin wrote them all down. He noticed that many of the boys on the list were the same boys who had taken part in the youth hunt with Sammy a few years earlier at Phil Colby's ranch.

Then Milstead said, "You want my advice, you need to

look outside Blanco County on this."

"Yeah? Do you have someone specific in mind?"

"No, but—do you know anything about how players like Sammy get recruited?"

"I don't follow that part of it real close. I played some ball for Southwest Texas State, but I wasn't quite to Sammy's level. Didn't get recruited."

"You were a walk-on?"

"Yeah."

"What position?"

"Linebacker."

"Okay, well, Sammy—as you know, he was as blue chip as they come. He could've picked just about any Division One school he wanted. Last I heard, he'd had something like thirty offers."

"Scholarship offers."

"Right. Let me back up. Coaches start going after some of these kids young—sometimes as early as their sophomore year, if they show a ton of promise. What a coach wants is for that kid to make a verbal commitment. Of course, my opinion, it's all sort of a waste of time, because the verbal commitment isn't binding. The kid can change his mind, and so can the coach, without any kind of penalty."

"How often does that happen?"

"Often enough. And even when a kid does verbally commit, it used to mean other coaches would respect that decision and back off, but even that has gone by the wayside in the past few years. There is a tremendous amount of competition between schools to get their claws into a kid like Sammy. I mean, you can build an entire offense around a player like him. I'm sure you've heard stories about boosters, or even coaches, slipping cash under the table to these kids. Buying them cars, paying their rent, things like that. All illegal."

"Does that still go on?"

"Some. And lately there have been more street agents around. You familiar with street agents?"

"I'm afraid not."

"It's a guy who pretends to be a scout or a trainer, or maybe he'll even worm his way into some recruit's inner circle, so he can claim to be a family friend. And then he'll try to influence which school that kid picks."

"For a price."

"Exactly. Scouting is totally legal, but once you start acting as a middleman between a recruit and a school, then it's crossing the line. It's hard to prove, though, because the school will say they were only paying the guy to be a scout."

"Pretty slimy."

Milstead leaned forward and placed his forearms on his knees. "Winning ballgames is one thing, but recruiting is a game in itself. Schools will try just about anything that gives them an edge. You know about hostesses?"

"I don't think so," Marlin replied.

"Most of the big schools have a group of girls—gorgeous young ladies, to be blunt—whose job is to show recruits around when they visit campus. The coaching staff is only allowed to spend so much time with any particular recruit, so these hostesses step up and have a lot of contact with these boys and make sure their needs are taken care of."

"The hostesses are an official school group?"

"Yep. Usually connected to the admissions office rather than the athletics department, but everybody knows their main task is to take care of recruits."

"When you say 'take care of...'"

"Use your imagination. Of course, maybe I'm generalizing, and I'd bet most of the hostesses stick to the job description, and that's as far as it goes. But there have been some that have offered more than a tour around campus.

Which is why a lot of these hostess groups have been disbanded in the past few years. Something that seemed quaint or charming thirty, forty years ago now seems pretty exploitive, doesn't it?"

"Very."

"Imagine being seventeen years old, having a dozen legendary football coaches interested in you, and when you show up to campus for a visit, you're greeted by a couple of the most beautiful young women you've ever seen," Milstead said.

"Hard to resist."

"Exactly, and sometimes a kid gets swept away by it all and makes a verbal commitment he later regrets. So he ends up changing his mind, like Sammy did. You have to wonder how many people that pissed off. That's the point I'm making."

"Did you advise him on all this stuff? His choices?" Marlin asked.

"In hindsight, I wish I'd butted in a little more. Some high school coaches are very protective of their players, and others prefer to stay out of the recruitment process entirely. I guess my style is somewhere in the middle. I let my boys—and their parents—know that I'm happy to give my guidance, if they want it. If not, that's fine too."

"I remember that Sammy committed to UMT back in the spring, but I never heard that he changed his mind."

"That's the other reason I'm bringing all this up. The timing just seems suspicious to me."

"How so?" Marlin asked.

"It wasn't just that Sammy decided he wanted to go to OTU instead of UMT, it was that he announced it on Facebook just a few hours before he died."

On his way through Johnson City after interviewing Milstead, Marlin spotted a cluster of trucks in the far reaches of the Super S Foods parking lot, out near the highway. Looked like an impromptu party—ten or twelve vehicles in total, with eighteen to twenty men seated on tailgates, leaning against fenders, standing in small groups talking.

Marlin switched lanes and pulled his green government-issued Dodge into the lot. He didn't recognize any of the trucks, but most of them were small and foreign-made—jacked up, with big tires and four-wheel-drive for off-roading. Some of the trucks had gun racks mounted in the rear windows. Several had light bars on their grills and whip antennas for CB radios on their roofs.

As Marlin got closer, he saw that he didn't recognize any of the men, either. They appeared to range in age from early twenties to mid-forties, and several of them discreetly held beer cans behind their legs as they noticed Marlin approaching. Some of them didn't bother hiding their beers, and one man even held his can up in a lazy salute.

Anyone from the city would say this was a rough-looking crew. Redneck all the way. Scruffy. Most of them needed a shave and, in some cases, extensive dental work. A few of the men wore camo, but most were wearing pearl-snap denim shirts and worn-out jeans with Justin Ropers or snake boots. At least half of them had black felt hats on their heads, with a feather tucked in the headband. It was a signature look, and Marlin had already realized who he was dealing with. But the final tip-off was that there was a dog box—basically a big aluminum crate—mounted in the bed of nearly every truck.

Great. Dog runners.

That was the name given to hardcore hunters who used Walker and bluetick hounds, beagles, Jack Russell terriers, and a few other types of working dogs to chase deer in the Pineywoods of East Texas. The dog runners' bloodlines usually went back many generations to the early settlers along the Neches River. Hunting with dogs was illegal, but it was sometimes hard to prove, because while a hunter couldn't use dogs to *pursue* a deer during an active hunt, he could use dogs legally to *trail* a deer that was already wounded. Except in East Texas. The problem with dog runners was so prevalent, and so concentrated, in that area of the state, it was illegal to even trail a deer with a dog in twenty-two East Texas counties.

These dog runners were obviously here to try to collect the pig bounty, and Marlin wasn't happy about it. Dog runners were notorious for breaking hunting laws. As far as the dog runners were concerned, they were just carrying on a tradition set by their daddies, and by their daddies before that, and so on. What right did the government have to tell them to quit doing what they had always done? It was their God-given right.

Not surprisingly, there wasn't a dog to be seen. The types of dogs used to hunt wild pigs would instinctively separate one pig from the herd. That's not what the hunters would want in this situation. They'd prefer to kill as many pigs as possible, as quickly as possible. So they hadn't brought any dogs.

Marlin stopped about forty feet away and studied the group. They watched him right back. More accurately, most of them glared right back. A few of them laughed, as someone no doubt had just made some sort of wise-ass remark.

What Marlin needed to do was get out and talk to them. Ask if he could join the party. Be friendly—but make his presence known. Get a good look at their faces. Take note of any names he heard. Sometimes these informal visits went just fine, other times he found himself in the middle of a pack of first-class assholes.

Just as he reached for the door handle, he happened to glance in his rearview mirror. Behind him, on the other side of the parking lot, was a similar cluster of trucks. As he was craning around to look, he saw several more trucks across the highway, parked in front of a convenience store.

He knew right then it was going to be a long night.

CHAPTER 10

Another side effect of Adderall—in addition to hives, breathing difficulties, blurred vision, change in sexual ability, irregular heartbeat, fever, anxiety, frequent urination, blistered skin, vomiting, slurred speech, and a host of other unpleasant possibilities—was "new or worsening mental or mood problems."

Many people would interpret that to mean the user might get depressed, irritable, or even aggressive—and that was true. Dexter Crabtree had experienced all three. But the "mood problems" could also include delusions and hallucinations. Scary stuff. Crabtree couldn't afford to have either of those.

He wondered: If you had a hallucination, would you know you were hallucinating? Say you walk into your backyard and see a green-and-pink zebra. Would you know it wasn't real, but still see it? Or would you see it and think it's completely real? Because it would be better to see it and know it's not real. Same with a delusion. If you were under the impression that you were the president of the United States, would you know deep down that you really weren't? On a similar note, if you began to have irrational thoughts, would you be aware that they were irrational, or would you think you were being perfectly reasonable?

For instance, here he was, in the Mercedes with Ryan, not even seven in the morning, driving south at eighty miles per hour to pay a visit to Colton Spillar. The idea was that they would not leave Blanco County until Spillar had changed his mind. Or, to be precise, until he had changed his mind about changing his mind. Dexter had already decided that he would do whatever it took to achieve that goal. Every option was on the table. Financial inducements. Expensive gifts. The promise of a starting position. Verbal coercion, including threats of humiliation. Even physical punishment, although Ryan would have his hands full with a kid as big as Spillar. But Ryan was talented. He could do all sorts of damage to ligaments, tendons, and—

Christ.

Was this line of thinking rational? What sort of man does these things, and at what possible personal cost? Obsessed by a goddamn game. Had to win. Whatever it took.

"Want me to call ahead for a hotel?" Ryan asked.

Dexter thought about it. For a long time. Then he said, "Turn around."

"Really?"

A mile passed.

"Dad?"

"No, don't."

"So call ahead for a hotel?"

"Well, we're not gonna sleep in the car, are we?"

"A hotel in Johnson City?"

"If you want to stay in some fleabag in Johnson City, be my guest."

"Then, uh, Blanco?"

"Austin, genius. Austin. It's fifty minutes away. Get a room at the fucking W Hotel in Austin."

Dexter hadn't always been so willing to put himself at such great risk. He used to stick with the basic money-under-the-table approach, knowing that if he were to get caught, his world wouldn't necessarily come crumbling down. People more or less expected those sorts of shenanigans from boosters in college football. Boys will be boys, right?

But these other things he'd been doing in the past few seasons, like yesterday's little visit with Adrian Lacy? How dumb was that? Crabtree knew he was being an idiot, but he couldn't seem to stop himself. It was like watching some character in a TV show making stupid decisions.

Was Adderall to blame? He should stop taking it. He knew that. He could stop anytime, of course, and he would. Soon. In February. Just make it to National Signing Day, when recruits had to commit on paper, with no backing out, and then he could take a breath. Wouldn't need as much energy.

Maybe by then, with his help, UMT would have landed a team that could win a national championship.

Fuck.

Why couldn't he stop thinking about college football, even for one goddamn minute?

Marlin poked his head into Bobby Garza's office doorway at eight-fifteen. The sheriff looked at him and said, "Yikes."

"Really? That bad?"

"You look like you got about two hours' sleep."

"That's two more than I actually got. Mind if I sit?"

"By all means. You haven't been home? Darrell told me you had a busy night."

Darrell Bridges was one of the dispatchers for the sheriff's department. Between Darrell's radio calls and the calls directly to Marlin's cell phone from various area residents, Marlin hadn't had a moment to catch his breath.

"Yeah, once the shooting started after dark, the calls were pretty much nonstop. But would you believe I didn't file on a single person last night?"

"No?"

"No road hunters, no trespassers, nothing. And here's why: You know that big bulletin board outside Super S? It's covered from top to bottom with little homemade ads and posters from landowners offering day leases for pig hunting. Same thing at every convenience store in town. Ads taped in all the windows."

Garza smiled. "Supply and demand. The locals are cashing in. What's the going price?"

"Generally about a hundred bucks per day, per hunter. But I noticed that the closer the lease is to Grady Beech's place, the higher the price gets. One of Grady's neighbors is asking a thousand a day."

"Wonder if he's getting it."

"Wouldn't be surprised. I have to admit, I'm thrilled. Makes my job easier. I must've checked a dozen camps last night, and even the dog runners had their hunting licenses. That's saying something."

"Yeah, they don't want to get busted and ruin their shot at the jackpot. See many dead pigs?"

"Some, but not as many as I would've guessed. Pigs are smart. Suddenly the woods are crawling with people, so the pigs are laying low."

Garza shook his head. "How do pigs lay low?"

"You'd be surprised. They get deep in a cedar break and you'd never even know they're there. You walk right past 'em. If you manage to shoot one pig, the rest of them hightail it and you won't see them again."

Garza said, "One thing that bothers me about this—I hate to see a bunch of pork go to waste."

Marlin said, "Same here, but I learned last night that about half a dozen butchers in the area are offering to cut the pigs up and donate the meat to charity."

"Nice."

Marlin leaned his head back and closed his eyes for a moment. "I could fall asleep right here."

"You should go on home."

"I will, but let me bring you up to speed first." Marlin proceeded to tell Garza everything he'd learned from Coach Milstead the afternoon before.

When Marlin finished, Garza said, "Interesting. When I spoke to Grady and Leigh Anne yesterday, they didn't say anything about Sammy switching his commitment to OTU."

"Well, it probably didn't seem relevant. I bet even now it wouldn't occur to them that backing out of a commitment would put Sammy in any danger. I was skeptical myself, so I asked Milstead to name some incidents where a recruit was beaten up or at least threatened after switching schools. I mean, if these boosters and street agents are as aggressive as they sound, that sort of thing must happen occasionally, or even routinely. Milstead couldn't come up with any examples."

"And of course that means…"

"We have to consider the possibility anyway. Even though it's a long shot."

"Yep."

Marlin rose from the chair. Time to get some sleep. But he asked, "How did Grady take the news, by the way?"

"I guess about the way you'd expect when you learn that someone chased your son to his death. He got pretty worked up. Unfortunately, he didn't have anything useful as far as who the pursuer might've been. He gave me the go-ahead to check Sammy's cell phone records, his email accounts, Facebook, all that stuff."

"Gonna interview his friends?"

"Bill and Ernie will handle that today. They'll go out to the school and pull some of the kids from class."

"Did they find any brass yesterday?"

"They did, but the problem is, they found too damn much. Three handgun shells and a couple of rifle shells—all different calibers."

"Okay, so one of those shells could be from the shooter, and the others were already out there from poachers or idiots shooting at road signs or whatever. That kind of thing."

"That's what we're thinking."

"The audio from that video is pretty crummy, but it sure sounds like a handgun to me."

"Me, too."

"Unless it's not," Marlin said.

"I love a man willing to stand by his opinions."

"What caliber were the handgun shells?"

"A mixed bag," Garza said. One nine millimeter, one .38, and one .357. I figure we can rule out the .357 since it's a revolver and the brass wouldn't eject."

"Makes sense. Also I'd say the audio sounds like just one handgun, or two guns of the same caliber, rather than two different calibers. But I figure just one gun."

Garza said, "I think so, too, and that helps. Wouldn't you agree that if it's a handgun, there's a better chance the shooter was alone? Because it would be damn difficult to drive and shoot a rifle at the same time."

"Absolutely. And any driver shooting a handgun, or even a rifle, would have to be shooting left-handed. Although I have no idea how that's helpful."

Garza frowned. "Wait a sec. If you're shooting a semi-automatic outside a car window—the way the brass ejects, it would likely end up inside the vehicle, don't you think?"

Marlin sat back down. "Maybe. Not necessarily. If the shooter had his arm extended out past the windshield—which seems likely to me—the casing would probably bounce off the glass and over the roof."

Garza thought about it, then raised his left hand, like he was holding a gun, trying to visualize shooting from a moving vehicle. "Yeah, I'd say you're right. And now that I think about it, if the shooter wasn't really trying to hit Sammy, he'd be shooting downward at the pavement or up into the air or across the road." Garza stuck his left arm straight out, like he was making a left turn. "Like this."

Marlin said, "Of course, there's the chance that none of the brass is from the shooter."

"Bite your tongue. Henry is processing those shells as we speak. All I want is one good fingerprint. Wouldn't it be great to have a solid suspect by day's end?"

"Hate to remind you, but it's rained a couple of times since then."

"You are a constant ray of sunshine and optimism."

"Glad to help."

They both went quiet for a minute.

Marlin said, "Find anything else useful on Sammy's phone?"

"Nothing obvious. Something might prove useful later."

Marlin stood up again. "I feel like I'm forgetting to tell you something."

"Will you be out again all night tonight?"

"I hope not. I've always got reinforcements, if it gets too crazy." Marlin had alerted game wardens in five neighboring counties about the situation with the pig bounty, and the subsequent influx of hunters. All of those wardens were ready and willing to respond to calls in Blanco County, as needed. In fact, some of the younger ones were envious that Marlin had so many calls to keep him busy. Marlin remembered the days when he was that gung-ho himself.

"Okay, then let's touch base later," Garza said. "When

you wake from your beauty sleep."

Marlin's phone rang. A rancher wanted assistance rounding up a loose bull on Ranch Road 3232. Marlin said he'd be there in twenty minutes.

When he hung up, Garza said, "You'd better turn that thing off for awhile or you'll never get any rest."

CHAPTER 11

Roy Ballard made sure that the man who was hiring him understood that he was *not* a private investigator.

"Then what are you exactly?" the man asked.

"I play the handsome stranger on various daytime dramas. Other times I play the handsome newcomer, or maybe the handsome bystander."

"On soap operas? You're kidding."

"Actually, yes, I am kidding. I'm a legal videographer."

The man—his name was Grady Beech—smiled. "Okay, gotcha. Good."

They were seated at a table in a building called the tasting pavilion at Grady Beech's winery. Grady Beech happened to know one of Roy Ballard's largest clients—a woman who worked in a large insurance firm—and she had given Beech Roy's name and number. Beech had called yesterday afternoon, and Roy had driven out from Austin this morning for this meeting. They were the only two people in the pavilion at the moment, but it was early. Not even eleven o'clock yet. Roy figured most people, even vacationers, didn't visit a winery this early.

"So you're familiar with the exciting and fast-paced world of legal videography?" Roy asked.

"Well, no, not even a little bit, but I'm guessing it involves videography."

"Indeed it does. I can explain it further if you'd like, but it's kind of boring, so I won't be offended if you say you'd rather plunge that corkscrew into your eyeball."

"I'll admit I'm curious, because Heidi said you were kind of like a private eye. And that you're very good at it."

"Well, Heidi is a sweetheart, but she hasn't been the same since she started smoking hashish."

Beech grinned at him. Nice to see a client—especially one in Beech's situation—who managed to retain a sense of humor.

"Let's hear it," Beech said. "What does a legal videographer do?"

"Brace yourself. What I do is videotape all sorts of stuff that might be used in a legal proceeding. Getting testimony from witnesses. Documenting the scene of an accident. Site and workplace inspections. But my specialty is catching people committing insurance fraud. In fact, that's pretty much all I do."

"Okay, now it makes sense. These people committing fraud—you follow them around until they trip themselves up, right?"

"Exactly. Some guy with a bad back might decide to go water skiing or do the hokey-pokey."

"I've seen videos like that. So that part's kind of like being a private investigator."

"Maybe, but I need to be clear that I'm not licensed for P.I. work, so I can't really—"

"This would be totally unofficial. Off the books. I could even pay cash, if you wanted."

"I prefer Kruggerands. But a personal check is fine, too."

Beech took a deep breath. It was obvious that he was struggling with something. "Okay, I might as well get to it—the reason I asked you to come out."

Roy said, "If it helps, I did some Googling, so I know a little bit about the situation with your son. The way he died, and the new developments. You have my condolences."

"I appreciate that—but I need you for something else

entirely."

That took Roy by surprise.

"It's not about Sammy," Beech said. "It's about Leigh Anne. My wife."

Just after seven o'clock that evening, Red O'Brien turned the corner onto Billy Don's street, saw a light-green Prius, and let loose with a long and colorful string of profanities commonly reserved for male members of the homosexual community. Many of the aspersions were hyphenated compound words. Some were Red's old favorites, others he created right then, on the fly.

Red didn't know the reason, other than the obvious, but he didn't like this guy Armando at all. Maybe it was because Armando said things that were almost insults, but not quite. Like he was goading you. Trying to see how far he could push it without getting punched in the face.

And, of course, there was the gay thing. Red honestly didn't have a problem with homos, as long as they had the common courtesy to keep it to themselves. Seriously, why did they feel the need to flaunt it in public? It wasn't like Red went around showing off how straight he was. But Armando was just so open about it. Like he expected people to just accept it and treat him like a normal person.

Nope, Red didn't like it, and he had been hoping he'd never see the florist again. But here was the Prius, parked in front of Betty Jean and Billy Don's house again.

Up until that moment, Red had been feeling pretty good—except for a mild yet insistent hangover. Last night, after sundown, he'd sat on his back porch with an ice chest full of Keystone Light and listened for rifle shots. Wasn't long before it sounded like a dadgum shooting gallery out there.

Of course, that much shooting was both good and bad. It meant there were a lot of hunters out there gunning for the pig. But it also meant he and Billy Don could hunt on the Kringelheimer Ranch and shoot as many times as they wanted.

Earlier today, Red had gotten out of bed at the crack of ten-thirty and driven out to the Kringelheimer place to set up for a hunt that night. Fortunately, Red had acquired a useful set of habits and skills as a poacher that he had refined over the years, and now he put them into use. For starters, he replaced the lock on the gate with one of his own. The day before, when Red and Billy Don had hunted on the ranch, Red had simply cut the lock and left it hanging in place, so it appeared to be undisturbed. Good enough to pass a drive-by inspection by the game warden, but obviously not good enough to pass a hands-on look-see.

Being a frequent trespasser, Red kept an extensive inventory of combination and keyed padlocks on hand—every common brand and model—for just this type of occasion, so he was able to replace the original lock with an identical lock. Granted, some landowners voluntarily gave the combination or a duplicate key to the game warden, so the warden could have access to the place even when the owner wasn't around. But Red was confident Kringelheimer hadn't done that, because the rancher was a proud Tea Party member, and the last thing he'd do is voluntarily grant some jackbooted government thug access to the ranch.

Next, Red drove to the tower blind where they'd hunted the day before, hammered a T-post into the ground, and mounted a solar-powered spotlight on it, aiming it directly at the deer feeder. The word "spotlight" made it sound more powerful than it really was. This light actually cast a beam no brighter than a regular flashlight—almost like moonlight.

Wouldn't spook the animals. Which was why Red had been using this particular type of spotlight for the past few years. He'd learned the hard way that a big old million-candlepower spotlight—the kind that could light up an entire oat field—did nothing but get you in trouble. Wardens could see those things from miles away, and they knew the county well enough that they could pinpoint exactly where the spotlighting was taking place. With this little solar jobbie, Red could pop a deer—or, in this case, a pig—with a .22 magnum and nobody would be the wiser. Stealth. That was the key.

After that, Red had scattered a five-gallon bucket of soured corn near the feeder, because pigs had powerful noses, and the gut-churning stench of soured corn could carry for miles. There were some other tricks you could do with the corn, like digging a deep posthole and dumping the corn down inside. The pigs would hang around that hole for hours, digging and eating, digging and eating. Of course, as soon as you popped one, any other pigs hanging around would generally run off. You had to be a pretty good shot to hit a running pig.

Red loved the thrill of the hunt. And tonight would be even more exciting, because $50,000 was on the line. So, as Red passed the Prius, he decided he wouldn't let Armando dampen his spirits. Or Betty Jean, either. She would probably be home by now, but Red could avoid dealing with her and Armando both by not even going inside the house. Easy solution.

So Red honked the horn once, good and firm.

Waited a minute. A very long minute.

He started to honk again, but then decided not to, because it was an almost sure bet that Betty Jean would appear at the door and tell him to shut the hell up.

So he waited, and before long the front door opened and

Billy Don appeared in the doorway. He waved at Red to come on inside the house. Red shook his head and waved for Billy Don to come on and get in the damn truck. Billy Don held up one finger, meaning *Give me a minute.*

Good. No going inside.

Red waited again. Several minutes. What the hell was Billy Don doing in there? Red was tempted to honk again, but why risk the wrath of Betty Jean?

Finally the door opened again, and here came Billy Don, carrying his rifle case and a small ice chest. And right behind him was Armando, carrying the camo-patterned canvas bag Billy Don used to tote snacks, binoculars, more snacks, extra ammo, and other crap. Wasn't it just like a gay guy to be all helpful and stuff? Red figured it was like some sort of mothering instinct. Whatever. It wasn't going to bother him. But he decided that if Armando made a single smart-ass comment, Red wouldn't put up with it. Gay or not, Red would bust him across the mouth. It might be like hitting a girl, but Red would do it anyway.

When Billy Don opened the passenger door, he had a mischievous grin on his face, like he was up to something. He said, "Hope you don't mind, but Armando wants to go with us."

After helping with the loose bull, then answering a call about some dove hunters shooting birds off a power line, Marlin had managed to go home, have lunch, then sleep for four hours. Then he'd taken a leak and slept for two more hours. When he woke, he grabbed his phone from the nightstand. Not a single voicemail. Outstanding. He'd received a text from Nicole.

Working late. Where are you?

She'd sent it twenty minutes earlier. He tapped out a reply.

Home. Just woke up.

She said: *Another busy night tonight?*

Quiet right now. Crossing my fingers. Meet me for supper?

He rose from the bed and went into the bathroom to brush his teeth. When he was done, she'd sent another text.

Love to. Where?

He was just about to respond when his phone rang. A widow living on five hundred acres not far from Grady Beech's place was calling. "I saw somebody moving around in that creek bottom on the west side of my place. I was over there checking the deer feeder."

Marlin heard from this elderly woman several times a year, and more often than not, she was mistaken about what she'd seen. She was a tough old gal—he'd seen her hoist a fifty-pound bag of corn onto her shoulder and carry it at least a hundred feet—but her senses weren't quite as sharp as they used to be.

"But you're not positive there's anybody there?"

"I saw 'em through my binoculars. Two or three of 'em."

"They're on your land and not across the fence?"

"That's right. Ten minutes ago."

"Did you talk to them?"

"Nope. Just turned around and called you."

"Have you leased the place out to anybody?"

"No, sir."

"Did you hear any shots?"

"What?"

"Have you heard any shots?"

"Of course I've been hearing shots. Between the dove hunters and this damn-fool pig contest, I've been hearing shots all day."

Marlin smiled. She got him on that one. "I'll be right

over," he said. "You stay in the house, okay? I'll check it out, and then I'll drive around and tell you what I found."

CHAPTER 12

"You sure are quiet, Red," Billy Don said.

Red was going to kill Billy Don. Murder him in cold blood, first chance he got.

They were sitting in the 12-foot tower blind on the Kringelheimer Ranch, all three of them crammed into the tight space. Even worse, Armando was in the middle. Red kept bumping arms with him, and that was giving him the willies.

"That's because we're *hunting*, Billy Don," Red whispered. "Everybody knows you're supposed to be quiet when you're hunting. Ask Elmer Fudd."

"Oh, come on. We always talk a little bit when we hunt. The feeder's a hundred yards away. Ain't nothin' gonna hear us if we keep it low."

When Billy Don had announced that Armando was coming along, Red had been struck speechless. Why would Billy Don want that? And even more odd—what kind of homosexual wanted to go hunting? It just didn't make sense. Homosexuals did things like, well, arrange flowers and listen to show tunes. While Red was trying to process the situation, Armando scooted into the truck, all prissy-like, and Billy Don piled in after him.

At that point, Red couldn't very well have told Armando to get out. That would've been just plain rude, and Red understood that gay people were extremely sensitive. Less like men and more like women. It would've created an ugly scene, and Red wasn't up to it.

The other irritating thing was that Red had no doubt that Billy Don knew exactly what he was doing. Trying to be clever. Like when you're at a party and you intentionally introduce your friend to the ugliest girl in the room, saying they have a lot in common, then you excuse yourself to get a cocktail, leaving your friend stuck with the uggo. Not cool, but it was sometimes pretty funny.

Regardless, Red had made one thing clear on the drive to the ranch—if they managed to shoot the right pig, Armando didn't get any of the bounty. Not one cent. He was simply along for the ride. Nobody had argued about that.

"I still don't understand whose property this is," Armando said. "Did you say it was your uncle?"

Red noticed that Armando had his legs crossed at the knees, and his hands were folded neatly on top of his thighs. The guy even *sat* like a gay man. Plus, the clothes he was wearing were all wrong for hunting. Slacks, loafers with silly little tassels, and yet another shirt that looked more like a woman's blouse.

"Yeah, he's my uncle," Red said. "He don't mind if we hunt here. Lives in Houston."

Nobody said anything for several minutes. Dusk was coming. The pigs would be starting to move. Red had already heard several shots in the past few minutes.

"When do the animals come out?" Armando asked.

"Can't never tell," Billy Don said. "Might see something in the next minute. Might not see nothing at all."

Armando nodded. "And then what happens?"

"What do you mean?"

"If an animal comes out, what happens next?"

"Well, that depends. We're hunting for pigs, so if we see a pig, we'll probably shoot it."

"Just like that? You just shoot it?"

"Well, yeah."

"You don't give it a running start or anything?"

Red couldn't help but let out a little snort.

"What?" Armando said. "Wouldn't it be more fair that way? If you just shoot it, that sounds more like an assassination than a fair hunt."

Red shook his head. *What an idiot.*

"We're not really innerested in making it fair," Billy Don said, "especially when you're talking about a pig worth fifty grand. Besides, even on a regular hunt, it's hard enough making a good shot at a hundred yards."

"I would imagine that's true," Armando said, "considering how much beer you two are drinking. Is that even legal? Drinking when you're hunting?"

Here we go, Red thought. *The man is nagging like a woman.*

"Uh..." Billy Don said.

"Who cares?" Red snapped. "Why are we even talking about this?"

Silence for ten seconds.

"It just seems dangerous," Armando said. "That's all I'm saying."

"I already got a mother," Red said. At this point, he didn't care if Armando was sensitive or not.

The blind was quiet for several minutes.

"I apologize," Armando said. "I didn't mean to sound critical. I do that sometimes, but I'm working on it. One of my many faults. *Many* faults. Just ask my ex."

Red had no idea how to respond to that, and apparently Billy Don didn't either. Several more minutes passed.

"What kind of rifle is that?" Armando asked.

Red was looking straight ahead, so he wasn't sure whether Armando was talking to him or Billy Don.

"Red?" Armando said.

Crap.

"Thirty-thirty."

Red knew exactly what Armando would ask next. It was unavoidable.

"What does 'thirty-thirty' stand for?"

Red let out a sigh.

Before he could say something mean, Billy Don said, "It specifies the caliber and such. Sure wish we knew what kind of pig to look for—at least what color it is. Something."

Red took a long drink of beer, then belched with conviction, just to irritate Armando. A few minutes later, the feeder went off, slinging corn in every direction. Red and Billy Don were used to the sudden sound, but Armando jumped and let out a little shriek. Red chuckled softly.

"Startled me," Armando said.

Red said, "How about we sit quietly for a few minutes on the off chance we might actually see a pig?"

Nobody replied.

After a few minutes, Armando whispered, "Something just occurred to me. What if there isn't a tattooed pig?"

"Huh?" Billy Don said.

"Well, the man who put the bounty on the pig… obviously, he hates pigs, and he wants as many of them killed as possible, hence the bounty. But he'd get the same result whether or not there was actually a tattooed pig scampering around."

Just that quick, Red suddenly felt sick to his stomach, like someone had shown him undeniable proof that Toby Keith was a socialist. Armando was right. There didn't need to be a bounty pig at all. And it was brilliant, really. It was exactly what Red would do himself. Who would ever know? Pigs would get slaughtered just the same, but Grady wouldn't have to part with fifty thousand bucks.

"I still don't get it," Billy Don said.

Red said, "Grady could lie about there being a tattooed pig. But as long as we all believe it, we're gonna hunt for it, and we're gonna shoot as many pigs as we can. And when nobody ever finds the pig, Grady can say, 'Well, it's damn sure out there. I turned it loose myself. Better keep on hunting, boys.'"

"Oh," Billy Don said. "Well, shit."

"Exactly," Red said.

"Wouldn't that be against the law or something?" Billy Don asked.

"Should be."

"I think it would constitute fraud," Armando said, "but I'm not an attorney. And how would anyone ever prove it?"

"I feel pretty dumb," Billy Don said.

"Business as usual," Red said.

"Huh?"

"Never mind. Bottom line—we don't know for sure there *ain't* no pig."

"That's true," Armando said. "I'm probably wrong. I mean, it would take a fairly corrupt person to go through with something that scummy."

Red didn't feel comforted by that at all.

The creek on the widow's property ran north to south, deep in a draw, with a steep slope up both sides. Running parallel to the creek, roughly one hundred yards to the west, was a county road that saw very little traffic. Marlin pulled his truck to the grassy shoulder of the road and killed the engine.

There were no vehicles anywhere in sight, and he could see another half-mile past where he'd parked. If anyone was going to trespass onto the widow's ranch, this was almost certainly where'd they'd enter—but the absence of vehicles didn't necessarily mean anything. Poachers weren't known for their brains, but they weren't necessarily stupid, either. They had their methods. For instance, in a situation like this, one man might drop another man off on the side of the road, then return later to pick him up. They'd stay in touch via cell phone.

The sun hadn't dipped below the horizon yet, but Marlin knew he'd likely be gone for twenty or thirty minutes, so he grabbed his flashlight and climbed out of the truck. He stopped at the fence for a minute and simply listened. Quiet. Not even a wind to rattle the leaves. Then he heard a shot— but it was well behind him, several miles away. He waited another minute and heard nothing more, so he eased over the barbed-wire fence, careful not to snag his khaki jeans.

Marlin had been on this ranch several times over the years. This was thickly wooded terrain, covered with cedars, oaks, mountain laurels, and even a few pecan trees down near the creek. He began to work his way slowly downhill, stopping every few yards to listen. Still nothing.

But Marlin was on high alert nonetheless.

Being a game warden meant dealing with subjects who were armed as a matter of routine. When you walked into a hunting camp, those people were carrying weapons, or they had weapons nearby at their disposal. Rifles, shotguns, pistols, knives, bows with razor-sharp arrows. And a game warden was almost always well outnumbered. A routine situation could turn deadly in the blink of an eye. Marlin knew that all too well, because his father, a warden before him, had been killed in the line of duty by a poacher when Marlin was still a boy.

Further, if the widow was right and there were trespassers on her ranch, they had already broken the law. Even the thought of getting caught for a minor infraction like trespassing could make a first-time offender panic and do something monumentally stupid. And the type of person who intentionally and knowingly trespassed was much more likely to have a history of illegal conduct—perhaps far more serious violations. So it was important to be wary.

On the other hand, you didn't want to behave as if every hunter you encountered was about to grab a gun and get violent, because those types of incidents were extremely rare. The overwhelming majority of hunters were cooperative, law-abiding types. Marlin tried to strike a balance of friendliness and caution when approaching any individual in the field.

After moving slowly downhill over rugged ground and through dense brush for ten minutes, Marlin reached the creek. The light was fading fast down here in the low areas. He hadn't heard or seen anyone. Maybe the widow was wrong again, or the trespassers had already taken off.

Marlin waded through the creek—it was no more than a foot deep, and the water was lukewarm at this time of year—and started up the slope on the other side, stopping every twenty yards to listen. When he reached the top, where it leveled out, the brush gave way to an empty pasture at least two hundred yards wide. Not a soul to be seen.

Marlin stood quietly for a solid two minutes. Heard a few shots in the far distance, but nothing anywhere near this ranch. Time to report to the widow. Reassure her that he hadn't seen anyone, without letting on that he was fairly certain there had never been anyone to see.

He was twenty yards down the hill when he glanced across the draw and saw a person—a trespasser—on the opposing slope, at least one hundred and fifty yards away. He was tucked in the shadows, with the setting sun behind him, so that the light was shining right in Marlin's eyes. Marlin tried to block the sunlight with one hand, but it didn't help much. A few minutes later and the sun wouldn't have been an issue.

Was the man wearing camo? Or just dark clothing? Male, most likely, because the person seemed tall. Very tall. The trespasser had plainly spotted Marlin and was simply standing in place, watching. Waiting. Then he gave a big, slow, exaggerated wave. But it wasn't a friendly wave. There was an attitude behind it. The guy was taunting Marlin, saying, *You're way over there, and I'm over here. So there's nothing you can do.*

"State game warden!" Marlin called out. "Stay where you are!"

Sound would carry across the draw, but the trespasser had no reason to comply. It would take Marlin at least ten minutes to traverse the rugged draw and reach the man. So he would almost certainly be long gone before Marlin reached that spot.

But the man didn't leave. Instead, he turned sideways, left shoulder forward, and made a familiar move with both arms. Marlin realized that the trespasser had just removed a rifle that had been slung over his shoulder. Marlin was astonished by what he saw next. The trespasser—who could have easily disappeared into the brush—calmly and methodically leveled the rifle and aimed it across the draw, straight at Marlin.

Marlin instinctively dropped, hitting the ground just as he heard the loud crack of a rifle shot.

CHAPTER 13

"Is that one?" Armando said softly.

"One what?" Billy Don asked.

"That thing over there in those trees. Is that a pig?"

Red couldn't see any damn pig, and he didn't want to be shown up, so he waited without saying anything.

"That real tall tree, to the right of your feeding machine..."

"That Spanish oak?" Billy Don said.

Now Red finally saw the pig. A small black one, solo. "About ten yards past the persimmon," Red said. "Don't you see it, Billy Don? I've been watching it for a few minutes."

He could feel Armando looking at him, even in the dim light. "Oh, really?"

"Oh, really what?" Red said.

"You saw the pig before I pointed it out?"

"Of course."

"Then why didn't you say anything?"

"Didn't want it to run off. Surprised it hasn't spooked already from both of you yapping."

"Well, why didn't you shoot it when you first saw it?" Armando asked, still unconvinced.

"Wanted to see if some others would show up, so we could shoot a bunch. But I'd say we've waited long enough."

He reached for his rifle.

Marlin was hidden by tall grasses—but he was far from safe. The man across the ravine could simply lower his aim about three or four feet and fire at will, right through the grass.

Before Marlin could decide what to do, there was a second shot. He thought he heard the bullet crashing through the brush. He rose to his feet and ran for the nearest cover—a dense cluster of cedar trees. He squatted behind them and tried to gather his composure. The trees shielded him completely from the shooter's view, but they provided about as little physical protection as the tall grasses.

His cell phone. He pulled it from his pocket—and saw that he had no signal on this side of the ravine. Not a single bar. No way to call for back-up. He put it away and drew his .357 instead. It wouldn't do much good—no accuracy at all at this range—but it was better than nothing. He fired a shot into the ground, hoping the shooter would think Marlin was returning fire. His palm was slick with sweat around the grip, and Marlin realized that he was breathing too rapidly.

Calm down. Deep, slow breaths. Don't let—

A third shot.

The shooter would be busy jacking another round into the chamber, so Marlin immediately rose to his feet and scrambled sideways to a nearby oak tree. The trunk was just large enough to give him total cover. But he was pinned down.

Now what?

"Too damn dark inside this pig's ear," Red said. "Gimme some light."

The pig had run about fifty yards and died in a cluster of cedar trees. Billy Don clicked on a large Maglite and aimed it.

"Well, crap," Red said. "Now the other ear. Well, crap." He let go of the pig's ears and the head thudded to the dirt.

"No tattoo?" Billy Don said.

"No, no goddamn tattoo," Red said. "If there'd been a tattoo, don't you think I'd be hootin' and hollerin' and dancin' around like an idiot? What a dumb question."

Armando, who was at least ten yards away, with his arms crossed, obviously disturbed by the pig carcass, said, "Give the poor man a break. You don't have to be so mean."

Red looked at Armando and smiled. "Really?"

"Really what?"

"I'm the mean one? After the way y'all teased me yesterday?"

"Yesterday? How did we tease you?"

"You kiddin' me? Acting like Billy Don and me were a couple? Saying how you might have to restrain yourself from copping a feel?"

"It wasn't...we weren't..."

"You were teasing me."

"Okay. Maybe a little. But if it bothered you, why didn't you say something?"

"I didn't say it bothered me. But you knew it could've, didn't you? That's why you did it, isn't it, *Armando*."

"You know, at this point, I don't even know what you're insinuating."

"Bullshit. It was obvious."

"Red, pray tell, *what* was obvious?"

"You were being as fruity as you possibly could be, just to irritate the small-town redneck. You're one of those guys who throws it in the face of people like me. Trying to make me uncomfortable."

"That is patently absurd."

"Exactly. Which is why you brought up your boyfriend

and some 'pig' you caught him with. You knew a guy like me wouldn't want to hear all that stuff."

Armando opened his mouth, stuttered a little, but nothing more came out.

Red pointed at him. "See. Gotcha. I ain't as dumb as I appear."

"I wish y'all would quit bitching at each other," Billy Don said.

"Armando started it," Red said.

"I have an idea. Maybe we should ask Emmitt," Billy Don said, referring to Grady Beech's foreman.

"Ask him what?" Red said.

"About the pig. What color it is, how big—all that stuff."

"Complete waste of time. He wouldn't tell us shit. Why would he?"

Armando said, "Wait. Emmitt Greene? Is that who you're talking about?"

"Yep," Billy Don said. "Grady's foreman."

"Huh. Small world. I play Bunco in a group with his wife Sharon. We are total pals. Of course, we *call* it Bunco, but instead of actually playing, we mostly just drink wine and gossip. And eat things we shouldn't. Our one night of the month to totally ignore our diets."

Red started to make the same "rat's hind end" comment he'd made to Billy Don the day before, but then he thought of something. Something that had exciting possibilities. He looked at Armando, there in the dim light, and grinned.

"What?" Armando said. "What'd I say? Am I being too gay again? Heaven help us all if a gay man actually says what's on his mind."

Red ignored the sarcasm in Armando's voice and said, "I'll bet your pal Sharon knows if there's really a tattooed pig. And if there is one, she knows exactly what it looks like, too."

A minute ticked by and no more shots came from across the draw. Marlin wondered—should he wait twenty or thirty minutes until it was good and dark? If he did, the chances of catching the shooter were almost zero. It would be too risky to look for the shooter, who could be lying in wait. Instead, Marlin would have to retreat, back up the slope behind him and through the pasture, and then at least half a mile to the widow's house. That would be the smartest way to go.

But he couldn't do it. He knew he should, but he couldn't. He wanted to nail the bastard. Didn't want to give him the chance to slip away.

Marlin leaned ever so slightly to his right and peeked around the tree trunk. Relief. The shooter was on the move, ascending the slope, with his back toward Marlin. Cool as can be. Not rushing. Like he was out for a late-afternoon hike to watch birds. Whoever the trespasser was, he had nerves of steel. Or he was just plain simple-minded.

It was tempting to lob a .357 round over at the man, but Marlin holstered his revolver instead, and began down the slope, picking his way carefully, but moving as swiftly as he could. Within thirty seconds, he was low enough in the draw that he was hidden by tall trees, so he didn't have to worry about any more shots. But it also prevented him from keeping track of the shooter above.

A few minutes later, Marlin reached the creek and waded across—quickly, but quietly. It was already considerably darker down here than it had been six or seven minutes earlier.

Now he began the uphill hike, weaving through the trees and brush. Pacing himself, so he wouldn't lose his breath.

Keeping his eyes peeled. Listening for the slightest sound. Halfway up, he stopped and waited. Nothing. Just as he was about to move again, he heard it. An engine. Far off at first, but growing louder. Sounded like a diesel—a truck, most likely, moving fast from the south. A vehicle on the county road, coming to pick up the trespasser.

The shooter was probably already on the shoulder of the road, waiting. Marlin hustled as fast as he dared, knowing that the shooter could be hiding in a hundred different places, his rifle to his shoulder, finger on the trigger.

Marlin was fifty yards from the road when he heard the diesel engine decelerate. Then a shout. Several voices. Marlin rested his right hand on his revolver and pushed himself harder, thighs burning as he climbed the hill.

Now he heard the slam of a door. Then the screech of tires as the vehicle gunned it.

Marlin was practically sprinting now, heart pounding, hoping to catch even a glimpse. The fence was thirty yards away. Twenty yards.

The roar of the vehicle was quickly receding.

He closed the gap and finally reached the fence. He could see up the road to the north in the dim light. Taillights, maybe three hundred yards away. He couldn't see any more than that. Couldn't tell the make or the model or even the color of the vehicle.

He sprinted for his truck to give chase, and as he approached from the front, he saw that the vehicle was sagging conspicuously.

Passenger-side tire was flat.

Son of a bitch.

The first deputy, Ernie Turpin, came roaring down the county road less than eight minutes later, siren screaming and cherries painting the surrounding countryside vivid red and blue.

By then it was fully dark. Marlin stepped well off the pavement, almost to the fence, until Turpin's headlights picked up the truck on the side of the road and the deputy began to hit the brakes. When he came to a stop, still in the lane of traffic, Marlin walked out to greet him.

"You okay?" Turpin asked.

"Yeah. You see any vehicles at all on your way down here?"

"Not a one. They must've made it to the highway before I turned off."

Marlin's hands were still trembling, and he could feel the moisture in each armpit. He was even a little light-headed.

"Well, damn," he said.

CHAPTER 14

Hostesses.

That was the topic Aleksandra Babikova had been researching for the cable TV sports program when the idea for her new career had struck her.

"Hostesses" was the term for friendly—and usually attractive—college girls who chaperoned football recruits during on-campus visits. There were rumors that some of these hostesses used sexual favors to obtain commitments from highly prized recruits, with the implicit approval of the athletics department.

Interesting. But what did the hostesses get in return? It appeared they got nothing at all. Aleksandra could not understand it. These young ladies were perhaps morally compromising themselves in a way that might haunt them for years to come—but at the same time, it was undeniable that they were offering a valuable service. If they were going to behave like prostitutes, why were they not asking for compensation, which they would surely receive? Then Aleksandra read that most of the hostess groups had been disbanded by the universities after the media began to question the propriety of such groups. That had created a void in the world of recruiting.

And thus Aleksandra's idea was born.

It was an amusement, at first. A daydream. But with each passing day, it had begun to seem more practical and plausible. She had discovered a market demand that was crying to be filled. Didn't it make sense to explore this opportunity?

But how to get started? Did it have long-term potential as a career? And—considering that she had no intention of actually sleeping with the players—would less licentious tactics suffice? She would have to know the answers to those questions before she could expect to be paid. Not only would she have to know the answers, her potential clients would also have to know the answers. She would have to prove herself beforehand.

So Aleksandra concocted a plan.

She paid a ridiculous amount for a ticket to the game between the University of Middle Texas and Oklahoma Tech University—one of the biggest rivalries in college football—and then she managed to locate one of OTU's most enthusiastic boosters in the bleachers. She had done her research on this man. Extremely wealthy. Outspoken. Brash. He visited Las Vegas often, where he drank large amounts of whiskey and enjoyed the companionship of many beautiful women. He had also been suspected many times of offering cash to key football players. He laughed about it in interviews. Did not deny it. Did not confirm it. The university itself publicly disassociated itself from the booster and condemned these sorts of practices. It was clear that the OTU coaches were not involved in any of this booster's alleged illicit practices.

But Aleksandra did not need the coaches to be involved.

During the game, she waited in the concourse. The booster was seated on the fifty yard line—in the shade, befitting a man of his stature, because even though the game took place in October, the temperature often hovered in the upper eighties or even the low nineties. Today it was eighty-seven, which gave Aleksandra an excuse to dress in a tight, revealing outfit—meaning she was dressed like most of the other young women in attendance.

Midway through the second quarter, the booster made a trip to the men's room. Aleksandra waited until he had relieved himself, because he would've been impatient if she had approached him beforehand.

When he emerged, she walked up to him and said, "Mr. Guthrie?"

"Yes, ma'am?"

She recognized the look on his face. *Do I know you?* He was an important man who met hundreds, or even thousands, of people every year, in a variety of social and business environments. She could be one of them. But he did not ask the question, because that would have been rude. He simply waited for her to speak.

And she did, getting right to it. "What if I told you I could get Duane Smith to commit to OTU within one week?"

He had been looking at her breasts, obviously enjoying what he was seeing, but this remark brought his eyes back up to hers. He laughed. "I'd say more power to ya, because that boy's been playing his cards close to his vest for months."

Aleksandra did not understand why he was talking about vests, but that was not a concern. She handed him a business card with nothing on it except her first name and a phone number.

"He will select OTU. This one I will do for free."

Up to now, he had appeared amused by what she was saying. Now he looked skeptical—and intrigued. "Free? Who are you?" he asked.

She had already begun to walk away, but now she turned and mimicked a gesture she had seen many Americans make. She held an imaginary phone to her ear and mouthed two words.

Call me.

Duane Smith committed to OTU four days later.

CHAPTER 15

Dexter Crabtree had seen a therapist once. Literally, once. This was five years ago, when he'd still been married to the she-devil named Gretchen, Ryan's mother.

She used to complain that he was totally consumed by college football—that it had become such an integral part of his identity, of his personality, of the fabric of his very being, that he couldn't live without it. The first thing he did every morning and the last thing he did every night was log on to various websites for the latest information on UMT specifically and college football in general. He checked player stats, injury reports, recruiting updates, conference standings, national rankings, pre-game analyses, post-game analyses, staff firings and hirings, and every little nugget or morsel of news that came from any legitimate writer, critic, or prognosticator.

He subscribed to eighteen glossy four-color magazines. He "liked" more than two hundred football-related Facebook pages. He received tweets from players, coaches, universities, athletic directors, even cheerleaders. He listened to more than a dozen sports-oriented talk radio programs.

One time, in an incident Dexter could only describe as perverted and sadistic, Gretchen had surreptitiously timed his activities on a randomly selected Saturday. The results: Thirty-six minutes eating. Forty-nine minutes showering, shaving, and taking care of other matters of personal hygiene. Thirteen hours and seven minutes dedicated to college football. And this was in the *off-season*, so it didn't include any actual watching of games.

He had to concede, he might have a problem. So when Gretchen badgered him into seeing a therapist—"Just go once and see what he says"—Dexter agreed. And, of course, after one fifty-minute session, the counselor concluded that Dexter might benefit by "broadening his interests and placing less of an emphasis on college athletics."

Dexter served Gretchen with divorce papers the following afternoon.

Such a relief. No more nagging. No more bitching and whining. Not long after that, Dexter realized that NCAA officials were just like an overbearing wife. They were always taking the fun out of everything, and wanting to regulate everyone's behavior. The NCAA classified Dexter, and other boosters like him, as a "representative of athletics interests" for the University of Middle Texas. Once you were identified as a representative of athletics interests for a particular university, that categorization stuck with you forever. You couldn't shake it. It followed you to the grave.

And along with that designation came a long list of recruiting no-nos. You couldn't offer cash to a prospective student athlete or members of his family. No loans, either. You couldn't promise employment after graduation. No free cars, no free housing, on and on.

Nag, nag, nag.

Another biggie: you couldn't even contact an athlete, or any member of the athlete's family, by any means—in person, by phone, email, letter, Facebook, Twitter, or any other social media.

But Dexter knew that becoming a national champion meant you couldn't always follow the rules. Just like in his playing days. Sometimes you had to say fuck it and take some risk. Not that you threw all caution to the wind. He and Ryan had spent the better part of the previous day trying to figure out a way to make contact with Colton Spillar. But he was in school, and after school he was in football practice, and after practice, he went straight home.

Fortunately, Dexter had another option.

"I know it's a pain in the ass, but let's go through it one more time. The shooter—describe him for me."

"Tall. Wearing camo or dark colors."

"How tall was he?" Garza asked.

"Well over six feet."

"Like six-two, six-three?"

"More like six-five. Maybe even taller," Marlin said.

"Hair color?"

"Wearing a hat, I think. Orange."

"Dark orange or light orange?"

"I don't know. Orange. Hard to tell for sure, because he was in the shadows and the sun was right in my eyes."

"Like the color of an actual orange?" Garza asked.

"Well, no, darker than that."

"Like burnt orange? Maybe it was a UT cap."

"Not quite that shade."

"Could you see his hair at all?"

"Don't think so," Marlin said.

"Fat? Thin?"

"Average. Not slender, not heavy."

"Age?"

"No clue."

Bobby Garza paused for a moment to take a sip of coffee. It was seven forty-five in the morning and they were seated on the porch of Marlin's house, enjoying a cool dawn. A team of deputies was at the widow's property—had been there since first light—looking for brass, boot prints, tire tracks, anything that might help track down the shooter. Marlin wasn't holding out much hope. The guy was too calm and collected to leave brass. The ground was too rough and rocky for prints. Tire tracks on pavement? Good luck.

"You said it was a diesel engine."

"No doubt about that. You know how distinctive they sound."

"So a truck, most likely."

"Probably several years old, because the newer diesels are quieter. The older ones you can hear coming from a mile away."

"Color?"

Marlin shook his head, but he knew it was necessary to run through all of this again. "Nothing's changed since last night. Still don't know."

"Dark? Light?"

"I'd be guessing. All I could really see is taillights."

"How about the voices?"

"Two of them, I think. Maybe three. All male."

"Deep? High?"

"Average."

"Could you make out any words?"

"Wouldn't swear on it, but it sounded like one guy said 'fucking idiot.'"

"That's new."

"I thought about it overnight, and I sort of replayed it in my head. It had that cadence. Two syllables, then three. Hard to explain, but I think that's what he said."

"Like maybe someone in the truck was telling the shooter he was a fucking idiot?"

"Could be. Or the shooter was saying that about me."

Bobby said, "Any chance there was a dog box in the bed of the truck?"

Marlin laughed. "That would narrow it down, huh? No, I couldn't see a dog box. Doesn't mean there wasn't one."

The door opened and Nicole stepped out onto the porch, dressed for work. Garza rose and gave her a quick hug. Then she held him at arm's length and said, "Bobby, will you do me a favor?"

"Catch the guy who shot at your husband?"

"Exactly. Then boil him in oil."

Garza grinned.

"We don't know that he shot *at* me," Marlin said. "In fact, I think he might've just been shooting *near* me. Playing head games." It was a theory that had crossed his mind in the middle of the night, when he couldn't sleep. After all, why had the man waved first? Why not just shoot? A 150-yard shot with a deer rifle wouldn't be difficult for an experienced shooter, especially if he rested the rifle in the crook of a tree.

"You don't know that for sure, and it doesn't matter anyway," Nicole said. "I don't care if he shot above you, below you, beside you, or around you, I still want him caught—and punished with extreme prejudice. Is flogging an option? Oh, the rack! We could build a rack!"

"Gotta catch the guy first," Marlin said.

"And it sounds like I'd better catch him before Nicole does," Garza added.

"Only if you want someone you can still question." She turned to Marlin, leaned down and gave him a kiss. "Gotta run. Call me later, okay? And *be careful.*"

After Nicole left, Marlin said, "Need anything else from me?" He didn't even ask if he could take part in the search for the shooter, because it wasn't an option. It wasn't easy for an officer who'd been shot at to remain objective. It would be too tempting to let emotions override protocol. So Marlin would step aside and let Garza and his deputies conduct the investigation.

"Just keep digging into the Sammy Beech case for me, if you can."

"Where does that stand?"

"Bill and Ernie interviewed a bunch of Sammy's friends yesterday and learned absolutely nothing. If Sammy had any enemies, or anybody even just a little bit angry at him, none of the kids knew about it. I'm starting to wonder if it was a road-rage incident. Maybe Sammy cut around somebody on his bike and they didn't like it."

"Boy, I hope not."

Neither man needed to state the obvious—that if Sammy had had a chance encounter with a dangerous stranger, the case would be much harder to solve.

Marlin said, "What about the shell casings?"

"Henry was only able to lift one usable print—from the nine millimeter—and it didn't get a hit. So nothing there. Meanwhile, I dug way back through Sammy's Facebook page, his email, his cell records, and there's nothing unexpected. Wait. There was one thing that raised my curiosity. Maybe. Don't know why. Sammy had all the usual teenager stuff on his cell phone. Hundreds of texts, songs, games, videos. A lot of pictures, too, mostly of his friends. But there was one photo that just seemed out of place. Maybe I'm wrong."

Garza removed his own phone from a holster on his belt. Turned it on and began thumbing through various menus.

He said, "Here, take a look."

He passed the phone to Marlin.

On the screen was a photo of a woman. An incredibly beautiful woman, with long, straight, black hair. Early or mid-twenties. And nude from the waist up. She was standing, in profile, wearing a snug skirt, and in the process of putting on or removing a bra. Red lace with black trim.

Vera Spillar, Colton's mother, worked as a cashier at the Wal-Mart in Marble Falls, about twenty minutes north of Johnson City. Dexter waited until her lane was empty of customers, then he approached with a single pack of Juicy Fruit gum. He chewed a lot of gum. It helped burn off some of the excess energy. In fact, his dentist had actually warned him to chew less gum, because he was wearing his molars prematurely. Dexter had tried going without gum for a few days, but he clenched his teeth all the time and ended up with a sore jaw.

"Is that gonna be it?" Vera Spillar asked with a fake smile.

She couldn't have been more than forty-five years old, but Jesus, what a hag. Gray hair that she'd apparently given up on. Very little make-up. Lifeless eyes. Wrinkles. Bags. Worry lines. A defeated slump to her posture. Perfect. Dexter was glad to see it all. This was a woman who needed something good to happen in her life. This was a woman who needed a bolt of wonderful out of the clear blue sky.

"Just the gum," Dexter said. He'd made Ryan wait in the car.

Vera Spillar rang it up and said, "Eighty-three cents." Still smiling. How did she manage that? If Dexter pushed cash register buttons for a living, he'd go home and swallow drain cleaner.

He smiled back and handed her ten one-hundred dollar bills.

Now she frowned. Total confusion. Didn't know what to make of the money in her hand.

He said, "Keep the change. But take a bathroom break and meet me out front in five minutes. There's plenty more where that came from."

There's plenty more where that came from. Wow. That might've been the corniest thing he'd ever said.

"Sir?" she said. Still not processing exactly what was happening.

"I'll explain out front. In five minutes. I have more money. For you."

She might've been stressed out and overworked, but she wasn't an idiot. She glanced around as she slipped the bills discreetly into the pocket of her jeans. Then she looked at Dexter. "Five minutes," she repeated.

CHAPTER 16

When the photo was taken, the woman hadn't quite gotten the bra over her breasts yet, so there was plenty to see. It was a snapshot, not a professional photograph. Totally candid, not posed, but surprisingly erotic. A pro might've taken a hundred shots and failed to get a photo as provocative.

Marlin got the sense that the woman hadn't known the photo was being taken. Sammy, or somebody, had snapped the photo quickly, sneakily, taking advantage of a split-second opportunity, while the woman was unaware. If Sammy had been able to shoot video while riding a motorcycle, sneaking a photo of this woman would've been a piece of cake.

The background of the photo was too dark and out of focus to learn anything about the location. Indoors, not outdoors—that was as much as you could ascertain.

"I assume you're studying that so closely purely for investigational purposes," Garza said.

Marlin pretended not to hear.

"Hey, John?"

"Oh, right." Marlin handed the phone back.

"She does have that effect, doesn't she?"

"No doubt. Any idea who she is?"

"Nope. And there weren't any other racy pics on the phone. No centerfolds, no bikini models, nothing."

"Did Sammy have a girlfriend?" Marlin asked.

"Yes, and this ain't her."

"Something he downloaded from the 'Net?"

"You'd think, but no. It was taken with the camera on his phone the day before he died. I'd say it's almost a given that Sammy took the picture himself, but the woman doesn't appear in any other photos, and nobody knows who she is. I didn't recognize her, and you didn't, and none of the deputies did, either. So I'm assuming she isn't from this area. I sorted through all Sammy's Facebook friends and didn't see her there. So, for now, she's a mystery woman. Next step is to show a copy—strategically cropped—to Grady and Leigh Anne. See if they know her. It's probably a dead end even if we can figure out who she is, but…"

"Gotta check it out," Marlin said.

"Right. Let's say Sammy *did* have something going with this woman, but she also has a boyfriend or husband…"

"And he finds out and gets pissed off, understandably."

"And so he decides to put a scare into Sammy by firing a few shots," Garza said. "Does it sound like I'm grasping at straws?"

"Not at all. Sounds like a pretty good theory. It even makes me wonder about Sammy's girlfriend. Wouldn't she have the same motive as this woman's husband or boyfriend?"

"Absolutely, but she was in Dallas with her family on the night Sammy died."

"Okay, then."

"Can you talk to Grady and Leigh Anne?" Garza asked.

"Sure. You'll need to email that picture to me."

"Don't let Nicole see it or you might be the one who'll wind up on the rack."

"You don't know me," Dexter said before Vera Spillar could even ask a question. "And I don't know you. Best if you just listen. Deal?"

She nodded, but now, outside, she wasn't looking quite as friendly. More like suspicious. They were tucked into an alcove near a stack of gaudy pink-and-purple kiddie pools. Too late in the season for those to sell, despite the greatly reduced price.

Dexter kept his voice low. "Your son made a verbal commitment to play football for the University of Middle Texas, but two days ago, he changed his mind. Now he says he's going to OTU."

"Well, I let him make his own decisions about football."

He noticed now that she had a thick hick accent. Sounded like a woman who should be washing sheets in a small-town motel. Or washing sheets in a hospital. Or a rest home. Washing sheets somewhere.

"Can't blame you," he said. "Best to let a young man like him steer his own ship. But there's also something to be said for keeping your word."

"'Scuse me?"

"I wish your son had kept his word."

"Mister, who the hell are you to judge my son about—"

"Ten thousand bucks. You get him to switch back to UMT—*and stick with it this time*—and I'll give you ten thousand bucks."

That shut her up. Momentarily. Looking at him now like he was crazy. "Bullshit," she said.

"No bullshit. Cash."

She looked left and right, wondering if this could be for real.

"Who are you?"

"Doesn't really matter, does it?"

"I guess not." Now she was studying him more closely.

"You on something?"

"Pardon?"

"You taking speed or something?"

"What? No. Why would you ask that?"

"Your eyes are all fucked up. Look at how you can't stand still."

Dexter did his best to stand still. It wasn't easy.

"I have an electrolyte imbalance. It screws up my metabolism. What about my offer?"

"Need to think about it."

"Sure. No problem. You have one minute. Then I go make the offer to another player. I *want* Colton, but I don't *need* him."

"When would I get the money?"

He raised a plastic bag in his hand. "Got it right here. You get half now, half when he switches back to UMT."

She started to speak again, but Crabtree cut her off.

"But you can't tell anyone. Ever. Not your son. Not your best friend. Not your sister. Not your mama. Not the guy you bang on Saturday night. You tell anyone and it could ruin your boy's eligibility. His career would be over before it even got started. On the other hand, if you keep it quiet—and you know damn well *I'm* gonna keep it quiet—nobody will ever know. How would they?"

She pretended to think about it, but Crabtree knew she was hooked. Ten grand in cash was hard for a world-weary Wal-Mart cashier to resist. Finally, she said, "Mister, you got a deal."

"One other condition," Crabtree said.

"What?"

"He's gotta make the announcement by noon tomorrow."

"Not a problem. He'll do it if I tell him to."

Crabtree opened the plastic bag and removed a stack of hundred-dollar bills. But rather than handing them over, he began methodically tearing each bill in half.

"What in the world are you doing?" Vera Spillar asked.

"Like I said. Half now, half later."

"So...what is this 'touchy subject' we need to talk about?" Sharon Greene asked.

For the past few hours, Armando had been rationalizing his behavior. Telling himself that he *did* have a delicate matter that he wanted to discuss with Sharon. It was true, wasn't it? Sort of? A little bit? So she had met him at the Pearl Tea Room in Johnson City, one of their regular haunts. Beautiful place with crisp tablecloths and hardwood floors. They were waiting on an order of scones, which were always delish.

"Okay. Brace yourself. Brad called a few days ago."

"No!"

"He did."

"That dog. What did he want?"

Armando always enjoyed his time with Sharon, and who would've guessed? On paper, as friends go, they should be a total mismatch. She was in her fifties and had been born and raised in Blanco County. Conservative roots. A church-goer. A ranch woman. Strong and opinionated. But equally warm and kind to everybody she met.

"He said he was just thinking about me and wondered how I was doing. Like he was just checking in, saying hi, but it was *so* transparent."

"And?"

"And then, right at the end of the call, he suggested we should get together for lunch. Or dinner."

Sharon unfolded her napkin and placed it in her lap. "Well..."

"Go ahead. Don't hold back."

"You already know what I think."

"Indeed I do. You've made it clear in colorful language many times. But I probably need to hear it again."

"If you do it, you'll regret it, and that's all I'm saying."

"I know. I know."

"Honey, you deserve so much better."

"That is so sweet. Thank you." He put one hand flat against his chest. "But I have weaknesses like everyone else."

"Send him to talk to me. I'll set that cheating bastard straight."

"No pun intended?"

Sharon let out a loud, deep laugh. "I always walk right into that one."

"Okay. I'm resolved. I will stay strong and not repeat the same old pattern."

"Attaboy."

"Thank you for listening," Armando said.

"Hey, who was it that listened when I caught Emmitt watching that smut on cable? Those girls couldn't have been twenty years old."

The waitress arrived with their scones and offered more tea. After she left, Armando said, "So…what's the story with this pig hunting thing? The bounty or whatever it is?" Trying to sound as casual as possible, and simultaneously wondering why he was even here, having this conversation. Why was he doing a favor for Red O'Brien? The man was an ignorant, backwoods bigot. Even Billy Don, with his somewhat narrow view of the world, was an enlightened, tolerant, open-minded sweetheart of a guy when you compared him to Red O'Brien.

So why was Armando doing this? He didn't know the answer to that question.

Sharon said, "Poor old Grady. He's still so brokenhearted about Sammy, although he tries not to show it. I guess he thinks this will make a difference somehow, but I suspect it won't. A bunch of wild pigs will die—and don't get me wrong, I don't have a problem with that—but it won't bring Sammy back. Grady has a strong will, and he's always been able to make things happen the way he wants them to happen. I think this is his way of exerting some sort of control over the situation. He's *doing* something about Sammy's death."

Armando nibbled on a scone and felt even worse about the situation. Grady Beech was dealing with his grief—this pig hunt was his way of working through it—and Armando was trying to help a cheater get the bounty. That was pretty low. Was that what Armando stood for? It certainly wasn't, so he decided that Mr. Red O'Brien could take a flying leap. Armando wouldn't help him at all. Okay, good. Now he was feeling better.

But...

Armando was still curious. After all, he had recognized a possible flaw in the contest. Had Grady and Emmitt realized that possibility themselves?

So Armando said, "You know, one thing occurred to me: What if the hunters start to suspect there isn't a bounty pig? What if they think Grady made it all up? Wouldn't some of them get pretty mad?"

Sharon chuckled. "Fortunately, that occurred to all of us before we turned the pig loose."

"*We?*"

"Yeah, I was there. I'm the one who darted the dadgum pig. I'm a better shot than Emmitt, especially now that his vision ain't so great. And Grady isn't much of a hunter himself anymore. Anyway, after we tranquilized it and marked its ear, Emmitt brought up the idea that someone might try to collect with a different pig. Of course, they'd have no way of knowing the number tattooed in its ear, so it'd be easy to spot any fakes. But that made us realize that we'd better have some proof of what our pig looked like, in case anyone did try to cheat. So we shot some video with my phone before we turned it loose. Here, take a look."

CHAPTER 17

As he had three days earlier, Marlin parked in front of the vineyard's visitors center and tasting pavilion. He saw Grady's truck, Leigh Anne's BMW, and a Chrysler Sebring convertible that screamed rental.

Just as Marlin reached the front door, it opened and a middle-aged couple emerged. Tourists. The man was carrying a case of bottled wine. They smiled and said hello and headed toward the Sebring.

Inside, Grady was behind the bar again, and Leigh Anne was seated at an out-of-the-way table, attention focused downward at the cell phone in her hand. Grady came around and shook Marlin's hand, and then Leigh Anne rose to give him a quick hug. Both of them seemed more subdued than they had on Saturday. Understandable, considering what they had recently learned about Sammy's death. For Grady, that had to be like a blow to the gut, just when he was catching his breath again.

They all sat at the table Leigh Anne had been occupying and Marlin said, "Thanks for meeting with me. This won't take long."

"Take as long as you need," Grady said. "Ask us anything."

"Absolutely," Leigh Anne said. "We want to help however we can." She was dressed more conservatively today. Khaki shorts and a mint-green button-down shirt with a white camisole underneath.

"Really just one thing I need to ask right now." He had

brought a manila folder with him, and now he removed the photograph inside and placed it on the table. The topless woman from the photo on Sammy's phone—just her face. "Do either of you recognize her?"

Both Sammy and Leigh Anne leaned forward for a better look. Several seconds passed.

"She's very beautiful," Leigh Anne said. "But I don't think I've ever seen her before. Who is she?"

Marlin didn't answer, but instead waited for a response from Grady, who reached out and picked the photo up. "I...maybe. She looks kind of familiar. But I can't place her."

"I'd kill for those cheekbones," Leigh Anne said. "She looks like a fashion model."

Marlin said, "We found this picture on Sammy's phone. Actually, there was more to the picture than this. I cropped it. Truth is, she was topless."

Grady looked up from the photo. "Maybe Sammy downloaded it off the Internet."

"No, it was taken with his phone."

"How do you know?"

"With a digital camera, every time you take a photo, it creates a little information record of that photo—what kind of device took the photo, the focal length, exposure, that sort of thing. It also records the date and time. Very convenient."

"I didn't know that. Were there other photos?"

"Not of that woman."

"Any other women?"

"None that we couldn't identify."

"But any other topless shots?"

"No."

"When was it taken?"

"The day before Sammy died."

Grady nodded and looked at the photo again. "This girl—this woman—looks a few years older than Sammy. She doesn't look like a high-school girl. Maybe college."

"I'd say she's mid-twenties at most," Leigh Anne said. "Definitely not any older than that."

Grady continued looking at the picture. "You know, I can't be sure, but I feel like I *have* seen her before. Somewhere. But I just don't know."

The door to the pavilion opened and four people came in. Two couples. More middle-aged tourists. Almost interchangeable with the couple who had just left.

"We'll be right with you folks," Grady called out.

One of the men waved an acknowledgment and the foursome gravitated toward the bar to wait.

Grady continued to stare intently at the photo, so Marlin remained quiet, letting the man think. But after a moment, Grady shook his head in frustration. "Maybe I'm wrong."

Marlin said, "The important thing is, now we know she isn't some regular friend of Sammy's or anything like that."

"No, she isn't," Grady said.

"I need to ask a fairly personal question," Marlin said.

"Ask anything."

"As far as you know, was Sammy sleeping around with a lot of girls?"

"You're thinking a one-night stand, huh? Maybe he got lucky with an older woman and wanted to have a little something to remember it by?"

"Well..."

"Sammy was a popular, good-looking kid. He had a lot of girls after him, but he had been seeing Tracie for four or five months. I don't know if he was exclusive with her or not. But I can tell you he wasn't a love-'em-and-leave-'em type—as far as I know, anyway. Kids surprise you sometimes."

"I'll be right back," Leigh Anne said, and rose from the table.

Grady had a pained grin on his face. "I second-guess myself a lot these days. It's somewhat of a hobby—to beat myself up and think about how I could've done things differently. Like with the drugs. Some people would say I was too lenient with Sammy, and I wasn't hands-on enough. Maybe that's true. I knew he had experimented with drugs on occasion—pot, mostly. If I'd had to guess whether he'd tried some harder stuff, yeah, I guess I would've said yes. Then I learned from the autopsy that he had. The Ecstasy. And he'd definitely been abusing booze. Not just that night, but in general. Sorry, my mind is rambling."

"That's okay."

"Obviously there was a part of Sammy's life that he kept hidden from me."

"That's true of almost all teenagers."

"I don't know where he got the drugs. Was there a whole other group he ran with? Maybe this woman was from that part of his life."

Marlin knew Garza and the deputies had looked hard into the drug angle. They'd come to the conclusion that Sammy, like a lot of teenagers, had done some experimenting, but it wasn't a major part of his life. He had probably gotten the Ecstasy from a classmate.

Marlin said, "Your son was a good kid, Grady. We saw no indication that he was into anything more than what we already know."

"Where did he get the money for the motorcycle? That bothers me."

"Isn't it possible he saved up for it?"

Grady didn't have an answer.

"Your son was a pretty average teenager," Marlin said. "Maybe he wasn't perfect, but none of us were at that age. Or any age. You shouldn't beat yourself up too much."

"I appreciate that."

Marlin glanced past Grady's shoulder and watched Leigh Anne at the bar, chatting with the two couples, and pouring samples of a white wine into glasses.

"Do me a favor, Grady. Keep that copy of the photo, but don't even think about it for a couple of hours, or until tomorrow. Then look at it again, with a fresh set of eyes. Maybe that'll help you remember if you've really seen her."

Just before two in the afternoon, after turning off A. Robinson Road and heading north on Highway 281, Bobby Garza spotted a blue diesel-powered dual-cab GMC truck in the parking lot of the Kountry Kitchen. It wasn't the only diesel truck he'd seen that day, but it was the first one with dog boxes mounted in the bed.

Earlier that morning, in Garza's office, Marlin hadn't seemed willing to conclude that it was a very good possibility that dog runners had been involved in the shooting yesterday evening. But Garza figured they deserved to be checked out just as closely as anyone else. Maybe closer.

He pulled into the parking lot and cruised slowly past the truck. Nobody in the cab. First thing he noticed was a faded bumper sticker that read: WHERE IS THE BIRTH CERTIFICATE? Another one said: GOT AMMO?

Garza stopped for a moment and jotted the license plate number down. Then he continued north into the lot next door, which served a liquor store and a dry cleaners. He whipped his cruiser around and parked parallel to the highway, facing south, giving him a clear view of the big truck.

He grabbed his microphone handset. "One oh one to Blanco County."

"Go ahead, one oh one." It was Darrell, the county dispatcher, replying.

"Need a ten twenty-eight and twenty-nine when you're ready."

"Ten four."

Garza recited the license plate number.

"Received, one oh one. Stand by."

While Garza was waiting, two men exited the Kountry Kitchen and walked in the direction of the truck. Dog runners for sure, from the black felt hats with a feather in the band, down to the scuffed Justin Ropers. They were both about six feet tall. Maybe thirty years old. Similar build. One had a goatee, one was clean-shaven.

"One oh one, that comes back to a GMC quad-cab truck. Registered owner is Dustin Bryant out of Jasper. Insurance is confirmed. Negative twenty-nine."

No wants or warrants.

"Ten four."

The men reached the truck, but instead of getting in, they stopped by the tailgate. One of them took out his cell phone and appeared to be checking messages, while the other one slipped a can of snuff from his back pocket and stuck a dip into his mouth.

Garza waited. Watched. A steady stream of traffic moved past the cruiser. A group of four elderly people exited the restaurant and got into a Buick.

The guy with the Copenhagen glanced northward and spotted Garza's cruiser. Now he was staring. No matter. Garza hadn't been trying to hide. The snuff user said something, and now the guy fiddling with his phone looked in the direction of the cruiser.

Garza could see a physical change in the demeanor of both men. Most people who suddenly realize they are being watched by a cop show it in their body language. Typically they become self-conscious. Or they go the other way, like these two men. They become cocky. A rookie might not be able to spot the difference, but Garza could, after all these years on the job. Even the way the men were standing by the truck now had a swagger to it. Arrogance. Similar to the way a drugstore cowboy leans backward against the bar on a Saturday night, scoping the place out, letting the ladies know he's the coolest guy in the room. Other signs weren't so subtle, like the man with the dip leaning forward slightly and spitting on the ground, all the while keeping his eye on the cruiser. Pure attitude. Letting Garza know what he thought of him.

Garza had become immune to that sort of provocation. These guys were just punks. Dime a dozen. *Spit all you want, dude.* It was almost comical that they thought Garza cared how they behaved. So predictable. And then the guy with the phone looked to his right, at someone else leaving the restaurant.

A very tall man. Probably six-five or more. Not slender. Not fat. With red hair. Or that's what most people would call it—"red." But like a lot of redheads, this man's hair color was actually closer to orange.

When the tall guy reached the other two men, they exchanged a few words and—just as Garza knew he would—the redhead turned and looked toward the cruiser. He smiled.

Then he gave Garza a big, slow, exaggerated wave.

CHAPTER 18

As far as Red O'Brien could remember, not once in his life had he ever been inside a flower shop. The few times he'd bought flowers for a woman, he'd ordered them by phone, like a normal American male. Or he'd grabbed a discount bouquet at the grocery store on the way back from the beer aisle. Nothing unmanly about that. He always figured the women in your check-out line thought you were being romantic, and the guys all knew you were just trying to get lucky that night.

But now here he was, inside a flower shop for the first time, and the first thing he noticed, being honest, was that it smelled pretty good. Like a bunch of flowers. Duh. And they also had some kind of music playing in the background. Not country or rock or pop. He didn't know how to classify it. Just soft, quiet music, with a woman singing, although he couldn't make out any of the lyrics. Or maybe she was just making sounds instead of words.

"I don't see Armando," Billy Don said.

"Me, neither, and this place ain't that big. You sure this is the right one?" Then he thought of a joke. "Oh, I bet I know where he is."

"Where?"

Red waited a beat, then said, "In the closet."

Either Billy Don didn't get it, or he didn't think it was funny, and maybe it wasn't, because Armando wasn't in the closet at all, was he? Or maybe Billy Don was distracted, because an old lady had just come out of a back room and she was headed their way.

"Good morning!" she said in a very sing-songy fashion. "How are you two today?" She glanced at her watch. "You're a little early, but if you'll give me just a few more minutes, I'll have your arrangement ready in a jiffy."

"Our what?" Billy Don asked.

"Your calla lilies?" the old woman said. She waited a second or two. "Well. Judging from your reaction, may I assume you aren't Matt and David?"

"We're Billy Don and Red."

"Okay. Then I'm guessing you aren't here to place an order for your commitment ceremony."

Red realized, with a sinking feeling, what had just happened. The other day, Armando had been joking when he acted like Red and Billy Don were a couple. But this woman had been thinking that for real, and Red was quickly beginning to regret coming in here. Sure, he wanted to know what Armando had learned from Sharon Greene, and since Armando hadn't returned their calls, they'd decided to make the drive to Marble Falls to see him in person. But there was only so much humiliation Red was willing to endure for a shot at a $50,000 pig.

"No, ma'am," Red said. "And no offense, but I think you need to get your eyes checked."

She blinked at him a couple of times. Then she grinned. "You may be right, young man. Judging by Matt's voice on the phone, I suspect that he and David aren't quite as stylish and well-groomed as you two fellows. Of course, I could be wrong, because the world is made up of all types of people who don't meet our preconceived notions."

Red didn't know if she was kidding or not, or even what she meant by that last part.

"Actually we're looking for Armando," Billy Don said. "We need to talk to him about something for just a minute.

Is he around?"

"He's in the back. I'll let him know you're here."

Marlin's first inclination was to speak to a couple of Sammy's friends. Ask them if they recognized the woman in the photo. Yes, some of the kids had already been interviewed by the deputies, but they hadn't seen this photo yet. Then he thought, *If I were a buddy of Sammy's, and Sammy had managed to get together with a beautiful older woman, would I tell an adult?* Probably not. Even under these circumstances.

But what if there was an adult who might've been privy to some details of Sammy's private life? It made sense to ask the adult first, then talk to the kids.

Marlin drove out to the high school and found Coach Milstead in his office, with some time to spare before football practice began after school.

"Have y'all made any progress?" Milstead asked, after shaking hands with Marlin and sitting back down behind his desk.

Marlin sat in one of two armless chairs facing Milstead. "Sometimes it's hard to tell. I think so. But I'm hoping you can help me out with something."

"Whatever I can do."

Marlin opened the manila folder and placed the photo on the desk, facing Milstead. "Do you recognize this woman?"

Milstead picked the photo up and studied it. Then he furrowed his brow. "Hmm. I think…"

Marlin waited.

Milstead said, "She *does* look familiar, but I'm not sure from where. Like I saw her out in public. Or…is she a celebrity of some kind?"

"I don't think so."

"I'm almost positive I've seen her. How old is she?"

"The general consensus is that she's in her early or mid-twenties, but that's a guess."

"Huh. She looks younger than that to me. I was starting to wonder if she was a student, but I guess not."

"She could be a former student."

"Yeah, but I probably wouldn't know her, depending on when she was here. I've only been here four years."

"Can you remember where you might have seen her?"

Milstead kept staring at the photo, obviously racking his memory. He was starting to shake his head when suddenly he said, "Oh! I got it. I was getting gas at the Super S and she was filling up her car on the other side of the pump. I'm pretty sure this is the same woman."

"When was this?"

"Quite awhile. Several weeks. Maybe more than a month."

"That long ago, but you remember her?"

"Well, not to sound like a dirty old man, but when you see a woman who looks like that in Johnson City, you tend to notice her. I mean, we have our fair share of attractive women, but this one was all dressed up and made up like a model. She just really stood out."

"And that's the woman in the photo?"

"I think so, yeah. Not positive, but pretty sure. Can I ask what this has to do with Sammy's death?"

Marlin was tempted to say, "Probably nothing," but that wasn't the way to keep a cooperative witness engaged. So he said, "That photo was on his phone. We'd just like to know who she is."

"You should show this picture to some of his friends."

"That was going to be my next request. If you don't mind."

"Not at all. I know the boys would love to help, if they can."

"Yes, I talked to her," Armando said. "This morning, before work. Sorry I didn't call you back. It's been crazy around here."

"And?" Red said. "What'd she say?"

They were behind the flower shop, in a small parking area, standing beside Armando's Prius. Armando was smoking a cigarette. Something called a "clove," which had an unusual smell to it. He was being careful to stand upwind of the cigarette, so the smell wouldn't get all over him.

"Sorry, guys, but Sharon didn't know anything. She wasn't involved in any of it."

"Damn," Billy Don said. "That sucks."

Red's heart dropped—but only for a moment. Because something wasn't right. Something about Armando's behavior. The way he wasn't making eye contact. The way he was being quieter than he had been the other times Red had been around him.

"Wait a sec. Sharon didn't help Emmitt round up the pig?" Red asked.

"Unfortunately, no," Armando said. "So she wasn't able to tell me anything."

"Huh. That seems weird, because from what I've heard, she's a hell of a shot. And a hell of a hunter."

"She said Emmitt tranquilized the pig."

"Really? Last I knew, he had all but given up shooting, because he could hardly see a damn thing. Even if the pig was in a trap, Emmitt would have to be able to see through a sight."

Armando shrugged and sucked on his cigarette. Still not

making eye contact. To Red, the signs were unmistakable.

"That really seems weird," Red said.

"Sorry, guys. Anyway, I need to get back to work."

"You know what I think, Armando?" Red said.

"I can only imagine."

"I think you're lying."

"Red!" Billy Don said. "What the hell's wrong with you? You don't just call a guy a liar like that. 'Specially when he was trying to do you a favor."

But Red wasn't listening. Instead, he was watching Armando's reaction closely. And all Armando did was give Red a weak roll of his eyes. That wasn't right, either. Armando was a big drama queen—no pun intended—so if he was actually telling the truth, his reaction would've been much different. He would've been more insulted.

"I guess I don't blame him, really," Red said. "See, I pissed him off yesterday when I called him on his bullshit, so now he's getting me back. Withholding information. Or maybe he's planning to sell that information to some of the other hunters."

Armando was glaring at him. "You are a horrible little person."

"Oh, did I touch a nerve?"

Billy Don said, "You're not lying, are you, Armando? Tell him to shut the hell up."

Armando said, "Grady Beech is in mourning. Do you understand that, Red? Can you wrap your mind around that fact? It's only been two months since he lost his son. This pig hunt is one way Grady is coping with his grief. I refuse to help anyone cheat."

"Aha!" Red said. "So you do know! Sharon told you."

"And what kind of person would I be if I violated my friend's trust?"

"You mean like you violated ours just now by saying

Sharon didn't know anything?"

"Armando?" Billy Don said.

Armando looked at him. "I am so sorry. I started out with good intentions, but as I was sitting there with Sharon, acting out this farce—being totally dishonest with her—I realized I just couldn't do it. That's not the type of person I am. I apologize for getting your hopes up."

He turned to Red. "And *you*. You are one of the most disagreeable and repugnant people I have ever encountered. As Oscar Wilde once said, 'Some cause happiness wherever they go; others, whenever they go.' I think he must've been foreseeing your very existence when he said that."

"I don't even know who that is. You might as well be talking about Oscar Mayer."

"You, my friend, are a rube. Look that word up when you have a moment, if you own a dictionary."

"Well, you know what you are?" Red asked.

"The anticipation of hearing your pronouncement is almost more than I can stand."

"You...are a bigot." Red said.

"Ha! Oh, my God! *I'm* a bigot? You're saying *I'm* a bigot."

"Exactly."

"Pot, meet kettle."

"What are you babbling about?" Red asked.

"That is laughable, and hypocritical, to boot. I can only assume you don't even know what the word 'bigot' actually means."

"Oh, I know exactly what it means. And right now, right here, I'm looking at a blue-ribbon bigot. You are a bigot against people like me."

Armando said, "My gosh, I didn't realize just how utterly un-self-aware you are until now. The irony is killing me."

"See? Right there. You're a bigot. You think you know

everything, and a small-town guy like me—I'm just an idiot. You think I don't even know what 'bigot' means. I drive a truck and like country music, so I'm a 'rube,' right? You said so yourself. And it's obvious you hate guys like me so much, you're looking for a reason not to tell me what that pig looks like."

"That is so not true. *You're* the one who's a bigot!"

"Yeah, that's original. 'I know you are, but what am I?' Now you're really sounding desperate."

"This is ridiculous! I am living in the Twilight Zone!" Armando screamed.

"That's what a bigot would say."

"I am not a bigot! People like me are the victims of bigotry almost every day from people just like you—and believe me when I tell you, I am not a bigot!"

"Prove it."

"I don't have to!"

"What's the pig look like?"

"Forget it!"

"Bigot."

"Stop saying that!"

"But it's true."

"No, it's not!"

"Bigot."

"Aaaahh! It's brown and white, okay? It's a small brown-and-white pig! Are you happy?"

Armando tossed his cigarette butt to the ground and hurried toward the back door of the flower shop. Red thought Armando might've even been crying.

"Jesus, Red," Billy Don said. "That was just mean."

"Boar or sow?" Red called out, but Armando was already through the door, which slammed behind him.

CHAPTER 19

It was tempting to confront the tall redheaded man immediately, but Bobby Garza resisted, and simply watched as the three dog runners climbed into the big diesel truck and went south on Highway 281. Garza followed at a distance.

After less than a quarter-mile, the truck took a left into the lot for the Hill Country Inn. Garza went past, then turned left and parked in the lot for Ronnie's Pit BBQ. If the diesel truck left the inn, he'd see it.

He scrolled through the contacts in his cell phone until he found the name he was looking for—Jerry Sharp, the sheriff of Jasper County for several decades.

"Bobby Garza! How the hell are ya?"

"Doing real good, Jerry, and you?"

"Quiet around here lately, and I think I have you to thank. I heard about the pig scramble going on in your neck of the woods. Anyone get the right pig yet?"

"Not so far."

"Boy, if I had an extra fifty grand, I believe I could go ahead and retire, and damn, wouldn't that be nice."

Garza smiled. "Come on over and give it a shot."

"Hell, I'm too old for that. Must be a madhouse over there."

"Believe it or not, things haven't been as crazy as you'd think. We figure most of these guys want the reward so bad, they don't want to blow their chances by getting busted. So they're staying out of trouble, for the most part. Plus, there's no need to trespass, because the locals recognize a gold mine when they see it."

"Meaning there's some high-dollar day leasing going on?"

"Exactly. Some of these ranches haven't been hunted in years, but now they're open for business."

"Well, something must've happened over there, or you wouldn't be calling me."

"Yeah, there's something I'm hoping you can help me with." Garza went on to describe Marlin's run-in with the man across the ravine on the widow's property.

"Your warden okay?" Sharp asked.

"He's fine. Thinks maybe the guy was playing mind games."

"Did he get a good look at the shooter?"

"Not so great, because the sun was in his eyes. But he knows the man was very tall. Six-four, six-five. Wearing an orange cap."

"Blaze orange?"

"Darker. More like burnt orange."

There was a slight pause. Then Sharp said, "Any chance the guy actually had orangish hair?"

Garza grinned. "I was hoping you'd ask that, but I didn't want to lead you. You know someone who meets that description?"

"Oh, you bet I do. Gilbert Weems. One of my best customers. And I'm telling you right now to be careful with that one."

"How so?"

"The man is about a full-on sociopath, if you want my opinion. Violent as hell. Gets in bar fights about once a month, usually beating up some poor son of a bitch pretty bad. His girlfriend filed a protective order against him last year for breaking her nose, but she dropped it later. He's a cruel dude, and he gets off on being a bad boy. This whole deal—taunting your warden, and sending a couple shots in his direction—that sounds exactly like something Weems would do. Just a matter of time before he kills someone."

"Sounds lovely. Who does he hang with?"

"That's easy. He ain't got but two friends—Dustin and Dylan Bryant. Twin brothers. They're no angels, but they ain't nearly as bad as Weems. Weems is always the instigator."

"How are these Bryant brothers on loyalty?"

"Meaning would they flip on Weems? Hell, yeah, if they were facing serious charges. In a heartbeat."

Roy Ballard, the legal videographer, considered it a bonus when the subject of his surveillance was a gorgeous woman. Was that sexist? Maybe. He could live with that. After all, if you were going to spend a lot of hours—if not days or even weeks—watching someone, it was undeniably a more enjoyable experience if the subject was female and easy on the eyes, like Leigh Anne Beech.

Right now, Roy was watching Leigh Anne's tail end— well, her BMW's tail end—as it cruised east on Highway 290 toward Austin. Ballard was about two hundred yards back. Barely a dot in her rearview mirror. A discreet distance. Didn't matter if he lost her temporarily, because the GPS tracking device he'd installed on the BMW would lead him straight to her via real-time maps on Roy's laptop or cell phone. It would also provide details if she went anywhere when Roy wasn't following her. Helpful, because he couldn't follow her 24 hours a day. Had to sleep sometime. And Grady Beech had agreed to alert Roy when he knew in advance that Leigh Anne was planning to leave the house.

"It's not about Sammy," Grady Beech had said the previous morning. "It's about Leigh Anne. My wife."

It was easy to predict what was coming after that, but Roy had asked anyway. "What's up with your wife?"

Beech didn't just spit it out right away. He had to work up to it. Hem and haw. Beat around the bush. Roy could understand that. He figured he'd do the same thing if he was in Beech's position. Hard to say something like that out loud to another man. What Beech eventually said was, "Well, I could be wrong about this. I probably am, and this will give me some peace of mind. Maybe I'm crazy or imagining things, or maybe there's an innocent explanation..."

"But..."

"Some things have happened in the past year or so that make me think Leigh Anne might be having an affair."

"What kind of things?"

"She's always been a big shopper, but now she's going several times a week. Always going to Austin or San Antone. I know she does actually go shopping sometimes, because she comes home with bags of stuff. Other times, nothing. She says she was just looking."

"Well, you know, women do that. They can shop for ten hours and come home with one item that cost three dollars."

"Oh, I know. And that's what I've been telling myself."

"Maybe she's just bored."

"Could be. I hope so. She doesn't answer the phone much when she's shopping, and that makes me wonder, too. What's she doing that she can't answer the phone? Speaking of her phone—that's something else that bothers me. She's always texting. Way more than she used to. And one time—well, I'm not proud of this, but she was in the shower, so I snooped around on her phone. Learned that she doesn't save any of her texts. Deletes them all."

Roy didn't say anything. It did sound a little fishy.

"And the last thing," Beech said, "is that she isn't much interested in sex lately. At least not with me." He gave a pained grin. "How's that for laying it all on the table?"

Roy said, "I don't want to pry, but—"

"Pry all you need to."

"Was she more interested in sex in the past?"

"Oh, yeah. Not like oversexed or anything, but she was interested. She's not inhibited. She always had what I'd call a healthy appetite."

"How long ago did her interest drop?"

Beech sort of shrugged. "It just slowly went away. Nothing abrupt."

"Has she had any affairs before that you know about?"

Beech looked away for a minute, then simply shook his head. "None that I know of, and none that I suspected."

So Roy had agreed to help Beech out. Roy's partner was working on a case of her own—a case that required only one person—so Roy's schedule was open. Roy had never conducted surveillance on a spouse suspected of cheating, but now, as he followed Leigh Anne Beech, he found himself hoping it was a misunderstanding on Grady's part.

When Leigh Anne Beech reached the west side of Austin, she went north on Loop 1. Way north. Past Research Boulevard, past Braker Lane, to an upscale shopping center called The Domain. She went inside Neiman Marcus and met someone—another attractive woman about the same age—and the two of them proceeded to shop for the next three hours. After that, she got back into her BMW and drove home.

The first player Marlin spoke to was named Eric. A junior. Second-string halfback. After asking a few questions—friendly, casual, putting the boy at ease—Marlin took out the cropped photo.

"I'm just wondering if you've ever seen this woman."

Eric leaned forward and looked at the picture. "Don't think so."

They were in Coach Milstead's office, with the door open. The coach had already begun practice, but had offered to send several of the players in for short interviews. These were some of the boys Milstead had mentioned on Sunday—Sammy's closest friends.

"She doesn't look familiar at all?" Marlin said.

"No. Is she supposed to?"

The boy was trying to be helpful. *Wanting* to offer something useful. Marlin hadn't told Eric where the photo had been found, and he wasn't planning to. At least, not yet. He also wasn't going to ask if Sammy was the type to have cheated on his girlfriend, Tracie. Better to see if one of Sammy's friends might offer that sort of information on his own. Marlin and Garza had no solid reason to conclude that Sammy had any kind of romantic or sexual relationship with the woman in the photo, so Marlin wasn't willing to ask questions that would start rumors spreading among the student body.

The next player was the placekicker. Name was Garrett. Marlin remembered him from the youth hunt on Phil Colby's ranch a few years back. Good kid. Bright. Treated adults with respect. The first to volunteer for various chores and tasks during the hunt. Garrett looked at the photo and shook his head. "Don't know her."

"Well, thanks for taking a look."

"That's all you needed?"

"For now."

"May I ask a question?"

"Sure."

"Coach told us someone was chasing Sammy that night. Firing a gun at him. Does this woman have something to do with that?"

Marlin took a moment to formulate a reply. "We have no reason to think that. It's just that we don't know who she is, and we'd like to find out."

"But where did the picture come from?"

"What I can tell you right now is that we think Sammy might've known her. We just need to identify her and ask her a few questions. Did you ever hear Sammy talking about any friends you didn't know yourself?"

"No, but Sammy and I hadn't been hanging out as much as we used to."

"Why's that?"

"Like I told the deputy yesterday—Sammy was partying too much. Not studying. He had all those scholarship offers and he didn't even know how lucky he was. If I'd had half the talent he had, man, I would've been focused. I don't mean to sound cold, talking about him like that."

"No, I appreciate you being straight with me. Would you say his partying was out of control? You probably heard he had Ecstasy in his system."

"I don't think that was a regular thing. Mostly he just drank. And, no, I wouldn't say he was out of control. I meant it more like he had this incredible opportunity that most kids don't get, you know? Why risk screwing it up?"

A few more players echoed that same thought; Sammy took his skills, and his future, for granted, and they were all a little worried that he wasn't committed enough to make it in college ball.

But nobody could identify the woman in the photo.

The last player Marlin talked to was an offensive tackle named Colton Spillar. The kid was huge—probably close to three hundred pounds, most of it muscle. In Marlin's high school days, his largest teammate had weighed about fifty pounds less than that.

By now, practice had been going on for close to an hour, so Colton was sweaty and very red in the face. When Marlin put the photo down on the desk, Colton's eyes got noticeably wider.

"You know her?" Marlin said.

"Uh-uh."

"Oh. I thought I saw a reaction."

Colton didn't say anything.

"You looked surprised or something," Marlin said. "Right when you looked at the photo."

"No, she's just kind of hot."

"That's why you reacted?"

"Yeah. And I'm tired from practice."

"You need some water or something?"

"No, I'm okay. Just need to catch my breath."

"So you don't know who this woman is?"

"No."

"Were you and Sammy good friends?"

"We hung out sometimes. We're, you know, teammates. *Were*, I mean. I wasn't his best friend or anything."

Colton seemed ill at ease—not making eye contact—but some teenagers behaved that way around adults.

"Who did Sammy hang out with the most?"

"Eric and Garrett. The other guys you already talked to."

Marlin slowly reached out and picked up the photo, wanting to see if Colton would steal another look at it. He didn't. Marlin slipped the photo back into the manila folder.

He said, "You know anyone who might've been mad at Sammy?"

"No, sir. Did that woman have something to do with Sammy dying?"

"We don't have any reason to think that. But Sammy

might've known her, and we'd like to ask her a few questions. That's all. So if anyone on the team knows who she is, that would be really helpful."

The flush in Colton's face still hadn't gone away. "Wish I could help," he said.

Marlin paused for a moment. Just let the silence settle in the room, to see how Colton would react. Would he get fidgety? Ask if they were done?

Colton said, "Sammy was a great player. We're missing him this year."

"From what I hear, you're a pretty good player yourself. Going to UMT on a scholarship."

"Actually, I switched to Oklahoma Tech."

"Oh, yeah? Didn't Sammy do the same thing?"

"Yeah."

"What made you change your mind?"

"OTU just seems like a better fit for me."

CHAPTER 20

Two solid-black pigs and one solid-white pig. That's what Red had seen so far. He and Billy Don were once again sitting in the 12-foot tower blind on the Kringelheimer Ranch. Red wasn't sure if Billy Don had seen those pigs, too, because the big man was being awfully quiet. Pouting. Or angry. Or something. Red didn't understand what the problem was. He knew that Billy Don had his panties in a bunch over the way Red had treated Armando at the flower shop. Weird. And it was getting tiresome.

They should both be thrilled that they knew something all of the other pig hunters didn't, because it gave them an edge. Most feral pigs were one color—black, white, or brown. Others were a combination—mostly black and white. Armando had said the pig was brown and white, which wasn't rare or anything, but in Red's experience, that was the least common combination. Very helpful to know that, and Red was glad he'd managed to get the information out of Armando. Billy Don should be glad, too.

Red retrieved a bulging plastic sack from the floor at his feet and began to root around in it.

"Pork rinds?" he asked.

Billy Don shook his head.

"Corn Nuts?"

"Nope."

"Slim Jim?"

"Uh-uh."

"Moon Pie?"

"Don't want nothin'."

Red dug even deeper.

"Teriyaki jerky?"

Billy Don didn't react at all.

"Peanut butter crackers?"

Still no response. Red put the sack back on the floor.

"So what's the deal?" he asked.

"Ain't no deal," Billy Don said.

"Something's going on. You're acting like a woman. Giving me the silent treatment."

Billy Don turned his head slowly and glared at Red. "Want me to toss you headfirst outta this blind?"

"Hell, no, but how about, instead, you quit moping around? That, or come right out and say what's on your mind."

"No problem. What's on my mind is that you treated Armando like shit earlier. You were a real asshole."

"Well, I'm not saying that's true, but even if it is—so what?"

"So what?"

"Yep. So what? Why do you care how I treat Armando?"

Billy Don was shaking his head. "Let me ask you something. Say some dude in a bar punched you in the face and you didn't deserve it. If I'm standing right there, would you want me to do anything about it?"

"I'd want you to do something even if I *did* deserve it."

"Zackly. And I would. That's what friends do."

"Wait a sec." Red had to take a breath. "You're saying you and Armando are *friends*?"

"Yeah. What of it? Why do you care if I'm friends with Armando?"

"I really gotta spell it out?" Red asked.

"Appears you do."

Red opened his mouth to reply, but he happened to

glance out the window of the blind, and there stood a small brown-and-white pig. Staring in this direction, because he and Billy Don had been talking more loudly than they should have been.

"Red, why are—"

"Shhh! Don't move."

The pig was still standing there, no more than fifty yards away. Red knew that pigs had poor eyesight, but he would swear that the pig was looking directly at him.

Red reached for his .30-30, which was leaning in the corner of the blind. He brought the rifle up slowly. Very slowly. Being oh so careful not to bang the muzzle on the metal roof.

The pig started to walk away to the left, while still keeping an eye on the blind.

By now, Billy Don had turned his head to see what Red had seen. Now he said, "He's heading for them cedars."

Red stuck the barrel out the window, then lowered it to rest on the window frame.

"Hurry up, Red."

He nestled his cheek against the stock, peered through the scope, and quickly found the little pig in the field of view. This would be an easy shot. Piece of cake. Like hundreds of other shots he'd made successfully over the years. Red put the crosshairs on the pig's shoulder, pulled the hammer back, took a breath, held it, and slowly squeezed the trigger.

There was a loud and very recognizable click.

Crap!

He'd forgotten to jack a round into the chamber when he'd first sat down. This business with Armando and Billy Don had distracted him too much.

Red quickly cranked the lever down and back up, loading a round into the chamber, but the noise it produced was just enough to send the pig into a trot. It reached the grove of cedars before Red could get off a shot.

Armando was working on a large arrangement—four dozen long-stemmed red roses, mixed with baby's breath and greenery—but his heart wasn't in it, because he was feeling so guilty. He'd betrayed Sharon's trust, all because he'd let that ignorant, repugnant, empty-headed, bigoted, insensitive hayseed browbeat him into spilling the beans. If only he had—

"Armando?" It was Grace, the owner of the shop, suddenly at his elbow. He'd been too preoccupied to even notice she'd come into the back room.

"Yes?"

"That's lovely."

"Thank you."

"But...which customer is it for?"

"Uh, the anniversary party this evening."

"Honey, those are supposed to be *yellow* roses."

"Oh, lord. I'm so sorry."

"Don't be silly. We have plenty of time to get another arrangement ready."

It was only a small mistake, but Armando had always prided himself on his meticulous attention to details. He had to clear his head and get his concentration back. Now it was obvious what he had to do. Confess to Sharon. Admit what he'd done. Then, in the future, avoid Red O'Brien at all costs.

Dexter Crabtree was in the process of stuffing Adderall— in the privacy of a filthy gas station bathroom stall, slacks hanging from a hook on the door—and he couldn't help gloating a bit. Clever what he'd done—the way he'd outfoxed Vera Spillar.

Giving her half of each hundred-dollar bill was absolutely brilliant. Just like Crabtree had said, she'd gotten half up front. Of course, that half was worthless without the other half. So she'd have to follow through with her side of the deal—or get nothing. Crabtree had seen that little trick in various movies over the years and had always wanted to use it himself. The only risk was that his half of the money would also be worthless if Vera Spillar didn't come through, or if Colton refused to do what she asked him to do. Fine. Crabtree could afford the gamble.

As soon as Colton Spillar announced that he was renewing his verbal commitment to the University of Middle Texas, that would be that. There would be no more opportunities for him to change his mind. He'd reached his limit—and there most certainly was one. Unspoken, but it was there. Most college coaches could understand how Colton might be lured away from his original commitment by a program as prestigious as OTU's. And they could understand how Colton might start to feel guilty later and switch back to his first commitment, to keep his word. But if he attempted to switch yet again, to OTU or anyone else, he'd be seen as a recruit who couldn't be trusted. A serial waffler. Coaches were patient, and they didn't mind stealing recruits from one another, but some of them had started drawing a line in the sand about all this switching around. They didn't want to waste time chasing a player who had about as much loyalty as a ten-dollar hooker.

Now all Crabtree had to do was wait.

Wait for the tweet—directly from Colton, or from one of the various media outlets that kept Crabtree up to date. And as luck would have it, just as he was pulling up his slacks, his cell phone emitted the alert for an incoming tweet. He pulled his pants up to his waist and—in a burst of giddy anticipation—yanked his phone from his front pocket.

That's when it happened.

He bobbled his phone. Clumsy. In too much of a hurry. The phone practically leapt from his hands, as if it had a mind of its own. Crabtree was already buzzing from the Adderall, but now his heartbeat jumped up a level, because in that fraction of a second while his phone was in midair, he knew exactly where it was going to end up.

And it did.

It landed in the toilet with a sickening splash.

The alert sounded again, but now it warbled from beneath several foamy inches of stagnant yellow pisswater. Crabtree hadn't flushed the toilet when he had come into the stall, and it appeared none of the previous ten occupants had bothered to flush, either. Crabtree simply stood there and watched until the alert stopped sounding and the screen on his phone went dark.

Fuck.

He couldn't just leave his phone in there. It was the most important thing he owned. It was loaded with all his important contacts—information that he hadn't backed up as frequently as he should have. It was his electronic lifeline to the world of college football. He didn't care about the actual phone, which was probably ruined, but maybe he could salvage the SIM card.

The good news was, he had Latex gloves.

He removed a glove from his pants pocket and tugged it on to his right hand, focusing on the fact that he was pretty sure urine was sterile. He had read that somewhere. So what he was about to do was gross, yes, but probably not dangerous. Then again, the bowl itself was crusted with all sorts of disgusting particles and remnants he'd rather not even contemplate. So, on second thought, there had to be billions of germs colonizing that water.

Think positive. He had a glove. The same kind surgeons wore. The germs were irrelevant.

He pulled the glove as high as possible up his wrist, then he slowly lowered his hand below the rim until it touched the surface of the water. He paused. Then he lowered it farther. He could feel the warmth of the water enveloping his fingers and creeping upward on his palm.

But he wasn't able to touch the phone yet.

He went a little deeper and his fingertips finally brushed the phone, but he couldn't actually grip or grab it. Ever so slowly, he lowered his hand a bit more, hoping to use two fingers like pincers. Still couldn't get it. Meanwhile, the level of the water was past the heel of his hand and almost to the lip of the glove.

He heard someone outside, trying to turn the locked doorknob. Then a light knock. "Dad?"

Ryan, wondering what was taking so long.

"Just a minute, goddammit!"

Crabtree reached still deeper, his eyes focused on the phone, and the way his two fingers could almost grasp it, clutching at it, so close, only to have it slip away each time, and then he reached too far, and the pisswater poured into his glove like water over the transom of a sinking rowboat.

No reason to be careful now. Crabtree plunged his hand all the way into the bowl, grabbed the phone, and pulled it out. He hustled over to the sink—feeling the pisswater running down his wrist and forearm—and quickly rinsed the phone off. Amazingly, it was still working.

He checked the incoming tweet, which had indeed come from Colton Spillar. But it had nothing to do with his verbal commitment. It simply said: *We're dedicating the rest of the season to our lost teammate, Sammy Beech.*

Crabtree read the tweet twice before the screen went dark again.

CHAPTER 21

Just after six o'clock in the evening, Sheriff Bobby Garza—accompanied by Chief Deputy Bill Tatum—knocked on the door of Room 115 at the Hill Country Inn. The blue GMC truck registered to Dustin Bryant was backed into a spot directly in front of the room.

Garza could hear the sounds of a TV playing loudly inside, but nobody answered the door. Garza knocked again. Now the curtain moved in the window to the right of the door and the TV went quiet. Then the deadbolt lock turned and the door swung open about a foot wide.

One of the Bryant brothers—the one with the goatee—was squinting through the opening. He was wearing jeans, but his torso was bare. His chest was pale and hairless, without much definition, a ring of fat around his waist. His hair lay flat against his skull from wearing a hat earlier in the day. He looked like a man awoken from a nap.

"Yeah?"

"Evening," Garza said. Friendly. All smiles. "I'm Sheriff Bobby Garza. This is Chief Deputy Bill Tatum. Which one are you—Dustin or Dylan?"

"I'm, uh, Dylan."

"Good to meet you, Dylan. We need to chat with you a minute. Mind stepping outside?"

"Uh...what's this about?"

"What's going on?" said somebody inside the room. And now the other Bryant twin appeared. "Oh."

"And you're Dustin," Garza said. "Great. I'm going to

ask both of you to come outside for a few minutes so we can ask a couple of questions."

"About what?" Dustin asked.

"Yeah, about what?" Dylan echoed. Their voices were nearly identical.

Garza noticed that Dylan's eyes were darting nervously over to Tatum every few seconds, and Garza could understand why. Tatum was an imposing figure. Not tall, but stout, with a weightlifter's torso and biceps that bulged like grapefruits beneath his uniform.

Before Garza could speak again, he saw the bathroom door swing open at the rear of the small motel room—and out came the tall redheaded man named Gilbert Weems.

"I don't know what it was," Marlin said, "but I couldn't shake the feeling that he knew something he wasn't telling."

"What's his name again?" Nicole asked.

"Colton Spillar."

"Mom's name is Vera?"

"Yeah. You know her?"

They were on opposite ends of the couch, relaxing for a few minutes before figuring out what to do for dinner.

"I answered a call at her place once. This was just a couple of weeks before I switched jobs, if I remember correctly."

"What was the call about?"

"Drunk live-in boyfriend making a nuisance of himself, which was a regular thing. She'd had enough and wanted him out of there, but he also paid half the bills, so she was going to have a tough time on her own."

"Did she boot him?"

"She did, yeah. I dropped in on her one time after I went

to victim services and it looked like she was getting along okay. Struggling a little, but that was better than living with an abusive jerk."

"Did you have much interaction with Colton?"

"None. But it could be you're reading too much into his behavior. He might outweigh you by fifty pounds, but that doesn't mean he wasn't intimidated by you, especially if Mom's boyfriend regularly put him down or picked away at his confidence."

Marlin thought about it. "You might be right."

"Especially considering the circumstances. You were showing these teenage boys a picture of a beautiful woman and asking if they know her. I imagine that might normally make them a little flustered, but then you add the fact that this woman might have something to do with Sammy's death."

"I would've sworn he reacted like he recognized her."

"But it's a sexy shot, right? Even cropped?"

"Well, yeah."

"Maybe that's why he reacted."

"That's what he said."

"Let's see it."

"Huh?"

She grinned. "I haven't seen the photo yet. I'm curious. This woman must be a drop-dead hottie."

"She's no Nicole Marlin."

"Ha. You're sweet."

Marlin went out to his truck and came back with the manila envelope. He removed the photo and handed it to Nicole.

"Wow," she said immediately. "She really is—" He was watching her expression and something suddenly changed. "Hey, wait a minute." She raised a finger. Her brow was furrowed. Recognition. That's what he saw on her face.

"We ain't done nothin'," Dylan Bryant said.

Weems was now standing behind the Bryant brothers, glaring at Garza and Tatum, and none of the three men had made a move to step outside the motel room. Garza had been careful to check Weems's hands, which were empty.

"You're Gilbert Weems?" Garza said.

"That's the name they give me."

"I'm going to ask all three of you to come down to the station."

Neither Bryant brother reacted. They were plainly going to follow Weems's lead.

Unfortunately, Weems said, "Got a warrant?"

"No, it's nothing like that," Garza said. "We just need to ask y'all a few questions."

"Sounds like fun, but we'll pass," Weems said.

"Won't take but a few minutes."

Weems stepped between the Bryant brothers and put one hand on the edge of the door, as if preparing to close it. Weems was knowledgeable enough on the law to know he wasn't obligated to step outside or to answer a single question. "Said we'll pass."

Garza gave up on Weems and looked at Dylan Bryant. "Where were y'all yesterday evening around sundown?"

"We—

"He ain't got to answer that," Weems said.

Garza said. "It's an easy question. What's the problem?"

"Ain't no problem."

"Don't you want to know why we're here?"

"Don't really matter, does it? It's always some bullshit deal with guys like you," Weems said.

Garza could feel his pulse picking up.

Bill Tatum said, "Somebody fired a couple of rounds at a state game warden yesterday. Y'all know anything about that?"

"No, but that sounds like a pretty good time. Was he hit?"

"No, he wasn't," Tatum said.

"Then you know it wasn't none of us. We all know how to shoot. Don't think we'd miss anything as big as a game warden. The question is, do you need a hunting license to shoot a game warden?"

Weems was grinning. Hoping to draw a reaction. Just as cocky and arrogant as Sheriff Sharp had described.

Garza turned to Dustin Bryant. "This is your truck behind me, right? Big diesel?"

"Yeah. So what?" Dustin said.

"The shooter yesterday hopped into a diesel."

"Lot of diesels around," Dustin said.

"True enough. But how many of them have dog boxes in the back?"

"Plenty."

"Maybe in East Texas, but not around here. How many are occupied by a passenger at least six-four or six-five?"

"How tall are you, Gilbert?" Tatum asked.

"I'm five foot eighteen."

"Clever. Six-six, huh?"

"You must've gone to college to figure it out that quick."

"The county is crawling with people right now, but I can't recall seeing anyone else as tall as you."

"Yeah, well, I'm sure I look like a giant to a short little guy like you."

Garza could see a trace of irritation on Tatum's face, but nothing to worry about. The chief deputy wouldn't be baited by Weems's weak insult.

Tatum said, "The warden said the shooter had red hair.

Wait, that's not exactly right. Orange hair."

"Dang, that's a freaky coincidence," Weems said. "My hair is kind of orange."

"That's true," Tatum said.

"No wonder you think it was me."

"Was it?"

"I think we're done for today," Weems said. "Time to go drink some beer and maybe get laid. Hey, do either of y'all have a sister?"

Garza said, "We *will* catch the shooter. I guarantee that."

"Yeah, well, good luck." Weems closed the door.

"Hey, Dustin," Garza said through the door. "You give me a call at the station if you want to stay out of trouble. You, too, Dylan. Don't let your buddy Gilbert drag you into a bad situation."

Nicole recognized the woman—that was clear—but she was trying to place her.

"You know her?" Marlin asked.

Nicole held her hand up, meaning *Be quiet and let me think.*

Marlin waited, while Nicole continued to study the photo.

"Damn it," she said. "Almost."

He could tell that it was one of those frustrating moments when the answer was dancing just on the edge of her memory.

He waited some more.

And then he saw her expression change again. A big smile. She had it.

"Wait right here," she said, rising off the couch.

"Do you—"

"Just a sec!"

She came back in half a minute with her iPad. He'd given it to her the previous Christmas. She sat down again and began to type something.

"I can't remember her name, but…" she said.

"You know who she is?" He was getting excited.

"Yes. Hold on."

He could see that Nicole was doing a Google search. She followed a link and studied the page. Shook her head. Followed another link. Then another.

"Got her!" she said.

"The name?"

"Yes."

Nicole typed in another search. She got a long string of results, but instead of following one of those links, she clicked on the "Images" tab instead. Dozens of small thumbnail photos filled the screen—all of the same woman. The woman in Sammy Beech's photo.

CHAPTER 22

"Her name is Aleksandra Babikova," Marlin said into his cell phone. "She played volleyball for the Russian Olympic team, then went pro for a few years."

Garza didn't reply.

"You there?"

"Yeah, I'm here. I just don't know what to say. The woman in Sammy's photo is a former Russian volleyball player?"

"Yep."

"I didn't know what to expect, but it wasn't that. You're sure of this?"

"Google her name and you'll see. She also did some modeling and acting, overseas and here in the States. That's how Nicole recognized her—from one of the movies she was in. She played the sexy Russian spy."

"Big stretch."

"Yeah, right," Marlin said.

"Aleksandra Babikova."

"That's it."

"Name doesn't ring any bells at all."

"Didn't for me, either. Not like she was a big star, but she had her moment in the sun."

"You know what I'm thinking?" Garza said.

"Huh?"

"That this is a dead end. Waste of time."

"Could be, but I should add that she lives in Dallas now. I saw something about that on the web, then checked to see if she has a Texas driver's license. She does. Seems a little coincidental that she lives in Texas, and Sammy Beech happened to have a photo of her on his phone."

"How long has she lived here?" Garza asked.

"Don't know."

"What does she do for a living nowadays?"

"Don't know that either."

"Okay, well..."

"I'll keep digging. See if I can get in touch with her."

"At least you have an address now," Garza said.

"Assuming it's current. But it'd be nice to find a phone number or email address, so I don't have to drive up there."

Garza switched topics and proceeded to tell Marlin about a man named Gilbert Weems, from Jasper County. Six-foot-six, with red hair. Found in the company of the Bryant twins, one of whom drove a diesel-powered truck. Garza said the men weren't willing to talk.

"This guy Weems has about eight nuts loose, according to the sheriff over there. Dangerous because he doesn't care. He was really trying to push our buttons. Talking all kinds of trash."

"Think he's our shooter?"

"Innocent until proven guilty and all that, but yeah, I do. He wanted me to think so, too, just to torment us. One of those jerks who thinks he's too smart to get caught."

"What about the Bryants?" Marlin asked.

"Not quite as out there as Weems. I'll flip one or both of them. Just you watch."

Unpredictability.

That was the thing about Gilbert Weems that always put Dustin Bryant on edge. One minute Gilbert would be having a good time, drinking a beer, telling a story, the next he might cold-cock some guy who jostled his elbow at the bar. No warning, either. Just…bam! And right after, you'd see this look in Gilbert's eyes, like he'd just as soon stomp the guy's head like a watermelon. Like he enjoyed hurting people.

Dustin himself didn't mind a little craziness now and again, but not the going-to-prison kind of craziness. That's why this game warden thing was a concern. Who the fuck takes potshots at a law-enforcement officer for no reason at all? Gilbert Weems, that's who.

Dustin and Dylan had dropped him off on the side of the road so he could scout that particular piece of property, and the plan was to pick him up ten or fifteen minutes later. Enough time for him to look around for signs of feral pigs. Gilbert would give them a call when he was ready. So Dustin had driven on down the road about a mile and parked on the shoulder.

Then they heard a shot from Gilbert's direction.

Then another.

And a third, but this one sounded different from the first two. More like a handgun.

Then another shot that sounded like the first two.

Then a few minutes later, Gilbert finally called. The cell signal was weak, and Gilbert's voice was breaking up, but it sounded like he said he'd been "having some fun" with a game warden.

Lord.

Dustin wondered at the time if Gilbert had just killed a man. No way to know for sure, because you couldn't always believe what he told you. But he said he didn't hit the warden, and there was nothing in the news later, no massive manhunt, so Gilbert must have been telling it straight.

But still—that kind of behavior was just plain nuts. The

local cops wouldn't let something like that slide. Which is why Dustin hadn't been surprised when the sheriff and his deputy had shown up at the motel. Fast, though, he'd give them that. Obviously, from what the sheriff had said, the game warden must have seen, or at least heard, Dustin's diesel truck. And the warden had probably gotten a decent look at Gilbert, too.

Dustin had wondered what the charges would be if they got caught. Attempted murder? Assault with a deadly weapon? A felony of some kind, for sure. He wasn't willing to take that kind of fall when it was all Gilbert's doing. Gilbert the troublemaker, dragging them into a clusterfuck.

And it was about to get even worse.

They stopped at a convenience store for more beer and some Cokes to mix with whiskey. Drink cheap before they hit some of the local beer joints.

Gilbert had been drinking hard ever since the sheriff had come by, and Dustin had been holding his breath. He recognized the signs that Gilbert could do just about anything at any given moment.

Dylan opened his door, but Gilbert said he'd do it, he'd go get the stuff. So he climbed out of the truck and went inside, and Dustin could see that he was unsteady on his feet.

Dylan, from the backseat, quietly said, "This ain't good, bro."

Dustin didn't reply. The way he saw it, he and his brother didn't have a lot of choices. See if they could ride it out. That was the way to go. Because the only other option was to snitch on Gilbert, and that would turn into a world of shit, no doubt about it. Dustin could only imagine what would happen if they pissed Gilbert off and turned him into an enemy. Gilbert had told them some stories about things he'd supposedly done in the past. Things way worse than taking potshots at a game warden.

"Maybe we should go back home," Dylan said. "Forget this stupid pig hunt. Before we really get in trouble."

They were parked on the side of the store, and Dustin could see Gilbert through the windows. Hard to miss the tall bastard. He was lingering near the beer cooler, too drunk to locate his brand.

"Push comes to shove," Dylan said, "we need to back each other up. You and me, I'm talking about. Screw *him*. We tell the truth in exchange for no charges."

"Well, duh, but let's wait and see what happens," Dustin said. "We might not have to do nothin'."

Gilbert finally found the right beer and was now making his way toward the soft drinks.

"We had no idea he was gonna do what he did," Dylan said. "So they shouldn't be able to bust us for it."

Dustin stayed quiet.

Dylan said, "But I'm guessing the longer we wait, the less likely the sheriff's gonna believe we wasn't part of it. We gotta come forward before they can prove it was us out there."

Gilbert was at the cash register, paying the clerk. A small green car pulled into the spot on the truck's passenger side.

"Ain't no reason to be afraid of Gilbert," Dylan said. "He's full of shit. Besides, it'd be two against one."

Gilbert exited through the glass door at the front of the store and turned right, then turned right again at the corner, coming back to the truck. He had a twelve-pack of Bud in one hand and a twelve-pack of Coke in the other.

The driver of the little green car, talking on his cell phone, stepped out and made his way toward the sidewalk.

Paying no attention to Gilbert at all.

It was about to get even worse.

Dustin would have stopped it if he had known what was going to happen. But that was the problem with Gilbert Weems.

Unpredictability.

Dustin was watching and saw the way Gilbert suddenly focused on the driver of the green car. The look that came over Gilbert's face. Disgust and revulsion, all in an instant. Dustin could tell that Gilbert wanted to do something. To lash out. But his hands were full. So he made a snap decision and used the only other weapon that was available to him.

Gilbert said something to the man. Then he leaned back at the waist, whipped forward, and brought his forehead crashing down into the other man's face.

It was the most savage head-butt Dustin had ever seen, and the driver of the little green car crumpled under the blow like he'd been shot by a deer rifle. His knees didn't even have a chance to buckle. The man was out cold before he hit the concrete.

CHAPTER 23

Marlin woke at six o'clock, brewed some coffee, and went straight to his computer. Just a few years earlier, he could hardly have conducted a simple Internet search. But he'd had some practice since then and had become proficient. Skilled, even. He'd learned that it wasn't that tough to track someone down online—if they could be tracked down.

He began with the most obvious step and checked a couple of telephone directories. Aleksandra Babikova wasn't listed. That would've been too easy. Like many people her age, she probably didn't even have a landline. Cell phone only.

He checked Facebook. There were a handful of Aleksandra Babikovas, but none of the profile photos showed the right Aleksandra Babikova. Either she did not have an account, or she had selected the option that excluded her from public search results. There was a page for fans of Aleksandra Babikova, but it said right up front that a fan ran the page and Ms. Babikova was not associated with it. Nearly three thousand people had "liked" the page. The last post had been three months earlier—a video clip from the movie in which Babikova had had a small part. Marlin watched it. Babikova looked great on screen, but she was a terrible actress.

The previous evening, before speaking to Garza, Marlin had completed a cursory Google search to confirm that the woman in the photo was in fact Babikova. Now he conducted another Google search, going deeper. He found a lot of references to her—and information about her—but nothing of value. Most of it was pretty old.

He checked the tax rolls for both Dallas County and Tarrant County. Nada. She didn't appear to own a home or any real estate in the Dallas/Fort Worth area. Probably rented.

This wasn't looking good.

There was a Wikipedia page for Babikova, but there was nothing there that indicated what line of work she was in now or how she might be contacted. However, it mentioned a sister named Tatyana. Back to Facebook, then.

A search gave half a dozen results, but it was easy to rule out most of them based on age. One young woman who lived in Saint Petersburg, Russia, had a profile photo that was encouraging. She looked a lot like Aleksandra Babikova. Marlin searched her friends list but didn't find Aleksandra. However, he saw several more photos of Tatyana that increased his confidence that he'd found Aleksandra's sister, or maybe a cousin.

"Wow. She's pretty," Nicole said, suddenly behind him in her nightshirt. "What are you doing in here? Cruising for chicks on the Internet?"

"Don't tell my wife."

She kissed him on the top of his head, then peered over his shoulder. "Russia?"

"You think this woman looks anything like Aleksandra Babikova?"

She leaned closer. "Hmm."

"Hold on. Look at a couple more." He clicked through the photos.

"I'd say yeah, she does. Almost certainly. Sister?"

"I don't know."

"Definitely a likeness."

"That's what I thought."

Nicole stretched and yawned. "Gotta go shower."

Marlin nodded. He clicked the Message button on Tatyana Babikova's profile and began to type.

"Problem is, I have this one place on my back I can never quite reach," Nicole said. "Very frustrating. If only there were a way to emerge from the shower with all of my parts properly scrubbed."

Marlin stopped writing. He could see Nicole grinning at him in the reflection on the computer monitor. He said, "I'd be more than happy to offer my services."

"Oh, you would? That is so generous of you. Give me five minutes first to shave my legs."

Shortly thereafter, Marlin heard the shower running.

He quickly finished writing the message:

Hello, Tatyana. My name is John Marlin. I am a game warden (a type of law enforcement officer) in Texas, in the United States. Is Aleksandra Babikova your sister? I am attempting to reach her regarding a routine matter. I understand she lives in Dallas now. Do you have a phone number or email address for her? Does she have a Facebook account? I appreciate your cooperation. Thank you.

In the morning, after Betty Jean had left for work, Billy Don stayed in bed and started thinking about everything that had happened with Armando—and he ended up feeling worse than he had the day before. He felt *guilty*. Yes, Red was the one who'd bullied Armando into spilling the beans about the pig, but what had Billy Don done about it? Nothing, really. He'd stood there and let it happen. He could've spoken up a little more forcefully, but no, he hadn't. Red had kept running his mouth, and Billy Don hadn't shut him up. And Armando had gotten upset.

It was weird the way Billy Don felt about Armando. Not weird in a bad way, but weird nonetheless, or maybe just different. It took awhile for Billy Don to figure out what it was, but he eventually realized that he felt inclined to treat Armando the same way he'd treat a woman. Just like Billy Don wouldn't put up with anyone saying mean things to Betty Jean, he didn't want to see Armando get his feelings hurt. He wanted to protect him.

If Armando had been just a regular guy, Billy Don would've let him fend for himself. That's the thing—most regular guys would've told Red to go screw himself, and Billy Don wouldn't have had to speak up at all. For instance, if Red had gotten into an argument or a disagreement with some other guy working on a construction job, not only would Billy Don have stayed out of it, it might've even turned into a good source of entertainment. Red and the other guy could call each other names, trade insults, maybe make idle threats, and Billy Don would stand back and enjoy the show.

But it was different with Armando. If you called him, say, a big dickhead, he wouldn't turn around and take a swing at you, and he wouldn't call you a gigantic horse's ass and then forget the whole thing. Instead, he'd reply with some insult you might not even understand. Or he'd act like he didn't really care, but you'd be able to tell that he was upset.

Billy Don didn't understand it, but he thought Armando was a pretty good guy—heck, a great guy—and it was really uncool the way Red had behaved. There were times when Billy Don was almost embarrassed to be associated with a guy like Red.

Bottom line, Armando deserved an apology—not just

from Red, but from Billy Don, too.

Billy Don grabbed the phone off the nightstand and dialed Armando's number. Four rings, then it went to voicemail. Billy Don hung up. He wanted to apologize to Armando in person, not in a voicemail. Maybe Armando was already at work.

So Billy Don called the flower shop. The old lady who owned the place answered, and when Billy Don asked for Armando, he could tell from the way the lady reacted that something bad had happened.

Sheriff Bobby Garza and Chief Deputy Bill Tatum rode downward in the hospital elevator, frustrated, because their visit had largely been a waste of time.

"Had to've been Gilbert Weems," Tatum said.

"I agree," Garza said.

"Do we have enough for a warrant?"

"I'll talk to the county attorney, but I don't think so."

Witnesses the night before had said that a tall redheaded man—appearing to be intoxicated—had been in the convenience store just moments before the victim was assaulted. Video from inside the store confirmed those accounts, and that the customer was indeed Gilbert Weems. But there were no video cameras outside the store.

Worse, nobody saw the actual assault. And the victim—a young man named Armando Salazar—had just confirmed that he had no memory of the event. Garza and Tatum had asked him questions for ten minutes, but it had proven futile. Salazar said that he had woken up that morning unsure where he was and why he was there. He couldn't even recall pulling in to the convenience store parking lot the night before. A nurse had told him he'd been assaulted.

But there were two small bits of good news. First, Salazar's memory might come back, either partially or completely. Might happen in a few hours, a few days, or a few weeks. Or it might not happen at all, but Garza preferred to remain optimistic.

Second—Garza had learned this last night—Salazar had been on the phone right before he was assaulted. He'd been speaking to a local woman, Sharon Greene, and she had heard the attacker use a slur against Salazar. Not a slur about being Hispanic, a slur about being gay. It was a hate crime, which meant the penalty would be more severe.

"Can we show Salazar a photo lineup?" Tatum asked. "Maybe that'll spur his memory."

"We could, but that's a risk," Garza said. "Right now, he remembers nothing. If we show him a lineup of redheads now, even if his memory comes back later, a defense attorney can say Salazar doesn't really remember anything, and that it was the lineup that made him 'remember' a redhead assaulting him."

Tatum let out a sigh. "I understand, but it's still tempting."

"It is, but let's give it a day or two. See if he remembers anything. In the meantime, I think it's time to put some major pressure on the Bryants."

CHAPTER 24

As Red and Billy Don rode upward in the elevator in silence, Red was starting to resent the many ways Armando was interrupting his life. Every day it was something new, and it was downright irritating.

Red had wanted to get some hunting time in this morning, because the pig he'd seen last night on the Kringelheimer Ranch was probably still roaming the immediate vicinity. Then, after lunch, Red had been planning to contemplate the possibility of laying the groundwork to prepare to look for some new paying projects today. Maybe call up some of his regular clients, or at least write all their numbers down on a handy list, so he could call them tomorrow, or later in the week. These things took careful planning. You had to be organized.

But Billy Don had called and insisted on going to the hospital to see Armando. And that meant the entire day was probably shot, even if they only stayed for an hour or so, because Red had discovered that once he'd lost his momentum, it was hard to get it back. Even something as simple as going to the bathroom could bring Red's workday to an early halt.

"The hell's wrong with him?" Red had asked when Billy Don had called.

"Got beat up outside the convenience store."

Which made Red wonder: What kind of man ends up in the hospital on account of a split lip or a black eye? Ridiculous. Take your lumps and get on with it. Who rides

in an ambulance for a bloody nose? A drama queen like
Armando, that's who.

"I ain't hangin' around long," Red said now. "Place
smells funny."

"Fine," Billy Don replied. "You don't have to come in at
all."

"But you asked me to come."

"Needed a ride. I knew you wouldn't be doing nothin'
important."

That was another thing Red was tired of—the way Billy
Don had been acting lately. Grumpy.

"You want me to come in or not?"

"Don't matter to me."

The elevator stopped on the third floor—the top floor—
and the doors opened.

"Well, hell, I've come this far," Red said. He gestured for
Billy Don to exit the elevator ahead of him. "Age before
beauty."

Dustin Bryant woke up in the motel room after nine.
They'd been out late the night before, first at some of the
bars, and then hunting with a spotlight on a lease—a place
not far from where Gilbert had taken potshots at the game
warden. No pigs to be seen.

Dylan was still asleep in the rollaway cot and Gilbert was
snoring loudly in his bed. Boy, he'd been hammered last
night. Dustin had been drinking, too. Not as heavily as
Gilbert, but he'd definitely been drunk, and that's why he
couldn't be sure if things had been as serious as they'd
appeared last night.

It had looked really bad, the way the little guy in the
green car had dropped like a deer shot in the head. Blood

everywhere. Gilbert so fucking proud of what he'd done. "Queers should stay in the city where they belong," he'd said when he got in the truck. They left the guy stretched out in the parking lot. Nobody seemed to have noticed anything.

Still, Dustin had expected the cops to be waiting at the motel when they got back from the hunt at about three in the morning. After all, the little gay guy would tell them a tall redheaded man had done it, and that would be an easy tip-off. But no. No cops. It looked like Gilbert might get away with this one, too. Maybe the gay guy hadn't gotten a good look at Gilbert. That was entirely possible, because it had all happened so quickly.

Dustin flipped onto his side, facing the nightstand, and noticed the little alert light on his cell phone was blinking. Voicemail waiting. He dialed in to retrieve it.

Hey, Dustin, it's Sheriff Bobby Garza. We know exactly what happened last night at the convenience store. The whole thing is on video. Gilbert is getting out of control, ain't he? But we can still charge you and your brother as accessories. We're talking a felony, or maybe several, depending on what the county attorney recommends. But we can probably work something out if you give me a call. Better yet, swing by my office and let's have a little chat. Bring your brother, but leave Gilbert at the motel. Better hurry, because this generous offer is only available for a limited time.

They stepped into Armando's room and Red immediately saw that he'd been mistaken. Big time. This wasn't a simple case of someone popping Armando in the nose or smacking him across the mouth.

Armando's face was heavily bandaged, but the parts Red could see didn't look good at all. In fact, it looked like

Armando had slammed his face into the dashboard during a car wreck. His nose was heavily taped, meaning it was most likely broken, and both eyes were ringed with black. Armando's lips were swollen, and there was a nasty split, closed with stitches, running between his top lip and his nose.

Armando slowly raised one hand about a foot off the bed in greeting.

"Jesus Christ," Red said, wanting to add, *They sure fucked you up good, huh?*

"Red," Billy Don said quietly, meaning, *Shut up or he'll know how bad he looks.*

They both moved over beside the bed.

"Hey," Armando said, wincing as he spoke. Red could tell that something was wrong with his mouth. It wasn't just swollen. Armando noticed where Red was looking, so he said, "Yeah, they're gone."

He opened his mouth just enough to reveal that his two front teeth—the upper ones—were missing.

Red badly wanted to make a remark about how Armando's boyfriend would appreciate the missing teeth during certain activities—but he managed to hold it in.

"Well, shit," Billy Don said. "What the hell happened?"

Armando did a slow head shake. "Can't remember. The deputy thinks I was either punched or head-butted."

"But why?"

"No particular reason."

On the one hand, Red couldn't help feeling a little sorry for Armando, but on the other hand, it was just a few days ago that Red felt like punching Armando himself. If Armando had been jerking someone's chain the same way he had jerked Red's, well, some people might get pretty angry about it. On the third hand, even if Armando had smarted off or made some comment to draw attention to his gayness, he didn't deserve to get clobbered as badly as he had been.

"Did you say something to the guy?" Red asked.

Armando started to answer, but Billy Don said, "Don't matter if he did."

"Hell, I was just curious."

Armando said, "I was on the phone to Sharon. She heard it. I didn't say anything to the attacker, but he said something to me."

"What'd he say?" Billy Don asked.

Red could tell that Armando was hesitant to answer, because he was obviously in pain with each word, or maybe he simply didn't want to talk anymore. But after a moment, he said, "He called me a faggot."

In the elevator on the way down, Billy Don said, "You know what I wanna do?"

"Stop at Sonic for a large order of tater tots?"

Billy Don glared at him.

"Jeez," Red said. "Ain't gotta lose your sense of humor. Relax. I ain't never seen you like this. What do you wanna do?"

Billy Don reached out into empty space with both hands and made a circle, as if strangling some imaginary person on the elevator with them. "I wanna find the guy who done it and beat him like a rented mule." He suddenly pointed a sausagelike finger at Red. "And you're gonna help me."

"Like hell I am."

"You are, too."

"I got a pig to kill. *We* got a pig to kill."

"Don't care. You're helping."

"If you think I'm gonna—"

"'Member when that dude came lookin' for you 'cause you banged his wife? Who was it that told him you'd been killed in a thresher accident? I did. Saved your ass that time."

Red didn't say anything.

"And who took you to the clinic when you had diarrhea so bad you had to ride in the bed of the truck?"

Red still kept quiet.

"And what about the time—"

"Okay. Enough. But we gotta make it quick and get back to looking for the pig."

"Then that's what we'll do."

The elevator dinged and the door opened.

Red said, "What exactly are you gonna do to this guy if we manage to track him down?"

"Don't know yet. Guess we'll cross that bridge when I break his goddamn face."

"Did we or did we not have a conversation with that little Spillar bastard's mother yesterday?" Dexter Crabtree asked Ryan, who was working out in the exercise room of Crabtree's Highland Park mansion.

The question sounded sarcastic and rhetorical, as Crabtree intended, but he honestly wasn't completely certain he *had* met with Vera Spillar. He was pretty sure he had, but the trip yesterday had a dreamlike quality to it that made Crabtree a little unsure whether the meeting had actually taken place. He remembered dropping his phone into the toilet. Then buying a new one. And being incredibly relieved that the old SIM card still worked, so he hadn't lost his contacts and other data. All of that was real.

"You sure as hell did," Ryan said, curling seventy

pounds with ease. He was shirtless, flushed, with beads of sweat streaming down his chiseled torso. Crabtree couldn't help but wonder sometimes why his son was so gifted physically and so sub-par intellectually. "The kid hasn't switched back to UMT yet?" Ryan asked.

Crabtree turned and left the room. Went into his office. Got online and looked up the phone number for the Marble Falls Wal-Mart. Dialed. Of course, he didn't get a person right away. Got some damn voicemail menu first, but he kept punching "0" and eventually a live human being answered. He asked for Vera Spillar. The woman started to hem and haw, saying Vera would have to return the call during a break, so Crabtree said it was a family emergency and he'd appreciate it if she'd move her ass. She put him on hold.

Maybe it wasn't smart calling Vera Spillar—leaving a trail—but it wasn't like he was calling her at home. And it wasn't like an NCAA investigation would ever go so deep as to subpoena the phone records of a Wal-Mart. And if it did, how could they ever prove that he was calling the Wal-Mart to speak to Vera Spillar? Of course, they had video cameras that would show her leaving her cash register at exactly the same time—

Damn. He was letting his imagination get away from him.

"Who is this?" a woman asked. That washerwoman hick accent again. Sounding suspicious. She wasn't buying the bit about a family emergency.

"Your old friend from yesterday. I bought some gum, remember?" He hoped he really had bought some gum.

"Oh. Yeah. I've been waiting for you to call."

"What's the hold-up?"

"I've been doing some thinking."

Crabtree couldn't remember a single time in his life when

a woman had said "I've been doing some thinking" and it had turned out well for him.

"Thinking? About what?"

"About my boy playing ball at your school. And how much that's really worth."

Crabtree didn't say anything. If he did say anything, he was afraid it would devolve into a raging, bile-spewing rant—possibly with a threat of violence. He could feel a sharp pain directly between his eyeballs.

"I done some research," Vera Spillar said. "Crazy how much money is involved in college football. The schools make big bucks. The coaches—hell, most of them is millionaires. The TV networks cash in, too. Then you got all them companies selling shirts and mugs and bumper stickers and whatnot. But what do the players get?"

"What about the scholarships? They get a free education."

She snorted. "That ain't much compared to the serious money everyone else is raking in."

Crabtree took a deep breath. *Calm. Have to stay calm.* "You don't consider ten thousand dollars to be serious money?"

"Oh, sure, it is to me. But it probably isn't to a guy like you."

"You don't even know me."

"You think I didn't figure out who you are? Do one of them Web searches for 'University of Middle Texas football' and your name pops up in half the posts."

Crap. Not good. But he wasn't going to be manipulated by a Wal-Mart cashier, for God's sake. "I don't have time for this. We got a deal or not?"

Her tone was all business. "Double it to twenty grand or Colton's sticking with Oklahoma Tech. And I want *all* of it up front. Send me the other half of those bills you got, plus ten grand in bills you ain't torn up."

"You sure are bossy all of a sudden. Maybe I'll just look for a different lineman."

"Fair enough. Good talking to you." He could tell she was about to hang up.

"Wait!"

"I'm listening."

"You want me to drive all the way back down there again? Screw that. You come and get it."

"Ever heard of FedEx, genius?"

CHAPTER 25

Seventy-three-year old J.D. Evans had been clerking at convenience stores from Florida to Texas for the better part of four decades, and truth be told, he enjoyed the work. You met all kinds of people on the job. Rich folks and poor folks. People from countries with names that J.D. couldn't pronounce. Tourists and locals. Assholes and salt-of-the-earth types. Drunk college girls who didn't mind giving an old man an "accidental" peek down their blouses. Illegal day laborers wanting beer and microwave sandwiches. Doctors, lawyers, Indian chiefs. Interesting bunch.

Of course, "interesting" wasn't always a compliment. You had people coming in that ended up creating a problem one way or the other—maybe intentional, maybe not. See a guy sprinting for the bathroom and you know there might be a nasty clean-up job later. A toddler trailing after his mom might bust half a dozen jars of applesauce on the floor. Kid wearing a loose jacket in warm weather was planning to shoplift. Man wearing a hoodie and sunglasses at night might stick a gun in your face and demand all the cash. J.D. had been robbed six times over the years.

People stopped to ask all kinds of questions, too. How do you get to the state park? Where's the best barbecue 'round these parts? Any strip clubs in the county? So it wasn't a surprise when an enormous, unshaven cedar chopper came into the store just before noon and asked several questions, starting with, "Was you working last night?"

J.D. had seen this big old boy before. Several times. Billy

Don was his name. Usually Billy Don was an easygoing fellow who tended to load up on beer, chewing tobacco, and assorted snack foods. But tonight he appeared gravely serious. He hadn't even glanced toward the pork rinds or the Slim Jims.

"I sure was," J.D. said. "Till closing at midnight."

"So you was here when the guy got decked in the parking lot?"

That was another "interesting" aspect of working at a convenience store: Fights in the parking lot. Seemed like there was at least one a month. Some of the stores J.D. had clerked were neighborhood hangouts, with punks and thugs and regular old kids gathering outside nearly every night. Lot of drinking and drugging going on, and the next thing you know, someone gets his ass whooped. Like the episode last night, with some guy getting clocked on the side of the building.

"I sure was," J.D. said again.

"You see what happened?"

"No, sir. Happened around the side."

J.D. glanced out the window and saw Billy Don's running buddy sitting in his old Ford truck, waiting.

"You ain't got any cameras over there?" Billy Don asked.

"No, sir. Wish we did."

The big man looked like he didn't know what to ask next. Finally he said, "Think any of your customers saw it happen?"

"Don't appear that way. Cops asked, but nobody said nothing." By now, Billy Don looked downright distraught, so J.D. said, "Was that poor feller a friend of yours?"

Billy Don nodded.

J.D. could only imagine what Billy Don might do if he caught up to the sorry son of a bitch who had cold-cocked the little guy in the Prius. Probably a lot worse fate than would happen to the man through the legal system. So J.D. was all for it. A piece of garbage like that needed to be dealt with.

"All I can tell you is what I told the cops," J.D. said. "I don't know who done it for sure, but I got a pretty good idea."

A customer entered the store—a man dressed in khakis and a golf shirt—so J.D. paused for a moment. After the customer had made his way to the back of the store, J.D. told Billy Don all about the tall, drunk, obnoxious, redheaded man.

Marlin was having lunch at the crowded Kountry Kitchen with his best friend, Phil Colby, when two things happened almost simultaneously: Marlin's cell phone vibrated with an incoming message from Tatyana Babikova, and a tall, redheaded man walked through the front door of the restaurant.

Marlin had just begun to read Tatyana's message when Colby—who had heard all about the incident on the widow's ranch two days earlier—said, "Oh, here we go."

There was a tone to Colby's voice that made Marlin glance up. He saw the redheaded man standing near the cash register, waiting for the hostess to seat him and the two men standing beside him. Twins, from the look of it, although one had a goatee. The Bryant brothers.

Marlin simply watched. None of the three men had spotted him yet. Marlin set his phone down. Tatyana could wait.

"Weems, right?" Colby said.

"Yep." Marlin had only seen Weems in person the one time—from a great distance. But he'd seen photos, and the redhead was definitely Weems.

"They look like rejects from one of those cable-TV hunting shows with a bunch of backwoods hillbillies," Colby said. "Where most of the locals have more guns than teeth. And their most valuable asset is an outboard motor."

Marlin waited. He could feel his shoulders tensing up. He wondered how Weems would react if he noticed Marlin.

"Look at the feathers in their hats," Colby said. "I'd feel like a major tool walking around like that. What is it, Halloween?"

Marlin was dedicated to his duties as a peace officer, and he knew he shouldn't be relishing a confrontation, but that was exactly what he was doing. Hoping Weems would come over. Hoping he would feel compelled to say something stupid and possibly incriminating.

The hostess hurried over to the waiting men, trying to keep up with the lunch rush. She grabbed three menus from the hostess stand and began to lead them through the dining area.

Weems was halfway through the room when his head turned, scanning the crowd, and his eyes settled on Marlin. For half a second, he kept walking and there was no expression on his face at all. Then something registered. Apparently it dawned on him that he was looking at a uniformed game warden. He grinned and immediately diverted his route toward Marlin's table. The hostess and the Bryant brothers continued on their way, unaware that Weems was no longer behind them. Weems stepped right up to Marlin's table without any hesitation at all.

"Howdy, Officer. How're you today?"

Marlin waited just a beat, then said, "Can I help you with something?"

"You're the county game warden, right?"

"Says so right on his shirt," Colby said.

Weems ignored Colby. His focus remained on Marlin. "Heard you had some trouble the other day. Somebody fired a couple of shots in your direction."

Stay calm, Marlin thought. *Don't fall for his bullshit.*

"That's true," Marlin said. "You know anything about it?"

The noise created by the other diners in their vicinity had virtually disappeared.

"Me? Heck, no," Weems said. "Sheriff asked me the same thing, and I can't figure out why. I wouldn't do nothing like that. Unless I thought I could get away with it." Weems let out a loud guffaw. "Just a joke. Everyone's so uptight around here. Y'all need to loosen up."

"So that wasn't you across the ravine? Sure looked like you."

"Then it must've been a good-looking guy, but it wasn't me."

"Glad I managed to snap a couple of photos. Grainy, but we're waiting to see if the lab in Austin can bump up the quality. Amazing what they can do nowadays."

"You wouldn't be bluffing, would you?"

"Guess we'll see soon enough. You know anything about the assault last night at the Speedy Stop?"

Weems knitted his brow—a purposefully exaggerated gesture. "Someone got assaulted? Well, shit. What's this county coming to? That's a shame, for sure, but I had nothing to do with that, either. Only thing I assaulted last night was a bottle of Jack Daniel's."

Colby said, "Sounds like the guy picked on a much smaller man. Someone who wouldn't fight back. An easy target."

Weems ignored Colby again. He said, "Anyway, I just wanted to come over here and tell you how much I appreciate the way all you law-enforcement types put your life on the line every day. I'd be a bundle of nerves if I thought someone might put a bullet in my back at any minute."

Marlin struggled to remain cool.

Weems continued. "Even worse, what if I was out on patrol, late at night, and someone stopped by my house and paid my wife a visit? I don't think I could—"

"You should stop right there," Colby said. There was no mistaking the threat in his voice and the change in his body language. Coiled tight. Both hands on the table's edge. He was saying, *You keep talking, I'm coming out of this chair to shut your mouth.*

Colby was five or six inches shorter than Weems, and maybe forty pounds lighter, but Marlin's money would be on Colby without question. Colby was hard as a rock from years of outdoor labor on his ranch, and he had a tenacity about him that meant he *always* finished what he started. Colby wasn't one to go looking for fights—despite his occasional temper—but, over the years, he'd been involved in a handful of brawls that were unavoidable. Marlin had seen several. Most of them were one-punch affairs. Colby was quick and amazingly powerful. He punched hard enough to do serious, lasting damage. Weems could end up with a broken jaw before he even managed to make a fist.

Maybe Weems had an intuition that told him to ease off, or maybe he wasn't quite as bold as he liked to appear, but he didn't accept Colby's unspoken challenge. Instead, he finally looked at Colby and said, "Aw, hey, I didn't mean nothin' by it. I was just letting this here warden know what a great job he's doing."

Now the entire restaurant was dead quiet. The Bryant brothers were on the far side of the room, seated at a table, staying put, not coming to back up their friend.

"Well, now, that's awful nice of you," Colby said. "And

since my friend *is* such a dedicated peace officer, he maintains a certain level of professionalism at all times. That means he can't just speak his mind whenever he runs across some asshole." Now it was Colby's turn to grin. "But I can. So let's be clear about something. Whoever fired those shots is the worst kind of coward. Total gutless scumbag. But it wasn't you, was it? You're not playing some sort of game where you're pretending like it wasn't you, but you really want everyone to think it *was* you, right? Because that would be even more cowardly than taking those shots in the first place. No, sir, with you being such a staunch supporter of game wardens, I'm guessing you agree that the shooter is a piece of human garbage, don't you?"

Marlin almost laughed. Colby had just called Weems a coward and a piece of garbage to his face, and everybody in the room knew it. It was obvious that Weems was trying to come up with a snappy reply, but it appeared he couldn't think of one. He had a pained smirk on his face, but the malevolence in his eyes, directed toward Colby, was unmistakable.

Finally, he said, "Guess I'll let you boys have your lunch in peace."

"That would be swell," Colby said. "And if you happen to hear anything more about the lowlife turd in question, I'm sure you'll let the sheriff know."

Weems didn't even respond, but simply turned and made his way to the table where the Bryant brothers were seated. After about a minute, the other customers resumed their conversations.

"That was fun," Colby said.

"I appreciate it," Marlin said.

"No problem."

"But you also just threw a rock at a hornets' nest." Marlin said. "No telling what he'll do."

Colby opened his mouth, then changed his mind. Marlin knew him well enough to know what he'd almost said. *That guy? All talk.* Or something similar. But Colby was smart enough to know that wasn't exactly true.

"Just watch your back, okay?" Marlin said. "You made him look like a jerk. Guys like that hold a grudge."

CHAPTER 26

Red could hardly believe he was about to say what he was going to say, but he said it anyway. "We don't know for sure it was the redheaded guy." Life would be easier for Red if he just assumed the redhead was responsible.

Billy Don said, "Sounds pretty likely. That clerk, J.D., said the cops asked a bunch of questions about that one guy. They didn't seem to care about any of the other customers that was in there right before Armando drove up."

"Yeah, but that don't mean the redheaded dude done it. Coulda been somebody that never even came into the store."

They were parked outside the Dairy Queen, with several bags of food on the seat between them. A Hungr-Buster for Red. Two Beltbusters, a chili cheese dog, a chicken wrap, and large tater tots for Billy Don.

"Look," Red said, "you know I'd just as soon get this whole business wrapped up, so it's tempting as hell to agree that it must've been the redheaded guy. Then we could track him down, you could whip his ass, and we could get back to hunting a fifty-thousand-dollar pig, which is way more important than this bullshit, if you want my opinion."

"I don't. Rarely do."

"Fine. But what if it wasn't him? I'm not saying it wasn't. Maybe it was. It *probably* was. All I'm saying is that you need a little more evidence before you go thump this guy's skull."

"Then I'll just get some more evidence."

Red sucked on his Dr Pepper, let out a soft belch, then said, "How?"

"Huh?"

"How you gonna get more evidence?"

"I'll just ask him."

"Really? Just ask him? And he'll confess?"

"Never know. Especially if he's been drinking. J.D. said the guy was drunk when he was in the store, and he was buying more beer."

"Drunk or not, what if he says he didn't do it?"

"Simple. I'll beat it out of him."

"And you don't see any potential flaws with that approach?"

"Nope. Fast and effective."

Billy Don was shoveling tots into his mouth a half-dozen at a time. Impressive capacity in that huge mouth of his.

Red said, "Think about it for a sec. If you was him, wouldn't you say you did it, just to make the beating stop?"

Billy Don stopped chewing for a minute and appeared to give that some thought.

So Red said, "No, what we need is someone who saw it happen, or maybe even someone who heard him bragging about it. Or better yet, maybe Armando's memory will come back. Of course, none of this even matters until we can find the guy."

"We'll run across him eventually."

"That's your plan? Just wait until we run across him?"

"Maybe drive around and look for him? This town ain't that big."

Red almost always had to do Billy Don's thinking for him, and it became wearisome at times. "How about if we visit some of the businesses around town and see if anybody knows who he is?"

"Which businesses?"

"Retail 'stablishments. Restaurants. Beer joints. Motels. Like that. Seeing as how the guy is a tall sumbitch with red hair, he'll stand out in people's memories. Someone's bound to have seen him. So if we—"

A Chevy truck Red recognized whipped into the Dairy Queen lot. The driver was Jack Chambers, a man who hired Red and Billy Don for various short-term projects now and then. He pulled up next to Red's truck, driver's door to driver's door, with his window down. Without so much as a 'howdy,' Jack said, "Y'all hear the news?"

Red said, "What's up?"

"Word is, someone shot the bounty pig this morning."

Red couldn't recall a time when his spirits had sunk quite as quickly.

"Well, fuck me," he said. "You sure?"

"That's what Jorge and some of his buddies told me."

"When?"

"'Bout an hour ago?"

"Where was the pig?"

"Out on McCall Creek Road, next door to the Kringelheimer place."

Son of a bitch! That made it even worse. Next door to the Kringelheimer place—where Red and Billy Don had been hunting for the past few days. Where they would've been hunting this morning if it wasn't for this mess with Armando.

Red turned and glared at Billy Don, who knew exactly what he was thinking. The pig they'd seen last night could very well have been the bounty pig. They might've had another real good chance at it if they'd been sitting in the blind instead of standing beside Armando's hospital bed a few hours ago.

"Don't you start bitchin' at me," Billy Don growled.

Jack gave a wave and drove off to kill the dreams of other hunters around town.

Red continued to glare at Billy Don, who said, "You ain't

gonna make me feel bad about this. We don't even know it was the same damn pig we saw yesterday evening."

Red slowly shook his head in exasperation.

Billy Don said, "Besides, you had your chance at it, and what'd you do? Dropped the hammer on an empty chamber, that's what. Easiest shot in the world—fifty grand just sitting there—but you blew it. So don't go blaming me on this. You want to blame someone, look in the mirror."

Red hated it when Billy Don was right.

"Everything, uh, okay?"

The voice came from above. The masseuse that visited Dexter Crabtree once a week. Janine. Beautiful young lady. Reminded Crabtree of some of the cheerleaders he'd partied with in his younger days. Nubile. Wholesome as a loaf of white bread. Or that's how she wanted to appear. But Crabtree had learned differently. Even Janine's ad on Craigslist had tried to maintain a sense of propriety, though it was obvious to anyone with a brain what she was really offering. She was not a licensed masseuse. Of course not. She was instead the kind of masseuse that made legitimate, professional, respectable masseuses angry.

"I'm…fine," Crabtree replied, keeping his eyes closed. Concentrating. Trying to enjoy himself. Take his mind off Vera Spillar and the money he was about to send her. It wasn't so much the money as the fact that he was giving in to her demands.

"You know I don't want to rush you, but I have another appointment soon," Janine said quietly.

The standard massage had ended at least twenty minutes ago, and she had been working on his member ever since. Normally it was a five-minute undertaking at most. Today, he couldn't seem to come to fruition.

"Please…don't stop."

Her free hand was resting on his chest. "Your heart is pounding."

"You have…that effect…on me."

"You're sweet, but it's really hammering. And you're sweating. You sure you're okay?"

The answer, of course, was no. For the past 24 hours, his heart had been beating so vigorously, he could feel it reverberating throughout his entire body. He was pretty sure he had also felt it skip a beat on several occasions. Palpitations? Arrhythmia? He didn't know the technical term for it. Along with a buzzing in his ears, a nagging headache that wouldn't respond to ibuprofen, and now this. He couldn't achieve an orgasm. His dick was rock hard, but he just couldn't get there. Was that a side effect?

"I'm fine," he repeated. "Can you…get on top?"

"You know I don't do that."

"Five hundred dollars."

"Sorry."

"If you'll just take off your top, I—"

"Shhhh. Just relax." She switched hands. Applied more massage oil. Suddenly he felt her hot breath on the side of his neck. She whispered, "Maybe this will help." And then she inserted her warm, moist tongue in his ear. Twirled it around. Licked his earlobe. Blew on it. Nibbled it. It felt fantastic. Heavenly.

But it was no use.

I believe there must be some mistaking. I have learned at the moment the meaning of 'game warden.' My sister is not a hunter or a fisher, nor does she do the boating. Perhaps there is the probability you seek a dissimilar Aleksandra Babikova?

That was the message from Tatyana Babikova, delivered on Facebook. Marlin read it while sitting in his truck outside the restaurant, trying to decide what, if anything, he should or could do about Gilbert Weems. The situation was tremendously frustrating. He'd need to talk to Nicole about it tonight. Tell her about Weems's veiled threat. Nicole was more security-conscious than average—not surprising for a former deputy—but Marlin wanted her to be even more cautious than normal.

On a positive note, at least he now knew that Tatyana was in fact Aleksandra's sister. He replied:

Tatyana, thank you very much for answering me so quickly. The reason I am looking for Aleksandra has nothing to do with hunting, fishing, or boating. Game wardens in Texas have a wide range of duties. Your sister might be able to help me with an investigation. It would be very helpful if I could speak to her. Can you provide a phone number, please? I would really appreciate it. I hope to hear back from you again very soon.

Then, just because he couldn't think of any reason why he shouldn't, he sent Tatyana a friend request. Maybe it would make her feel more comfortable communicating with him if she could see his profile. If she accepted, and if Aleksandra was on Facebook, and if Tatyana was friends with Aleksandra, friending Tatyana might give Marlin a peek at some of Aleksandra's comments that would otherwise remain invisible to a complete stranger. Lot of ifs. But it couldn't hurt. Maybe he'd learn what Aleksandra did for a living, or whether she ever traveled to central Texas.

Or maybe he wouldn't learn anything at all.

Crabtree idled his Mercedes in the far corner of a parking lot that served a small business complex. Rental offices for white-collar professionals.

His heart was still racing. His testicles ached.

The torn bills, plus ten thousand additional dollars— untorn—were in a sealed cardboard box resting on the passenger seat. A UPS box, not a FedEx box. Hell if he was going to let Vera Spillar dictate which delivery service he used. Ten feet away, between his car and the street, was a UPS drop box. Only ten feet, but it might as well have been one hundred.

So lightheaded. Woozy, even.

Did he really want to do this? Give in to that bitch's demands?

When he reached for the cardboard box, he noticed that the tremor in his left hand was more pronounced than it had been yesterday, when he'd first become aware of it. He had to grin. Gene Wilder in *Blazing Saddles*. The drunk gunfighter with an uncontrollable palsy. His hand would flop around like a fish on a pier. *Steady as a rock,* says Sheriff Bart. *Yeah, but I shoot with this hand,* says the Waco Kid. Floppity-flop.

Crabtree grabbed the cardboard box and opened the Mercedes door. Why did he have an indeterminate sense of impending doom? He felt the grip of something almost like panic, for no reason that he could identify.

Left foot on the pavement. Now the right. Up and out of the car. Wobbly. No balance. Something was definitely wrong. Vision fading in and out.

Was he falling?

There was a tremendous jolt, and then darkness. A pain. Time passed. He heard a voice. Someone shaking his shoulder. More darkness. Quiet. More time passed.

Then he came awake like a swimmer bursting to the surface, hungry for air. He was facedown on the pavement, gasping. The left side of his face felt like it was on fire. He struggled to raise up on his knees and palms. Warmth running down his cheek, dripping off his chin. Blood. Not a constant flow, but a persistent one, and it wasn't stopping.

He reached with one hand to explore his face and ascertain the extent of his injury. He found the wound and jerked with a jolt of pain. A gash on his forehead, above his right eyebrow. He had touched the bone underneath the skin. Small gravel pebbles were stuck to his cheek.

But his eye was not injured. Thank God, his vision was fine. He could see. What he saw, when he swiveled his head, was that his Mercedes was gone. Just gone.

So was the box of money.

CHAPTER 27

In the early afternoon, a beautiful auburn-haired woman visited Armando in his hospital room. She was dressed well, but casually—pressed jeans and a nice blouse. She had warm, friendly eyes.

She came to his bedside and said, "Mr. Salazar, my name is Nicole Marlin. I'm the victim services coordinator for Blanco County. How are you feeling?"

"I've been better." His voice was raspy.

"I understand. Can we talk for a few minutes, or should I come back later?"

"We can talk."

"I want you to know I'm very sorry for what happened to you. Have you ever been the victim of a violent crime before?"

"No, ma'am."

"Please, call me Nicole."

"Only if you call me Armando." His mouth still hurt, but it wasn't quite as bad as it had been earlier. Maybe it was the pain meds. He was self-conscious about his missing teeth.

She smiled, and it was lovely. "It's a deal," she said. "Are you familiar with what a victim services program is?"

Armando said that he wasn't, and Nicole proceeded to give him a description of various services that were available to him as an individual affected by a crime. The list was quite impressive—ranging from counseling to crisis intervention to guidance through the legal system. Armando had had no idea that type of program even existed.

"Almost anything you need, you can ask me," Nicole said. "I am here to help you in any way that I can."

She was so sweet and genuine, Armando almost began to cry.

"Maybe it's time to hit the road," Dustin Bryant said as they waited for the waitress to bring the check. "Head on back home." He said it quietly, casually, trying to keep the worry out of his voice. Trying to sound like the whole Blanco scene had grown boring and Dustin was ready to move on. Like he wasn't pretty damn terrified that the sheriff would show up any minute and put them all in cuffs.

After Gilbert had joined them at the table, Dustin had noticed that just about every customer in the café was taking sideways glances at the three of them. Dustin and Dylan hadn't been able to hear what Gilbert had said to the game warden, but it couldn't have been good. Gilbert had told them he was "just saying howdy," but Dustin wasn't buying it. Gilbert had never just said howdy to any law-enforcement officer in his life. What he did instead was taunt and tease them, like he'd done with the sheriff and his deputy the day before.

"That might not be a bad idea," Dylan said, backing Dustin up.

"Jesus Christ, y'all need to quit being pussies," Gilbert said. "Cops around here are clueless and those voicemails are just bullshit. They're trying to rattle you, 'cause they ain't got nothin'. Get it?"

"I'm not even talking about all that shit," Dustin said.

But those voicemails were exactly why he was ready to leave town. The sheriff had left a second one an hour after the first, saying he was trying to get arrest warrants for all three of them, so Dustin's time for making a deal would run out soon. A couple of other times, the sheriff had called without leaving a message at all. Dustin had told Gilbert that the sheriff was calling and hassling him, and now he was wondering if he should have kept that between him and Dylan.

Did the sheriff really have video of the assault last night? On the way to the café, Gilbert had insisted on driving past the convenience store to see if there were any exterior surveillance cameras, but they hadn't seen any. Didn't mean there weren't any, as far as Dustin was concerned. Maybe they were concealed.

Of course, Dustin hadn't shared everything with Gilbert. He hadn't revealed that the sheriff was offering a deal to Dustin and Dylan—if they would rat on Gilbert. When Gilbert had asked to hear the voicemails, Dustin said he'd deleted them already. He hadn't.

"Then what are you talkin' about?" Gilbert asked now.

"This pig hunt."

"What about it?"

"Waste of time. I gotta get back to work in a couple days. Besides, what're the odds we even have a chance at it?"

Gilbert grinned. "Getting better by the minute."

Last night, he'd started a rumor. Everywhere they'd gone, he'd spread the word that the pig had been shot yesterday evening. "God's honest truth," he'd said to the doubters. See, he'd seen the dead pig with his own eyes. Saw the tattoo in the ear. He'd been standing right there when the TV news crew had come out and interviewed the man who'd shot it. The story hadn't aired yet, but it would soon. So the contest was over. Ain't that a bitch? Might as well pack it up and go on home. Gilbert was a great liar. Most everyone he'd talked to had believed him. And the traffic around town *had* seemed lighter this morning, like some hunters had already cleared out. Dustin would never have thought of a trick like that, but it came natural to Gilbert. Kind of funny that it was working.

The phone on Dustin's hip vibrated again. He ignored it.

When they came outside, the man who had been having lunch with the game warden was sitting, boots dangling, on the opened tailgate of a truck parked with its nose toward Highway 281. The man hopped to the pavement and immediately headed their way, with a deliberacy to his stride that was unmistakable. Dustin didn't know why, but just like last night at the convenience store, he had the distinct feeling that something was about to go terribly wrong. He was tired of having that feeling.

Apparently, Gilbert saw the man coming, too, because he simply stopped and waited where he was, fifteen feet from the restaurant's front door, squinting, with a toothpick nestled between his lips. It was a clear day and the sun was beating down with a surprising intensity for September.

The man stopped five feet away, locking eyes with Gilbert.

Gilbert spoke first, saying, "You need something, sport?"

"Just to be clear, since you don't strike me as the most intelligent guy I've encountered this week, when I was talking about the shooter being a coward, I was referring to you. You were the shooter, so you're also a coward. Am I wrong on either count?"

Jesus, Dustin thought. *This guy doesn't fool around. Comes on strong, right from the get-go.*

Dustin glanced over at Gilbert, who had a smirk on his face, as usual. Like he was amused, but not worried in the least. Gilbert slowly pulled the toothpick out of his mouth and casually flicked it into the parking lot. "Who the hell are you again?"

"My name is Phil Colby."

"You really this dumb, Phil Colby?"

"Who can tell? I've never had my IQ tested. You gonna answer my question?"

"You ready to take on three guys at once?"

Colby said, "What, you three? There won't even be one to take on. I'm a good judge of people, and I'm pretty sure about that. Your two friends aren't gonna back you up. They don't think you're worth the trouble. Anybody can see that, except you, I guess. That leaves you, by yourself, and you don't really concern me."

Gilbert gave a fake chuckle. "Why's that?"

"Cowards aren't much of a threat, except for shooting people in the back."

Gilbert looked at Dustin and said, "You believe this guy?" Dustin didn't say anything. He was so tired of Gilbert and all the trouble that seemed to follow him around.

"Of course, you're welcome to prove me wrong," Colby said.

"Yeah? How would I do that?" Gilbert was still smirking. "Just for conversation's sake, tell me."

"Kick my ass."

The tension was ratcheting up so high, Dustin could hardly stand to watch. He could feel perspiration trickling from underneath his armpits. He was tempted to walk away, get in his truck, and drive home to East Texas without stopping. But he couldn't move.

Gilbert said, "That's all it would take? Kicking your ass?"

"You bet. A coward wouldn't have the guts to even try."

"You're a feisty little booger, aren't you?"

"A better question is: Why are you still talking when you should be kicking my ass?"

Dustin had never seen anyone deal with Gilbert this directly, and without the slightest detectable trace of fear.

"I guess because it don't really matter to me whether you think I'm a coward or not," Gilbert said. "You're nobody. You're some game warden's jack-off buddy, that's about it."

"See, you're still talking. Still mouthing off. That's what cowards do. Easier to talk than to take action. By now, your friends are starting to understand what a coward you are. Their respect for you—if they ever had any—is gone now."

"Fuck you." Now the smirk was disappearing. This man had definitely gotten under Gilbert's skin.

"More talking. Easier than proving you're not a coward."

Dustin had lost track how many times Colby had said the word "coward." He was repeating it, Dustin knew, because there weren't many worse things to call a man.

"Listen, asshole," Gilbert said. "I don't have to prove anything to you. Besides, how do I know you aren't setting me up? That game warden probably asked you to do this so he could arrest me for assault."

"He doesn't know I'm still here. And you and your buddies can say I started it, because it's true. I did start it. That means you won't get arrested."

"I will be if I throw the first punch."

"So that's what's holding you back? You want me to throw the first punch instead?"

The four men were standing in front of a plate-glass window that gave everyone inside the restaurant a clear view of the parking lot. Dustin glanced through the glass and saw that virtually every customer was watching the scene that was unfolding outside.

Gilbert hadn't answered the question, and Dustin didn't blame him. There was something about this man that was intimidating as hell. He reminded Dustin of some of the pit dogs he'd seen—the ones that would keep fighting, injured, bleeding, it didn't matter—until they'd destroyed their opponent. Relentless determination. Once they started, it was almost impossible to make them stop.

"I'll do it," Colby said, leaning closer, his voice low. "Just say you want me to. That's all you gotta do. Just say it. But you should know that I won't stop with the first punch. That man you shot at? The game warden? He's my best friend. Known him since I was six years old. I love him like a brother. So if you tell me to throw the first punch, you better believe I will, and I'll try to do as much damage to you as I possibly can. One or both of us will be leaving here in an ambulance. So go ahead. Say it."

Dustin realized he was holding his breath—and trying to decide what he'd do if the shit hit the fan. Cover Gilbert's back? Not a chance. No, the only question was: Stay and watch or get the hell out of Dodge?

Gilbert looked like he was just about to act. A punch, a headbutt, something. But he couldn't bring himself to do it. The moment passed.

"Well, I guess that answers my question," Colby said.

He turned and walked to his truck without a backward glance.

Another day, another shopping excursion. Apparently. This time, Leigh Anne Beech went south on Highway 281 out of Johnson City, as she'd done the day before, but she bypassed the turnoff on Highway 290 to Austin.

Going to Blanco?

Nope. She passed through and kept going.

Forty minutes later, she entered the northernmost outskirts of San Antonio. Turned right—west—on Loop 1604. Exited at Blanco Road and took the turnaround over the highway, which put her going east on the access road. Turned into a shopping center called Ventura Plaza and parked in front of a restaurant called Silo.

Roy Ballard parked several rows away and watched Leigh Anne Beech enter the restaurant by herself. He had binoculars, and he was lucky that the restaurant was fronted with a wall of windows. He watched from seventy yards as she was shown to a table where two women—attractive, of course, and about the same age as Leigh Anne—were already seated. They rose to greet her and air kisses were exchanged all around.

Roy grabbed one of his cameras—one with a superzoom lens—and took several shots of the women. Chances were good he would never need the photos for anything, but taking photos didn't cost anything.

While the threesome had lunch, so did he: a turkey-and-avocado sandwich he pulled from a small ice chest, plus a bag of chips and a can of root beer. He was done in about ten minutes, whereas the ladies stretched their lunch to an hour and a half. Then they appeared to request that the waiter provide separate tickets for each of them.

Finally, out they came for some animated chat on the sidewalk, followed by more air kisses, and then Leigh Anne Beech got back into her BMW and went west once again on Loop 1604. Not going home just yet. She exited a few minutes later and pulled into a shopping center called the Shops at La Cantera.

It was only when a Lexus parked next to the BMW that Roy realized one of the other ladies from lunch had followed Leigh Anne Beech over to the shopping center. She had to have been behind Roy on the way over, and that made him feel sloppy. He could have been spotted. Fortunately, these women weren't trained surveillance experts, and Roy's aging beige minivan was all but invisible to anyone in these ladies' tax bracket.

They shopped for about two hours, which resulted in Leigh Anne Beech carrying one small bag from a place called bebe. All lowercase letters. Marketing geniuses. Roy noticed that the women lingered in front of Victoria's Secret, looking into the windows, but they didn't go inside. Darn the luck.

Just before rush hour, the ladies went their separate ways. Leigh Anne Beech drove her BMW straight home.

"This asshole is really starting to piss me off," Nicole said.

She and Marlin were sitting on the porch swing, beer bottles in hand, an hour before dark. Geist was lying in the yard, twenty feet away, enjoying a patch of weak sunlight. Marlin had just finished recounting his experience at the café that afternoon, including Weems's veiled threats.

"I don't think I've ever come closer to losing my cool," Marlin said.

"That's what he wanted you to do."

"Yeah."

"I'm proud that you didn't."

"Thanks. Both of us need to be careful. Keep our eyes and ears open."

"We will."

"I have to admit, I'm feeling a little, I don't know—like I should've..."

"Broken his nose? Kicked him in the teeth? Ruptured his kidney?"

"Well, yeah."

"I know you know better than that. That would've been a disaster."

Marlin took a long drink from the bottle of beer in his

hand. "Sure would've felt good."

"Besides," she said, "if it comes to that, I get first crack."

He looked at her. "You're really worked up, huh?"

"What he did to Armando Salazar should put him in prison for years. That poor guy absolutely did not deserve what happened to him. Gilbert Weems is an animal and he should be locked up."

"Agreed—if it was him." She whirled toward him with her mouth open and her eyes wide, and he said, "Hold on, take it easy. I'm not saying it wasn't him, but we still need to prove it."

CHAPTER 28

The next morning, Marlin met Bobby Garza and chief deputy Bill Tatum in the conference room at the sheriff's office. Garza had texted them both the evening before to arrange the meeting. The sheriff arrived a few minutes late, but he was carrying a box of glazed donuts, which he set in the center of the table.

"Breakfast of champions," Tatum said.

"Only the best," Garza said.

Marlin took one and set it on a napkin. He already had a mug of hot coffee.

"Okay," Garza said. "I wanted to sit down and talk for a minute about both the Sammy Beech case and the walking crime wave known as Gilbert Weems. Both of these cases are going nowhere, and frankly, it's starting to piss me off. So let's do some brainstorming and see if that gets us anywhere."

"Can't hurt," Tatum said.

"John," Garza said. "Tell Bill about your run-in yesterday with Weems."

Marlin had called the sheriff the previous afternoon and given him the highlights of his encounter at the café, but now he described it in detail for the chief deputy, including the veiled threat about paying Nicole a visit while Marlin was on patrol.

"Kudos for keeping your cool," Tatum said. "I bet you wanted to knock him cold."

"It crossed my mind."

"He just loves to provoke, doesn't he?" Tatum said.

"Nice of Phil Colby to say some of the things you couldn't," Garza said. "You talk to him since then?"

"Phil?"

"Yeah."

"No."

"Apparently, he had a few words with Weems in the parking lot," Garza said.

"Huh. I hadn't heard about that." Marlin remembered now that Phil had seemed to linger in his truck after lunch. Obviously, he wanted Marlin to leave so he could confront Weems by himself.

Garza said, "At this point, I gotta be honest—unless something shakes lose, Weems is gonna skate on two felony charges."

"Still putting pressure on Dustin Bryant?" Marlin asked.

"Yeah. He hasn't gone for it yet. I'll keep after him, but I really thought he'd break by now. I said we had video of the assault, but in hindsight that might've been a mistake. Easy enough for him to go back to the store and see if there are surveillance cameras, at which point he'd know I was lying."

Marlin said, "Did you say the video was from a surveillance camera?"

Garza paused, thinking, then smiled. "No, I said it was all on video, that's all. So it could be video from someone's phone. That's where you were going, right?"

"Exactly."

"So maybe I give him one more push, saying not only is it on video, but we have a witness to boot. I mean, we'd have to have a witness, if someone shot it on their phone."

"The only flaw with that," Tatum said, "is why would someone be shooting video of Weems or Salazar prior to the assault? We know from Sharon Greene that the assault was sudden. There wasn't an argument or confrontation beforehand. So why would someone be recording the scene? Just random coincidence? That seems like a stretch. And if we did have video, why wouldn't we have already arrested Weems?"

"Yeah," Garza said, deflating. "Those are good points."

"On the other hand," Marlin said, "if Bryant thinks you lied to him about having video, what's the harm in pushing it further? You come right out and say it's a cell-phone video, but it's not that great, so we're working on getting it cleaned up. That means now's the time for Bryant to come forth as a witness himself, while he still has a chance. Maybe that will push him over the edge. With luck, he won't even wonder why anyone was shooting video. Or maybe he'll think you're stretching the facts—that you do have video, but it's of the moments right after the assault. He'd have to call your bluff to find out."

Armando jerked awake from a nightmare and the sudden movement made his head throb. But he hardly noticed it, because the content of the nightmare was lingering as he woke, and he was trying to prevent it from slipping away.

Armando had just been assaulted again in his dream.

By a redheaded man. *The* redheaded man, theoretically.

It seemed so real. Armando had pulled into the convenience store, parked, then dialed Sharon's number. He stepped from his Prius, phone to his ear, and began to go inside. He wasn't paying much attention to his surroundings, but this was Johnson City, not some big, dangerous city. Nothing to worry about out here, right?

Sharon answered, and Armando said hello, and then—

Fucking faggot.

Armando heard it, looked up, and—
WHAM!

A massive jolt, and then he was on the pavement, head spinning. What in the hell had just happened? It had had the startling force and impact of a car wreck. He put his hand to his face to staunch the flow of blood that was dripping from his face. He could feel split skin. Teeth missing.

He realized there was a man towering over him.

Armando looked up—way up—and there he was. The redheaded man. Armando saw his face. Not clearly, but he got a sense of it. The shape, the proportions, the angle of the jaw.

Lying in the hospital bed, Armando concentrated on that face. Trying to hold on to it. Memorize it as best he could. And he was wondering—was this entire dream, including the face, something his imagination had conjured up to fill in the blanks? Or was it an accurate memory? Could he trust it? After the assault, had he come to just long enough to see the man's face? More important, if his memory was coming back, would the details become sharper and crisper over time? Would that face come into focus?

"What's the latest with the mysterious Russian woman?" Garza asked.

"Aleksandra Babikova," Marlin said. He was tempted to grab another donut, but he resisted.

"Right."

"Don't know anything new about her, but I managed to track down her sister on Facebook. She got back to me once, and now I'm waiting to hear back again. With luck, she'll give me a phone number."

"Does the sister live in Dallas, too?"

"No, still in Russia, according to her Facebook account."

"Didn't you tell me the other day that you have an address for Aleksandra in Dallas?"

"Yeah, if it's current."

Marlin knew what Garza was thinking. He'd been thinking the same thing himself. Like it or not, it might be time for a road trip.

Red O'Brien was acutely aware of his own shortcomings. His IQ landed in a disappointing part of the bell curve. He had very few unique professional skills or qualifications. Neither his looks nor his personality had ever garnered him any great success with the ladies. He was admittedly a slacker in the area of personal hygiene. He couldn't sing, dance, write, draw, or even tell a joke particularly well. He tended to associate with persons of questionable character. Hell, his own character was questionable—which explained the dozens of citations, fines, garnishments, indictments, levies, and other assorted penalties and sanctions imposed on him by various federal, state, county, and city agencies and organizations over the years.

But he did have a finely honed bullshit detector.

He saw this as a major strength that he had grown to heed and respect. Whether this ability was borne of an innate skepticism or a learned distrust, Red could identify bullshit like nobody's business. Which wasn't to say that he could spot every last bit of bullshit he ever heard. That was nearly impossible. Some bullshit slipped past him, but that bullshit tended to be trivial.

For instance, if someone mentioned that Keystone Light was on sale at the Super S, it was doubtful that Red's bullshit detector would go off, because why would someone make something like that up? And if they did, what would they gain? And what would it matter if Red believed them? So, yeah, someone could bullshit about that if they really wanted to, and Red might not know it.

But if that same person said they were selling a 15-year-old Ford F-150 with only seventy thousand miles on it—and that person wasn't a little old lady, a shut-in, or a hermit—Red's bullshit detector would go on high alert. If one of Red's friends said they'd hit three doves with one shotgun blast, another alert. If a drunk in a bar bragged about the time he whipped two bikers at once without even spitting out his cigarette, Red could almost hear the bells and whistles going off.

Conversely, someone could have a fantastic reason to bullshit, but Red would think they were telling the truth—and later he'd learn that he was right. Like with Grady Beech and the tattooed pig. When Armando had pointed out that the whole thing might be bullshit, Red was concerned. But they had later learned that it wasn't bullshit, and Red had realized in hindsight that his bullshit detector hadn't gone off.

Honestly, Red didn't know why it worked. He wasn't sure why some things set the detector off and others didn't, but he figured it was a complicated formula having to do with the level of plausibility of the alleged occurrence, minus the incentive for someone to make it up, divided by the reputation of the person making the claim, multiplied by the personal price Red might pay for believing it. Or who the hell knows, but it worked, and that was the important thing.

So, the previous afternoon and evening, after Jack Chambers had said that the bounty pig had been shot, when Red's bullshit detector began to give a faint but persistent ping, Red listened. And he began to think. Wouldn't it make sense that someone would spread that rumor eventually?

Red had been listening to the local and regional radio stations ever since, waiting to hear it from a reliable source, but nobody had been able to confirm it. Lots of talk, but no details. *Why isn't the winner coming forward?* everyone was asking. *Why wait?* Red figured that was because there wasn't—

"Where the hell you going?" Billy Don asked.

They were in Red's truck on Highway 281 heading south. They'd passed the sheriff's office and El Charro Mexican Restaurant and Whittington's Jerky, and Red had kept on going past the city limits, because he was preoccupied, and because he was growing tired of the search for the redheaded man.

"Jesus, how long do you wanna keep driving around?" Red asked, pulling into the left lane for a U-turn at the next crossover.

"As long as it takes," Billy Don replied. "He's gotta be around here somewhere."

They'd visited nearly every retail business in town, and quite a few waitresses and cashiers had reported seeing the guy. But Red and Billy Don hadn't seen him yet themselves. Red had had the smart idea to visit the only two motels in Johnson City, but that was a dead end. At the first motel—the Best Western—the clerk said they didn't have a guy like that staying there. At the second motel—a little mom-and-pop place called the Hill Country Inn—the clerk, a kid no older than twenty, said, "Sorry, but it's against policy to reveal information about our guests."

"So he is a guest?" Red said.

"I didn't say that."

"So he isn't a guest?"

"Didn't say that either."

"Well, it's one or the other," Red said.

"Obviously."

Smart-aleck punk.

Red tried another tack, slipping a bill from his pocket and discreetly placing it on the counter. "How 'bout you blink twice if the guy is staying here?"

The kid looked at the bill and laughed. "Is that a joke?"

A dollar didn't go as far as it used to. Red dug around and came out with a five, but the kid said, "Look, I'm not taking a bribe. I could lose my job. I'm the interim assistant day manager."

"Whoop-de-doo," Red said, because by now it was apparent that the kid wasn't going to cooperate. "I think that's how Donald Trump got his start."

"It sure wasn't by taking dollar bribes from rednecks."

Red hadn't been able to think of a good comeback, so he'd snatched his money off the counter and left.

Now, as he drove through Johnson City for the umpteenth time, he said, "He could be staying in Blanco. We haven't even checked there yet. All the motels are full up here, so maybe he's staying down there."

Red didn't really want to drive the fourteen miles to Blanco and start the search all over again, but Billy Don was set on finding the guy, and if that's what it was going to take before they could start hunting the pig again, Red was resigned to getting it done as quickly as possible.

"Don't forget Dripping Springs," Billy Don said. "Marble Falls. Wimberley."

Jesus. They could be chasing this jerk for days.

CHAPTER 29

Dexter Crabtree was still in a fairly deep mental fog when he called the Wal-Mart in Marble Falls for the second time. Had to deal with the damn automated menu again, but he finally got a real person. A woman who sounded like she was chewing food while she talked. She said Vera Spillar wasn't working this morning. Great. *Does she work this afternoon?* The woman didn't know.

Dexter hung up and swiveled—slowly, so as to avoid vertigo—toward his computer. Lot of people nowadays didn't have a landline, preferring a cell phone only. But he got lucky and found a listing for her in one of the online directories.

He dialed.

She answered after three rings. His name had obviously popped up on Caller ID, because she said, "Isn't this kind of stupid, calling me at home?"

Well, shit. She was right. That's how out of it he was. Big mistake. He blamed it on the fact that he was still reeling from the blow to his head yesterday when he'd hit the pavement. The ER doctor hadn't wanted to let him leave, saying he might have a concussion, and because Dexter's vital signs were all over the place. Dexter hadn't told the doc about the Adderall, of course. He had no intention of submitting to a battery of tests to figure out what was wrong with him—especially when he knew exactly what the problem was. He just needed to dial his usage back a bit, that's all. No big deal. Didn't need to listen to a lecture from some young doctor.

"I had no other way to reach you," he said to Vera Spillar, trying to put some attitude in his voice, because he didn't like this woman talking down to him.

"That don't make it any smarter. I've been doing some reading on the Internet, and we both could get in major trouble. I didn't realize this was such a big deal."

"Didn't I already tell you that? But as long as you keep your mouth shut…"

She laughed. "I ain't got a lot to keep it shut about so far. You send that money or what?"

His head was throbbing, and this raging bitch was making it worse.

"That's why I'm calling. Ran into a little delay."

"What kind of delay?" She sounded suspicious.

So he told her exactly what had happened. Sort of. Instead of saying he fainted and cracked his head, he said somebody came up from behind and waylaid him. The robber stole the cash and his Mercedes, which was still missing. Probably in some chop shop by now, or inside a trailer headed for Mexico. Cops said they'd call if they found it. He wasn't holding his breath.

When he finished with the story, Vera Spillar said, "Rough break."

"Nine stitches," Dexter said. "They got me on hydrocodone." And now he was wondering, for the first time, if the painkillers would interact with the Adderall. He should check into that. Could be dangerous.

"I thought you were a tough guy," she said. "Some kind of stud back in the day."

My fucking god, this woman was a ball breaker.

"I'm just telling you what happened."

"I feel your pain," she said, being sarcastic, "but it ain't my problem."

"I never said it was," he said, gritting his teeth, and starting to lose his patience. "But you won't get a package today. That's what I'm saying."

"You got one more day," she said, "or our deal is off."

"I'll send it this afternoon, overnight express. You'll have it tomorrow."

"Don't need to know the details. Just send it."

She hung up, and that was a good thing, because that meant she didn't hear the long and colorful string of verbal abuse that followed.

"I might have to run up to Dallas," Marlin said into his cell phone, after he returned to his office within the sheriff's department. He'd noticed lately that he tended to use his cell phone even when a landline was available. Funny, because for years he had resisted owning a cell phone.

"Oh, yeah? What for?" Phil Colby replied.

"Need to track down a possible witness on a case."

"When?"

"Haven't decided yet. Maybe tomorrow. Or I might go ahead and leave this afternoon."

There was a silence on the line for a moment. Then Colby said, "And considering some of the things that shithead said at the café yesterday..."

"Yeah. Would you mind checking on Nicole?"

"Of course not."

"Does that make me a sexist pig?"

"Well, considering that Nicole is probably more capable of taking care of herself than either of us are at taking care of ourselves, then yeah, probably."

"True."

"Plus, I've seen her shoot. She puts us both to shame."

"Agreed."

"And she's generally smarter than both of us, don't you think?"

"Almost certainly."

"In fact, now that I think about it, maybe you should be asking Nicole to check on me instead."

"That might be right, based on the rumors I'm hearing," Marlin said.

"What rumors?"

"That you mouthed off to Weems in the parking lot after we had lunch."

"Mouthed off? When have you known me to mouth off?"

"Just about every waking moment."

"Okay, but I didn't mouth off to Weems."

"What would you call it?"

"Uh, attempting to reason with a man of limited intellect."

"What a coincidence. That's what I'm doing right now."

"I see what you did there, you clever bastard."

Marlin paused for a moment. After his meeting with Garza and Tatum, he had hoped to find a message waiting from Tatyana, with contact information for Aleksandra, but Tatyana hadn't responded. He said, "Seriously, Weems is not a pushover. He's dangerous."

"Hold on a sec." A few seconds later, Colby said, "Hear this?"

A sound followed. Recognizable. Colby had just racked the slide on his nine-millimeter Glock semi-automatic.

"I don't know whether to be comforted or concerned," Marlin said.

"Everything will be fine. Go to Dallas. I can crash at your place if you want. That is, if you can trust your wife to keep her mitts off me."

"I'm pretty sure she could control herself, but no, I don't

think that's necessary. Just maybe give her a call at some point. Or swing by."

"You got it."

"And if it turns out I'll be coming back home tonight, I'll let you know."

"Deal."

When they hung up, Marlin checked his Facebook account, just to make sure he hadn't received any messages. He was alerted by email anytime someone sent a message, but he'd noticed there was sometimes a delay of several hours.

There was no message. In fact, when he checked, he couldn't find Tatyana's previous reply, or any of the communication between them. He checked his friends list and Tatyana Babikova was no longer on it.

She'd unfriended him. Not just unfriended him, but blocked him, too.

Dustin Bryant was lying in his bed in the motel room, watching mindless crap on TV and trying not to think of anything at all. But it was hard. He hated mornings in the motel room, because it meant being cooped up with Gilbert for so damn long. And Gilbert was always massively hungover, which made him surly.

But there wasn't a good reason to leave the motel room until lunchtime, was there? Do what? Drive around? No sense hunting pigs during the daytime, because pigs moved mostly at night. Can't hunt around the clock, so it made sense to hunt after dark, when the odds were the best. Rest up during the day.

"Turn the damn channel," Gilbert said from his own bed. "What is this shit we're watching?"

Dustin had thought Gilbert was snoozing, but no such luck. In response, instead of changing the channels, Dustin tossed the remote in Gilbert's direction. It landed on the mattress beside him.

Really, fuck all this.

Dustin was starting to lose all respect for himself. Why was he still scared of Gilbert? Dustin was honest enough to admit to himself that, yeah, he was scared of Gilbert. But why? The man outside the café yesterday had proven that Gilbert wasn't necessarily as tough as he thought he was. You could back him down if you stood up to him. If you had the balls. Maybe that man had been crazy to test Gilbert like that, but it had worked.

Dustin, on the other hand, always caved. Always did what Gilbert said. That's why they were still here, in Johnson City, instead of back home. Dustin wondered why he couldn't just face up to Gilbert and say, "Me and Dylan are hitting the road. You can come with us, or you can stay here, it don't matter to me. But if you're coming, pack your bags, 'cause we're leaving in ten minutes."

He imagined saying those words, but they just wouldn't come. The man yesterday had called Gilbert a coward, but Dustin figured Gilbert wasn't the only coward in the room.

Now Dustin could feel his phone vibrating again on his hip. Crap. He didn't react. Didn't want Gilbert to know.

"I'm going to the Coke machine," he said a few minutes later, lifting himself off the mattress. "You want anything?"

"Ginger ale," Gilbert said. "Couple of cans." Ginger ale was Gilbert's favorite mixer, which meant he'd be drinking whiskey soon, and it wasn't even noon yet. Great.

Dustin rose from the bed and walked over to the closed bathroom door. Dylan had been taking a shower, but the water had cut off a few minutes ago. "Want a Coke?" Dustin said.

"Yeah. I got some quarters on the nightstand."

The moment Dustin stepped outside, he pulled his phone from his hip and listened to the new voicemail from the sheriff.

CHAPTER 30

Third day in a row, Leigh Anne Beech was in her BMW and on the move. Grady Beech had called Roy Ballard earlier to say that Leigh Anne was planning to meet a friend for lunch in Wimberley.

Roy waited at a rest stop and tracked her on GPS as she took McCall Creek Road in a northeast direction to Highway 290. But then, instead of going east, she turned west. Not the way to Wimberley. She hit Highway 281 and went north to Johnson City. Then she went west again.

By then, Roy was trailing in his Caravan. Way back, because he didn't want her to become suspicious. Even a beige minivan could become conspicuous if you saw it in your rearview mirror for three days in a row.

Roy had learned that Leigh Anne Beech was not a prudent or attentive driver. She tended to talk on the phone a lot. Roy could tell simply by the way she weaved out of her lane at times and her speed would drop. Other times, she cruised along at 80 to 85 in places where the limit was 65 or 70. Roy didn't want to get pinged for a ticket, but he had to take that chance. If he laid back and lost sight of her, he could always find her vehicle later via the GPS unit, but what if he'd missed a good photo op in the meantime?

She passed through a tiny community called Hye, home of Garrison Brothers Distillery, then through a larger community called Stonewall, home of Stonewall Motel, Stonewall Body Shop, and Stonewall Smokehouse. Roy wondered how they came up with such creative names.

Fifteen minutes later, Leigh Anne Beech reached the edge of Fredericksburg. Great little town with a German heritage. A tourist destination. Lots of unique little shops and restaurants. Leigh Anne Beech filled up with gas, then she stopped at a shop that sold Amish furniture, food, and gifts. She was in there for about twenty minutes, but when she exited, she had no packages or bags.

Then she got back into her BMW and drove to a motel called the Big Buck Inn.

Gilbert surprised Dustin by saying, "Let's take a drive."

"Where to?"

"Anywhere, for fuck's sake. I'm tired of lying around this shithole."

So they climbed into Dustin's truck and headed out.

"Go west," Gilbert said from the passenger seat. He had a large Styrofoam cup filled with ice, whiskey, and ginger ale between his thighs.

Dustin went west on Highway 290. What did it matter which direction they went? They were just out for a drive, right?

But then Gilbert said, "Take a left up here."

Now Dustin was starting to wonder. Dylan, in the back seat, caught Dustin's eye in the rearview mirror and shot him a look that said, *What the hell is Gilbert up to now?*

Dustin turned left on Avenue F, drove past the headquarters for the Pedernales Electric Cooperative, past some small, neatly maintained homes and trailers, and then the structures gave way to open ranch land. Avenue F had turned into County Road 203, also known as Miller Creek Loop.

Now Gilbert had his phone out, checking something.

"Where are we going?" Dustin asked.

Gilbert didn't reply.

The road curved sharply west, then south again. Gilbert was looking at a map on his phone.

"Gilbert?"

"Not much further."

"Where are we going?"

Silence. Then Gilbert said, "Slow down. Slow down. Yeah, right up here. Pull over."

"Where?"

There was nothing but a gated ranch entrance with limestone columns on either side.

"Here," Gilbert said.

Dustin simply stopped where he was, on the pavement. They had passed no other cars on this road, and it wasn't likely they'd see anyone traveling in either direction. Gilbert set his drink in a cup holder, then opened the door and got out. He went to the bed of the truck and started rummaging around for something.

"What the hell are we doing?" Dylan said quietly.

Dustin shook his head, and then his eyes came to rest on a nearby mailbox. COLBY was stenciled on the side. The man in the parking lot outside the café—the game warden's friend—had been named Phil Colby. Gilbert had managed to track him down.

And now Gilbert was coming around the side of the truck, and Dustin saw that he was carrying a scrap of two-by-four about three feet long.

Gilbert walked toward Colby's gate but angled to the left, where an electronic keypad was mounted at the top of the metal post. This was how visitors got onto the ranch—by punching a code into the keypad. Gilbert drew back with the piece of scrap lumber and smashed it into the keypad. Again. And again.

"Goddamn it," Dylan said.

Dustin looked straight ahead through the windshield. Nobody coming. He checked the rearview. All clear. Dustin decided that if a vehicle approached from either direction, he'd take off, leaving Gilbert standing on the side of the road.

"This is so stupid," Dylan said.

Gilbert finished up with the keypad and let out an excited whoop. Then he went after the mailbox.

Leigh Anne Beech drove to the rear of the motel, out of Roy's sight, and he wondered if she was meeting someone who already had a room. But less than a minute later, here she came, walking around to the front of the building, to the office. She checked in, which took no more than a minute or so, then returned to the rear of the motel.

Discretion. That's why she'd parked first, so that her BMW wouldn't be sitting in plain view from the road. And it was obvious she'd done this before. She knew she'd get a room in the back, because that's what she always got.

Roy parked at a bank next door, which would give him a good view of any other vehicles that might pull into the motel lot. Just to be sure, Roy checked Google Maps and saw that there was no exit from the parking lot in the back of the property. So he stayed where he was. And waited. For a long time—thirty minutes—nobody came or went. Whoever Leigh Anne was meeting couldn't already be in the room, because then she wouldn't have needed to check in.

Oh, hell. What if they were on foot? Roy checked Google Maps again, using street view, and saw that a six-foot privacy fence followed the entire perimeter behind the motel. Unless somebody wanted to climb that fence in broad daylight, they'd enter through the front of the property.

A little while later, Roy realized a full hour had passed. If Leigh Anne was meeting somebody, they were very late. Roy was beginning to wonder if Leigh Anne might have some other reason for renting a motel room. Maybe she simply needed some time alone, and this was the best way to get it. Maybe she had some strange hobby that her husband wouldn't like. Maybe she was a Santería priestess and she needed solitude to conduct animal sacrifices. Maybe she had a lover, but they were strictly into phone sex.

Then a white Chevy truck swung into the motel parking lot and drove around to the back.

"Turn around!" Billy Don shouted suddenly, just about giving Red an aneurysm, because they'd been riding in silence for the past few miles.

Now Billy Don was attempting to twist his massive torso and look back over his right shoulder at a vehicle they'd just passed—a blue GMC truck that was waiting to enter Highway 281 from Miller Creek Loop. The intersection was roughly halfway between Johnson City and Blanco.

"The red-haired guy!" Billy Don thundered.

"In that truck?"

"The passenger! He's getting away!"

Red had instinctively slowed down, but now he gave it gas again, because he could see in his rearview mirror that the truck was going straight across the highway, crossing the median to go north. The opposite direction. Red had no choice but to go to the next crossover, several hundred yards down the road.

"Hurry!" Billy Don was twitching and jerking, still looking out the rear window.

"How do you know it was him?" Red switched into the left-hand lane.

"'Cause he was taller'n hell and had red hair."

Red started to argue but changed his mind, because tall and redheaded pretty much summed up the person they were searching for. And if, somehow, against the odds, there happened to be two tall redheads in the area, would it really matter if Billy Don kicked the shit out of the wrong one? Sure wouldn't matter to Red. And there would be no way of knowing, since the redhead would almost certainly deny beating up Armando, even if he'd done it.

"We're gonna lose him!" Billy Don said.

"Just hold on, dammit." Red finally reached a crossover and whipped the truck left, but there was oncoming traffic, so he had to wait.

"Shit! Go!"

"You want me to get hit by a semi?"

Finally there was a break in traffic, and Red gunned it, which meant his old Ford crept forward at a painfully slow pace.

"I don't even see 'em anymore," Billy Don said.

Red kept the accelerator mashed, and eventually the Ford began to pick up some speed. Sixty miles per hour. Then seventy. And eighty. Red wasn't crazy about the idea of getting pulled over, but he figured if he got stopped, he'd tell the cop he was trying to apprehend a man who'd committed an assault.

Red had it up to ninety when Billy Don pointed toward a vehicle on the horizon and said, "I think that's them."

CHAPTER 31

Roy Ballard had to take a calculated risk.

He needed to know whether the person in the white Chevy truck was going to Leigh Anne Beech's room, and there weren't many ways to accomplish that.

Since there was no exit from the parking lot back there, he couldn't pretend to be driving through. The privacy fence would prevent him from being able to see the rear of the motel from the next street over.

That left one viable option: Drive to the rear of the motel and pretend to be another customer. If he'd been thinking, he would've actually gone ahead and rented a room himself—providing perfect cover—but it was too late for that now. He would be conspicuous, especially to someone who was having a secret rendezvous with a lover. But the alternative was to give the man time to enter the room, then wait to see which room he exited, which could be overnight, or at least several hours. So Roy decided to take the gamble.

He counted to twenty after the Chevy disappeared from sight, then followed. When he turned the corner, he saw that the Chevy was already parked in a spot right next to Leigh Anne Beech's BMW. There were no other vehicles back here. Not a one. A man had just emerged from the white truck, and he was about to close the driver's door. But when he saw Roy's van rounding the corner, he stopped. He leaned into the truck to get something. Well, to pretend to get something. It was bad acting. The man was stalling. He didn't want to go into Leigh Anne Beech's room until he knew that Roy wasn't a danger.

So Roy went with his plan. Act like he was just another customer. He backed into a spot in front of the room at the near end of the building, a fair distance from the two other vehicles. He did not look in the direction of the Chevy. But in his peripheral vision, Roy could see that the man was still waiting.

Roy got out of the van and popped the rear hatch. Fortunately, he had a gym bag filled with some spare clothes back there. He slung the strap over his shoulder, closed the hatch, and turned toward the room. Just another traveler, checking into his room.

The man was still standing beside the Chevy, with the door open, now pretending to be checking his cell phone.

Roy had worked himself into a tight spot. He had to keep the ruse going. He took a credit card out of his wallet and slipped it into the door slot. Pulled it out and waited for the green light. Didn't get one, of course. Jiggled the handle. The door remained locked. So Roy went through the steps again. No use. And once more. Jiggled the handle even harder.

He said, "Goddamn it," just loud enough for the man to hear. Then Roy walked around the corner of the motel, as if he were returning to the front office to get a key that actually worked.

What he really did was simply stand there and wait. Sure enough, in just a few seconds, he heard the closing of the man's truck door. Half a minute later, he heard the closing of a motel room door.

Okay, so he hadn't actually seen which room the man had entered, but based on the man's behavior and where he had parked—and the fact that there were only two vehicles back there—it was obvious the man had just entered Leigh Anne Beech's room. It looked like Grady Beech was right.

But Roy would need additional evidence.

He waited another five minutes, then he returned to the van and quietly got inside. One of his best video cameras was mounted on a tripod, so now he aimed it toward the front door of Leigh Anne Beech's room, just a few feet from the BMW's front bumper. He kept the shot wide, so that it included both vehicles. He started recording. Anyone glancing toward the van, with its tinted windows, wouldn't notice a thing. The camera could record for hours.

Roy grabbed his laptop and walked to a coffee shop next door to the motel. Might as well be productive while he waited. He'd jotted down the license plate number on the Chevy when it had first entered the motel lot, and in just a few minutes, Roy would have the name of the registered owner, thanks to a website to which he paid a monthly fee. Worth every penny.

A waitress came and took his order—coffee and a slice of apple pie. Before she came back, Roy had the name. Now he just had to wait until the BMW and the Chevy were no longer parked behind the motel.

Dustin Bryant was waiting for the stoplight in Johnson City to turn green when a truck—an old red Ford with dents on every panel and paint missing in spots—pulled up on the driver's side. The passenger—a huge dude—motioned for Dustin to roll down his window.

The dude looked past Dustin at Gilbert. "Ain't you the guy that put a thumping on that queer the other night?"

"What's it to you?" Gilbert replied.

"Hell, don't get uptight. I just wanna shake your hand, if you're the guy. We don't need that type of perverseness around here, that's for sure. We got family values and such."

"Yeah, well, you should tell your sheriff that," Gilbert

said. "He's pretty uptight about it."

"So you *are* the guy?"

The big man was pushy. The driver—a skinny dude wearing a feed store cap—was leaning forward and watching.

"Why do you think it was me?" Gilbert asked.

"We heard it was a tall redheaded guy. Someone that don't live around here. Figured that was you. Y'all got dog boxes in the back, so I figure you're from East Texas."

The light changed, but there wasn't a vehicle behind either truck, so Dustin stayed where he was.

"Well, I ain't saying nothin' either way," Gilbert said, "but I can say if I was the guy, I wouldn't have no regrets about what I done."

Now the big man looked puzzled. "So...wait. You saying you did or didn't do it?"

Gilbert laughed. "You ain't too swift, are ya?"

The light turned red again.

The man's expression changed to a scowl. "Ain't no reason to get nasty."

The driver said, "Of course he's the guy, Billy Don. But he can't admit it, because someone might tell the cops."

"Bravo," Gilbert said. "You musta been the valedictorian of your class."

"Well, fuck you too, buddy," the driver said.

"Back at ya," Gilbert said.

Billy Don said, "If you're gonna mouth off, why don't y'all pull over and say it to my face?"

Dustin was so sick of this. Everywhere they went, Gilbert created trouble.

"Get bent," Gilbert said.

Billy Don pointed a meaty finger at Gilbert. "Listen, you gangly sumbitch. That guy you beat up was a friend of mine. That means you got a serious ass-kicking coming your way."

"A friend? Ain't that sweet. You one of his butt buddies?"

"One of his what?" Billy Don asked.

"What about you?" Gilbert said, addressing the driver. "You a rump ranger, too? Bet y'all have some nice three-ways, huh?"

Now the big passenger was red-faced and fuming, and he began to paw for the handle to open the truck door.

The light turned green and Dustin stomped on the gas. The red Ford tried to keep up, but it wasn't long before Dustin couldn't see it in the rearview mirror.

Roy gave it three hours, just to be safe. He finished his pie and his coffee, then he browsed through several of the quaint little shops along Main Street. When he returned to the motel and peeked around the corner to the rear lot, the BMW and the Chevy were both gone.

He went straight to his van, got in, and drove to a Sonic Drive-In less than a mile away. He ordered a Dr Pepper and a burger, and while he waited, he reviewed the video from the motel.

About an hour and a half after he'd started the recording, Leigh Anne Beech had exited the motel room by herself, hurried to her car, and drove away. Ten minutes later, the man from the Chevy had emerged. Roy was finally getting a good look at him. His hair was slicked back, wet from a shower. Decent-looking guy. Some might even say handsome. Mid-forties. Apparently Leigh Anne liked older men. The man glanced toward Roy's van, then climbed into the Chevy and drove away. Didn't take a genius to know what had happened in that motel room.

"Sir your fee linno, Kay?"

What? What did that mean?

Ryan was speaking gibberish. Dexter Crabtree could not understand his own son. It was unsettling.

"Huh?"

"Sure you're feeling okay?"

"Oh. Yeah. I feel fine."

"Yule ookalit tulpail."

What the hell? Dexter played it back in his mind. Then he got it. *You look a little pale.*

They were in Ryan's car, driving, and for a moment, Dexter couldn't remember where they were going. It was almost like an alcoholic blackout. Suddenly he's in the car, and he can't remember why. But he kept quiet, thinking, until it came to him. The rental car. They were going to pick up Dexter's rental car. A Mercedes CLS500. Not nearly as nice as his own, but it would have to do for the time being, until the insurance company agreed that his car was long gone.

Dexter had a to-do list:

Get the rental car.

Go to the bank and get cash.

Box the cash up and send it to Vera Spillar, overnight express.

Had to stay sharp and get it done, without any mistakes—but the fog in his brain was almost too much to bear. He wanted to blame it on the hydrocodone, but he knew better. He knew what the problem really was.

Two Adderall tablets weren't cutting it anymore. Not even close. It was time to admit that. Truth was, even three tablets weren't getting the job done. The last few times

Dexter Crabtree had stuffed, he'd gone with four tablets. That did the trick, but just barely. Was it time to go with five? Or even six? Was that what it would take to give him that edge again? That mental clarity?

"Jew breengyer dry verslie since?"

Dexter couldn't stand this much longer. Something was seriously wrong inside his brain. He was having to translate everything that Ryan said to him.

"Yeah," Crabtree replied. "I brought my driver's license."

CHAPTER 32

Marlin stopped in Hamilton, Texas, for a go-cup of coffee, but other than that he drove straight through to Dallas, making good time, hitting the outskirts before five o'clock, which, unfortunately, put him in the middle of rush hour. What a mess. Sometimes he forgot what life was like in big cities.

He crept along in bumper-to-bumper traffic toward the address he had for Aleksandra Babikova, which he knew from Googling was a unit in a loft complex near the campus of Southern Methodist University, just outside the municipality of University Park. Nice place to live, according to the website. Real nice. Health club. Olympic-size rooftop pool. Twenty-four-hour security team. If Aleksandra Babikova was still a resident, she was paying nearly three grand a month in rent, based on the prices Marlin had seen online. Whatever it was she did for a living, she must do damn well. That, or she had managed to turn her fifteen minutes of fame into a decent amount of money a few years back. Maybe she got royalties or something for that movie she'd been in. Marlin didn't know how it worked.

He finally reached the loft complex—an impressive four-story building in what was obviously one of the nicest areas of the city. Everything was clean and well maintained. He pulled in and found a guest parking spot easily enough.

He entered through the double glass doors and immediately came face to face with a guard behind a long counter at a reception area. Younger guy. Thirties. Neatly clipped black hair. Wearing a blue blazer adorned with the logo for the loft tower. A small sign written in ornate script read: *All Visitors Must Sign In.* Past the counter, to the left, was a bank of two elevators.

The man, wearing a telephone headset, offered a big smile. "Good evening, sir. May I help you?"

Marlin gave him a smile right back. "I would appreciate that. I'm here to see Aleksandra Babikova."

The smile cooled off a bit. Nothing dramatic, but there was definitely a change in the guard's demeanor.

"Miss Babikova?" the man asked. He seemed to be eyeing Marlin up and down. "Is she expecting you?"

Excellent, Marlin thought. Now he knew he had the right address. "No, she's not."

"I'll check to see if she is here. Whom may I say is visiting?"

"My name is John Marlin."

"Is this professional or personal?"

That was an odd and rather pushy question to ask, but maybe it was because Marlin was in uniform.

One of the elevators dinged and the doors opened. A second security guard, wearing an identical blue blazer, stepped out.

"Uh, professional," Marlin said. "She doesn't know me, but it's important that I speak to her."

Another small change in demeanor. The man's smile warmed up again. Now Marlin realized what was going on with the guard. He got his hackles up when he thought the visit might be personal, but relaxed when he learned it was professional.

"May I tell her what it pertains to?"

"I'm afraid not."

"Oh. Okay. One moment, please." The guard pressed a

button on a console and focused on nothing in particular.

Now the second guard—another young guy, but with blond hair—had reached the reception area. He walked behind the counter, took a seat in a rolling chair, and began to type on a keyboard in front of a computer.

Marlin waited.

Several moments later, the first guard said, "Good evening, Miss Babikova, it's James at the front desk."

At the mention of "Miss Babikova," the blond guard stole a discreet glance at Marlin, who almost had to laugh. These two guys were so hung up on Aleksandra Babikova, they couldn't resist checking out any man who came to see her. Maybe they were jealous or simply curious. Or James was jealous and the blond guy was curious.

James said, "His name is John Marlin and he appears to be a…" He looked at Marlin.

"Game warden from central Texas."

"A game warden from central Texas," James said into the phone. Pause. "Yes, that's right. A game warden." Pause. "From central Texas."

The blond guy was openly staring now. When Marlin looked at him, he smiled and said, "How ya doing?"

Marlin nodded a greeting and turned back toward James. He expected James to say something like, "Miss Babikova is wondering what this is about," but instead he punched a button on the console, ending the call, and said, "She'll be right down."

"That means ten or fifteen minutes," the blond guy said, grinning.

The dark-haired guard scowled at him, but the blond guy didn't notice.

Grady Beech agreed to meet Roy in the parking lot of the Super S in Johnson City. This was after Beech had asked, on the phone earlier, if Roy had learned anything.

"Yeah, I have," Roy replied. "We should talk in person."

Beech didn't respond right away, but Roy could hear him breathing. Then Beech said, "I was right, huh? Otherwise you'd say you hadn't learned anything yet."

At the time, Roy couldn't think of a reason to hold back. The man was going to learn the truth sooner or later. So Roy said, "Yeah, you were. I'm sorry to tell you that."

Another silence. Then Beech said, "You got video? Pictures?"

"Video."

And Beech had let out a long, sad sigh. Roy expected Beech to immediately ask for details—Who was Leigh Anne cheating with? Where? When?—because that's exactly what Roy would've done—but instead, Beech had asked Roy to meet him at the Super S.

So they'd set up a time, and now Beech opened the passenger door of Roy's Caravan and climbed in. They didn't shake hands or exchange any sort of greeting. Beech simply gave Roy a rueful grin and said, "Sucks to be right."

"Yeah, I imagine so. Wish I had better news."

"Me, too. It's disappointing, more than anything. Just so damn disappointing. I realize there's an age difference, but I always hoped that wouldn't be a problem. Or maybe it's something else entirely."

Roy waited, then said, "I know you don't know me well, and I'm no expert on this type of situation, but I'm willing to bet you'll look back on this someday and realize that it was all for the best. Maybe a little bad news now will lead to something better than you ever imagined."

"One can hope, huh?"

Roy shrugged. "You never know."

"I appreciate that."

They were parked to the far right side of the parking lot, closer to the Dollar General and the Subway. Plenty of privacy over here.

"Okay, well," Beech said, "I guess we should take a look at this video."

Roy had contemplated whether he should insist that Beech wait a day or two before viewing it. Roy didn't want Beech to learn the identify of Leigh Anne's lover, then get angry and do something stupid or impulsive. But Beech didn't appear volatile. Instead, he seemed defeated and resigned—like he'd been expecting this outcome, and had already come to terms with it.

So Roy opened his laptop and played the video. Beech watched with a grim face as Leigh Anne emerged from the motel room. Roy fast-forwarded, and then the man exited the room a few minutes later. Simple as that. Roy closed his laptop.

"You know that guy?" he asked.

Grady Beech shook his head.

"You sure?" Roy thought he'd seen a trace of surprise or recognition cross Beech's face when the man had appeared.

"Never seen him before. Doesn't really matter who it is, does it?"

The blond guard was right. It was a full twenty minutes before the elevator dinged and Aleksandra Babikova appeared. And when she did, she stepped into the lobby with the same self-possessed flair of a top actor stepping from a limo onto the red carpet at an awards presentation.

She was even more beautiful than any of the online photos had captured. Possibly the most eye-catching woman

Marlin had ever seen in person. She was dressed in a dark blue skirt that reached mid-thigh, heels, and a white silk blouse with a deep V neckline. She turned to face him but remained where she was, expecting him to move toward her. He did.

"Miss Babikova?" he said as he approached, extending a hand.

"Yes?" She shook his hand. She wasn't smiling, but she wasn't frowning, either. Her expression showed nothing except perhaps the faintest trace of curiosity. He had been wondering all along whether Tatyana had alerted Aleksandra that a game warden was looking for her, but if she had, Aleksandra wasn't showing any signs of it.

Her eyes were incredibly blue. Mesmerizing. She had to be close to six feet tall, and she was wearing heels, so her eyes were almost level with his.

"My name is John Marlin. I'm a game warden in Blanco County, west of Austin. Can we talk for a few minutes?"

"For what is this regarding?"

Marlin had no doubt that the two guards at the reception area were doing their best to eavesdrop on the conversation.

"I just need to ask you a couple of routine questions, and it would probably be best if we could speak somewhere more private. I noticed a Starbucks on the corner…"

She was studying the badge on his chest and the patch on his arm. "A game warden. Is this not a deputy of the deers and fishes?"

"Well…" He laughed. "Sort of. We enforce hunting and fishing laws, yes, but other kinds of laws, too. I help the sheriff in my county with many different investigations."

"Interesting."

"It can be."

"But mysterious, yes? You mention no details. What you investigate now is large secret?"

"Not at all. I'd be happy to tell you more. Just, uh, not here."

She didn't say anything right away. Instead, she was looking him in the eye. Holding his gaze. And now a slight smile slowly played across her lips. Whether she intended it or not, it was one of the most seductive things Marlin had ever seen.

In a low voice that the guards probably couldn't hear, Aleksandra Babikova said, "Perhaps we should maintain this conversation into my apartment."

CHAPTER 33

They'd done more driving—hours of driving, covering almost every square inch of pavement in Blanco County—but Red wasn't as impatient about it as he'd been before. In fact, now he was fully on board with it. He'd drive as far and as long as it would take to find the redheaded man again and shut his damn mouth.

Rump ranger?

Red sure as hell wasn't no damn rump ranger, and he wasn't going to let some inbred, banjo-strumming dog runner imply that he was. Red had every intention of giving that jerk a good old-fashioned beatdown, or at least watching with enjoyment as Billy Don did it.

"Maybe we should just park somewhere and wait for them to drive by," Billy Don said, as Red maneuvered the curves of Cypress Mill Road. They'd been cruising the northern end of the county, since that was the direction the redhead and his pals had headed from the stoplight in town. "If we keep moving and they keep moving, we might not ever see 'em. But if we stay in one spot and they keep moving, eventually we're gonna see 'em. Don't ya think?"

Normally, Red would've argued, simply based on the fact that—historically speaking—most of the things that came out of Billy Don's mouth were incorrect. But what he'd just said actually made some sense, and it would save a lot of money on gas, too.

"I was just gonna suggest that," Red said.

"Where ya think we oughta park?"

"Since we saw 'em in Johnson City, I'm betting they're staying there. So we should park somewhere in the center, like the Super S."

Billy Don agreed, so Red returned to the highway and went south, back to town. Just as he turned into the Super S parking lot, Billy Don said, "There's Grady Beech."

And he was right. Grady was just getting into his truck as a beige Dodge Caravan drove away. Red pulled up beside him and said, "Hey, there, Grady."

"Oh, hey." Grady started his truck.

"Listen, I'm glad we saw you. Nobody got the pig yet, right? There was a rumor going around, but I didn't believe it."

"The pig?" Grady seemed distracted. Even puzzled. How could he not know which pig Red was talking about?

Red laughed. "The *bounty* pig, Grady. Remember?"

"Yeah, it's still out there. Guys, I don't mean to be rude, but I have to go."

And Grady drove away without another word.

"That was weird," Billy Don said.

Armando woke again, in the late afternoon, and he felt even more clear-headed than he had that morning. Sure, there was still some pain, but his strength was returning, and he wasn't nearly as groggy or confused as he had been the day before. Almost back to normal.

And the image of the redheaded man had gelled even further.

Now Armando could see him sharply—the high forehead, prominent cheekbones, thin lips—and he knew that it wasn't just an apparition from a dream. This was a real memory. This was the man who had assaulted him.

It made him nervous. Palms sweaty. Heartbeat accelerating. Was he ready to do this? Wouldn't it be easier to let it go? Why create more trouble for himself? More drama?

But how would Armando feel if it happened to someone else? Or worse—what if the redheaded man killed someone because Armando had failed to stand up and do what was right?

He flipped slowly onto his left side and reached toward the small rolling nightstand beside his bed. His cell phone was resting there, along with a slip of paper with various phone numbers printed on it. He found the one he wanted, took a deep breath, and dialed.

After two rings, a woman answered, and Armando said, "Nicole, this is Armando. I'm sorry to bother you this late in the day, but can you help me with something? Can you let the sheriff know that I'm ready to look at a line-up?"

"I am investigating the circumstances revolving around the death of a high school boy—a young man—in Blanco County," Marlin said. "Great football player. All the big colleges wanted him."

They were seated on a couch in Aleksandra Babikova's loft apartment. It was a very large, open space, and everything in it spoke of money. The leather furniture. The contemporary art on the walls. Even the light fixtures. Where did all her money come from?

Marlin continued, saying, "His name was Sammy Beech. Did you know him?"

"Sammy Beech? I do not recall him."

"Do you recognize the name?"

"It is possibility. From news reports about his tragic

death. You are confident you would not enjoy coffee?"

"No, thanks."

"It is no trouble."

"I had some on the drive up here. Let me ask you this: What is it that you do for a living?"

"I am consultant."

"That covers a lot of ground. What kind of consultant?"

There was a slight pause. "Sports consultant."

Marlin felt a faint buzz in his chest—his body responding to the first sign that he might be on the right track. He said, "Okay, what exactly does that involve?"

She made a gesture with her hands—like *Where to start?*—and said, "Is very complicated. I provide services to an ample range of clients."

That was meaningless fluff. She seemed to be dodging his question. The buzz in his chest grew more pronounced. "Who are your clients?"

"My clients?"

"Yeah, just name a couple, if you don't mind. It's not a large secret, is it?"

She smiled. "You repeat back to me what I say earlier. You are clever man."

"Thanks."

She crossed her legs and leaned backward, spreading her arms in either direction to rest them along the top of the couch. As a result, the front of her blouse, which was unbuttoned to mid-chest, opened wide. She was trying to distract him. So obvious. He refused to look down.

"Have you at all times been this clever?" she said.

"No, only on rare occasions. Can you name a couple of your clients?"

Another pause, this one longer than the earlier one. Then she folded her arms, abandoning her distraction attempt, and said, "I'm afraid that subject must continue with confidentiality."

And Marlin immediately knew that the photo on Sammy Beech's phone was not a dead end. What kind of sports consultant needs to protect her list of clients?

"You won't tell me?" he said.

"American law gives me that alternative, yes?"

"It does."

"My clients value their seclusion."

"You mean their privacy?"

"Yes. Thank you."

Marlin decided to push harder. He pulled his phone from the holster on his hip and tapped the screen, bringing up the photo from Sammy's phone. He showed it to her, watching her face closely. "Ever seen this photo before?"

Practice had ended an hour ago. Kurt Milstead was in his office, which was in the same building as the gymnasium, detached from the rest of the high school. He was meeting with one of his assistant coaches, discussing some defensive adjustments for the game the following night, when Grady Beech opened the office door and stepped inside, without a greeting of any sort. He left the door open behind him. The hall outside was quiet, because all the players had already showered and gone home.

"Well, come on in, Grady," Milstead said sarcastically but jovially. "Don't mind us."

Grady didn't respond to Milstead's remark, but instead turned to the assistant coach and said, "Cliff, can you give us a few minutes alone?"

"Everything okay?" Cliff said. "You look like someone pissed in your corn flakes."

"Just need a few minutes with Kurt."

Cliff looked at Milstead, who nodded that it was okay. When the assistant coach had stood and left the office, Grady closed the door behind him. And he locked it. Then Grady swung back toward Milstead, and now he had a revolver in his hand, which he aimed directly at the coach's face.

"Jesus, take it easy, Grady," Milstead said, holding his hands in front of him.

"I caught you," Beech said.

"Caught me?"

Grady pulled back the hammer. "You are about the lowest of the low, you know that?"

"What—"

"Don't lie, Kurt. Whatever you do, don't lie."

"I won't, Grady."

"Good."

"Just tell me—what did I do?"

Beech aimed just inches above Milstead's head and pulled the trigger.

CHAPTER 34

Aleksandra Babikova was definitely surprised, maybe even shocked, by the photo on Sammy Beech's phone. She tried to cover it with a joke. "I have never seen her, but she is very beautiful woman."

"Hey, no argument there," Marlin said. "This photo was found on Sammy Beech's phone. Not just on the phone, but *taken* with the camera built into the phone. That means Sammy, or someone carrying his phone, was with you at some point and took this picture. Seems weird, especially since you said you never met him."

Now she wasn't just shocked, she was shaken. He waited for her to respond. She didn't.

"Miss Babikova, have you heard anything about this case in the past few days?"

She shook her head.

Marlin said, "When Sammy died back in September, we thought it was a motorcycle accident. But we recently learned that someone was chasing him, shooting at him. Whoever it was, they caused Sammy's death."

Her eyes grew wider. "I did not know. That is horrible."

"I need you to tell me about your interaction with Sammy—especially since the photo of you on his phone was taken the day before he died."

Now her arms were wrapped tightly around her torso, as if she were suddenly cold. "Perhaps I need attorney?"

"You have a right to an attorney, but that doesn't mean you need one. Were you involved in the death of Sammy

Beech?"

He saw a sudden fire in her eyes. "Certainly not."

"Do you have any knowledge about it at all?"

She said something quickly in Russian, then caught herself and switched to English. "I know nothing of this! You insult me with these declarations!"

He sensed that he was on the verge of losing her. That she would stop talking and ask him to leave. At the same time, he believed her. Her outburst was genuine. It appeared she had known that Sammy had died, but she hadn't learned about the circumstances. But still, she was one of the last people to see Sammy alive. She might know something useful. He needed to know all about her dealings with Sammy. He remained silent for a few moments to allow her to regain her composure.

Then he said, "I apologize. I didn't mean to insult you."

He waited again, and eventually she nodded her acceptance.

"However," he said, proceeding slowly and carefully, "I still need to ask you some questions. You might be able to help me—and I need all the help I can get. So does Sammy Beech's family. They deserve to know the truth about what really happened that night."

He gave her a chance to speak, but she wasn't ready yet. So he continued. "I don't know why Sammy had that photo of you on his phone, or what your relationship with him was, but I'm going to go out on a limb here and try to fill in some blanks myself. I'll take a guess that your main job as a sports consultant is to steer a player like Sammy toward a particular school. I imagine a woman like you could be awfully persuasive."

She didn't raise any objections or deny what he was suggesting. She didn't say a word.

Milstead flinched at the gunshot, but he remained seated, with his hands in the air.

"Christ, Grady!"

"Be a man, Kurt. I won't shoot you—as long as you tell the truth. It's so simple. Just tell the truth."

There was a firm rap on the door.

"Go away!" Grady shouted.

"What's going on in there?" It was Cliff.

Grady said loudly, "Everything will be fine unless you try to come into this office. You understand? You try to open that door and Kurt's in big trouble."

"Kurt?" Cliff said.

Grady nodded at Kurt, who said, "I'm okay, Cliff."

"Now go away," Grady said.

No response. Fine. Grady knew Cliff would call the police, or maybe he already had. Nothing he could do about that.

Grady returned his attention to Milstead.

"Let's hear it. The truth. Everything."

Milstead didn't look like the confident, charismatic football coach that viewers often saw on TV interviews. His lip was quivering. He looked like a small child who had just been scolded by a stranger in public. Afraid and ashamed, but trying to hold it in.

Marlin said, "If I'm right, I don't really care. Let me rephrase that, and please don't get angry. If I'm right—and you weren't having sex with underage players..."

Her eyes flashed again. "Never. Of any age."

He didn't ask why the photo on Sammy's phone showed her in her bra only. Maybe that was the deal—she let them get a good look, but no contact. He wouldn't be surprised if an offer like that was effective. Besides, Sammy had reached the age of consent at the time, and she wasn't that much older. There was nothing illegal about the photo.

"Okay," he said. "Then all I care about is finding out who was chasing Sammy. Maybe it had nothing to do with football. But if it did, there might be something you know that will help. Regardless, whatever you tell me, as long as you weren't involved in Sammy's death yourself—and I believe that you weren't—I can virtually guarantee that you won't get into any trouble yourself."

Technically, he hadn't said she would receive immunity if she had taken part in any crimes, but it was highly likely, especially if she hired a decent attorney. If she had helpful information in this case, any NCAA recruiting violations would be almost meaningless in comparison.

Aleksandra Babikova didn't move or speak for half a minute. It was obvious she was deciding what to do. She didn't have a lot to gain, and depending on what she said, she might have quite a bit to lose. Finally, she let out a deep breath and said, "I had meeting with Sammy Beech. He was nice young man." She bit her bottom lip. Marlin waited. "I stimulated him to play football at OTU."

Despite the circumstances, Marlin almost laughed. He assumed she meant *encouraged* or *motivated*, but she'd gotten her synonyms mixed up. He kept a straight face and forced himself to remain quiet. Let her keep talking.

"No more stalling," Grady Beech said. He raised the gun again. Milstead had no alternatives. None. "Talk, Kurt.

Now."

"You'll kill me," the coach said. He was sniveling—snot running from his nose.

"I won't," Grady said. "I give you my word. As long as you tell the truth. I need to hear it from you. Tell the truth and you get to walk out of this room."

"You promise?"

Grady was starting to lose his temper, but he reined it in. He kept control. "I promise."

Milstead began to shake his head. "I'm so sorry. I didn't mean for it to happen. How could I have known something like that would happen?"

What? Grady Beech was confused. You don't sleep with someone's wife and then ask, *How could I have known something like that would happen?* It just didn't make sense.

After another pause, Aleksandra Babikova said, "Sammy agreed that OTU was better program for him. He was enthusiastic. But he said his coach would be angry that he change his mind."

His coach. Kurt Milstead.

Marlin said, "Why would his coach be angry?"

And now there was the longest pause yet.

"Spit it out, Kurt," Grady Beech said. "How could you have known what would happen?"

Milstead wiped his nose with the back of his hand.

"How could I have known that Sammy would run into a pig?"

Aleksandra Babikova had to be wondering how wrapped up in this mess she wanted to be. Even if she wasn't prosecuted for anything herself, her own involvement in the case—every titillating detail about her career as a "sports consultant"—would be discussed and dissected in the tabloid press. It had to be a tough decision for her.

"Why would his coach be angry?" Marlin repeated.

And that was enough.

"Because he paid Sammy large money to select UMT."

CHAPTER 35

Grady shook his head, confused. What had he just heard? *How could I have known that Sammy would run into a pig?*

Oh, Lord. The son of a bitch. Milstead was the one. He'd been chasing Sammy that night. He was responsible for Sammy's death. He'd just admitted it.

The coach must've seen the puzzlement on Grady's face.

"You didn't know?" Milstead said.

Grady started to squeeze the trigger, feeling the resistance, knowing that just another half-pound of pressure might be enough. It was the greatest temptation he had ever experienced in his life. Vengeance for Sammy.

"I don't understand," Milstead said.

"I was talking about the fact that you've been sleeping with my wife, you enormous asshole."

Milstead blinked. "Oh."

Neither man spoke for several seconds. Grady hadn't heard sirens yet, but he guessed the deputies would drive silently so as not to alert him.

Grady said, "I want so badly to shoot you. I've never wanted something so much in my life."

Milstead was cringing. "Please, Grady, let me explain. Don't shoot me. Please."

"Start talking."

Milstead took full advantage of the opportunity to ward off death, even for a few minutes. "A booster paid me some money to steer Sammy toward UMT. I know it was wrong, but I gave some of that money to Sammy. That's why he verbally committed to them. It's the only time I've ever done anything like that, I swear. And I'll never do it again. Oh, my God, I screwed up. I'm so sorry."

He was sobbing now.

"How much money?" Grady asked.

"Twenty thousand."

"How much did you give Sammy?"

"Five thousand."

"You know what that means, Kurt? Not only did you corrupt my son and put his football career in jeopardy, you gave him the money to buy the motorcycle he was riding when he died."

Milstead didn't reply. What could he say?

Grady thought he might've heard a noise outside the closed door. Maybe it was Cliff, or maybe it was the cops. Or maybe he hadn't heard anything. The lock on the door was a deadbolt, which was better than a knob lock, but even a deadbolt wouldn't keep out a team of deputies if they decided to bust the door down. Grady knew he didn't have much time.

"Why did you chase him?" he asked.

Milstead was starting to show some relief in his eyes—like he was thinking he might get out of this alive, if he kept talking.

"I saw what Sammy had said on Facebook—that he was switching to OTU—so I sent him a message. Had him meet me at the school."

"The cops didn't find that message."

"I deleted it later."

"Did you know that Sammy was drunk? He'd been at a party."

"I know, but he seemed okay. I swear. If I'd known he was drunk, I wouldn't have let him drive."

"So what happened?"

"We argued. I told him that if he switched to Oklahoma Tech, I'd have to give the entire twenty thousand back to the booster, and I didn't have it anymore. I'd already spent it."

"On what?"

Milstead appeared sheepish. "My truck."

Grady resisted another strong urge to shoot. "What was the booster's name?"

Milstead hesitated. "Can't we keep him out of this?"

"His name!"

"Okay. Okay. It was Dexter Crabtree."

Grady blinked. *Dexter Crabtree?* "The football player?"

"Yeah."

This story was almost too crazy for words. "Okay, continue," Grady said.

"With what?"

"You said you argued with Sammy. Where was this?"

"Right outside, in the parking lot. I tried to be reasonable. I wanted him to switch back to UMT, but he wouldn't. He was just so...headstrong. Then he said if I kept pressuring him, he was going to tell everybody what I'd done. I don't blame him, Grady. I really don't. That was a pretty smart way to get me off his back. But it also would have ruined me. I'd never coach again. All because I'd made one little mistake."

"It wasn't a little mistake, you moron."

"No, you're right. I didn't mean it that way."

"What happened next?"

"He took off on his motorcycle," Milstead said.

"And you chased him."

Milstead nodded.

"And you decided it would be a good idea to fire a gun at him."

Milstead was afraid to answer. He stalled. Then he said, "Not *at* him, Grady. You have to believe me. I fired at the side of the road. I never meant for him to get hurt. I was just trying to scare him."

Grady didn't respond.

Milstead said, "He didn't scare easily, I'll tell you that. He was a tough kid."

"He wasn't a kid, he was a man. More of a man than you'll ever be."

Milstead nodded. "God help me, that's true. It really is."

"And when my son died—right in front of you—you drove off and left him there."

Milstead was cupping his face in his hands. "I couldn't do anything for him. He was already gone."

Grady pointed the gun away from Milstead. He had to, because he knew if he kept aiming at him, he couldn't resist the urge to shoot.

"You are a pathetic excuse for a human being," Grady said.

"I know I am, Grady. I know."

"Bobby?" Marlin said. He was in his truck, back on the highway, talking to Garza along the way. The cell phone connection wasn't great. He probably should have called before he'd left the outskirts of Dallas, but he wasn't comfortable talking and navigating the heavy traffic at the same time.

"John, good timing," Garza said. "Major development going on down here." The sheriff sounded rushed and distracted.

"What's up?"

"We're on our way to the high school. Apparently Grady Beech is holding Kurt Milstead at gunpoint, and I have no idea why."

"You will in a minute. Aleksandra Babikova is a hired gun of sorts. She gets paid to entice players like Sammy to pick a particular school."

"Entice how?"

"I didn't dig too deep on that—didn't want to scare her into silence—but I assume it was mostly a peep show, hence that photo on Sammy's phone. She said she didn't have sex with any of them."

"Do you buy it?"

"I do."

"Think she slipped them any money?"

"I didn't ask."

"What did she say about Sammy?"

"That she met with him on the day before he died, and he said Milstead gave him a lot of cash to commit to UMT."

A pause. Then Garza said, "Damn."

"I'm guessing a booster paid Milstead to influence Sammy, and Milstead used some of that cash to do it."

"Jesus. So when Sammy changed his mind, Milstead was pissed."

"Exactly. Which makes him a good candidate for being the person who was chasing Sammy that night."

"I have about thirty seconds. How would Grady have learned all this?"

"No idea. Maybe he found a note or something in Sammy's belongings. Does it matter at this point?"

"Probably not. I gotta go. I'll call you later. Good job."

Phil Colby was on his way to Marlin's house—a casual drop-in visit to make sure Nicole was okay—when he spotted the dog runners' truck in the parking lot at El Charro. He drove past, resisting the urge, but he couldn't help himself, and he turned around.

When he'd found his smashed mailbox and gate keypad earlier in the day, he'd known immediately who'd done it. No question in his mind at all. He hadn't reported it. What was the use? This was a man suspected of taking potshots at a state peace officer and assaulting a civilian, so a charge for destruction of property was meaningless.

Colby pulled around the side of the restaurant, backed into a parking spot, and waited. And the more he thought about, the more comfortable he became with what he was about to do—because afterward, John and Nicole Marlin would be the last people on Gilbert Weems's mind.

"Does Leigh Anne know about any of this?" Grady asked.

"No, nothing," Milstead replied. "None of it."

"She didn't know about the money you gave Sammy?"

"Absolutely not. I didn't tell a soul—not even my wife. Leigh Anne wouldn't cover something like that up. She *loved* Sammy."

Those words stabbed Grady in the heart. Leigh Anne did love Sammy. Grady knew that. But there had been a time when he'd wondered what kind of love it was. For several weeks, he had wondered if the two people he loved most were betraying him. Turns out it was only one.

Grady could think of dozens more questions related to the affair—*When did it start? How often did you meet? How could both of you do something like that?*—but in light of what Grady had just learned, Leigh Anne's cheating was all but irrelevant. Grady honestly didn't care about the answers to those questions.

Mostly, Grady was just tired. Emotionally drained. He

wanted to go somewhere far away, all by himself, and forget all of this. Start over. But that wasn't going to happen—at least not anytime soon.

Grady kept his eyes on Milstead, but he turned his head slightly toward the door behind him. "Who's out there?"

Tatum looked at Garza with an expression that said, *Do we answer?*

Garza wasn't sure whether they should. That would give up the element of surprise. On the other hand, it was usually advisable to make contact with a hostage taker as soon as possible. He'd learned that several years earlier, when a murder suspect had taken a Blanco County deputy hostage inside the sheriff's department. He'd also learned that it was sometimes best to trust your instincts.

"It's Bobby Garza," he called out.

"And who else?"

"Bill Tatum," Garza replied. He didn't mention that every available law-enforcement officer in the area had responded, which was standard during an active-shooter situation, especially on school grounds. Garza said, "What's going on in there?"

"Kurt Milstead is about to come through that door. Would you do me a favor and shoot him for me?" Before Garza could reply, Grady Beech said, "That's just a joke, but you can take it seriously if you want. He's a piece of garbage, but I'm going to let him go anyway. Then I'm gonna need about ten minutes to myself. You promise to give me that, Bobby?"

When someone says they are about to release a hostage, you say yes to just about anything. That would leave Beech alone in the office with no more hostages. When Garza and

Tatum had first arrived, the assistant coach had stated that he'd been keeping an eye on the office door the entire time. So there couldn't be anyone in there except Beech and Milstead.

"Sure thing, Grady," Garza said. "Go ahead and send him out. We'll sit tight."

"Back away from the door."

"No problem. Give us a minute."

"Look who it is," Dylan Bryant said after they'd exited the restaurant.

Dustin looked to his right and saw the rancher, Phil Colby. He was headed straight for them again, just as he had at the café the day before. Walking with purpose. Like he had a score to settle, which, of course, he did.

"Jeez, I might have to kick this guy's ass," Gilbert said.

The three of them stopped and waited. Colby kept coming, now less than ten yards away.

Gilbert put on his fake smile and said, "Fancy seeing you again. Did you get my letter in your mailbox?"

Colby was five yards away. Then three. Then he was front and center, and without saying a word, he drove his fist into the center of Gilbert's face. It was a massive right-hand blow, delivered with the full thrust of Colby's pivoting torso, and it produced the sickening thud of knuckles against flesh and cartilage.

Gilbert grunted in pain and fell backward onto his ass, with his long legs splayed out in front of him. Blood immediately began to gush from his nose. He cupped his face with both hands, saying something at the same time, but the words were unintelligible.

Colby leaned over him, his fist drawn back, as if

preparing to strike another blow. Gilbert flinched. Dustin was having a hard time keeping the smile off his face. This was downright awesome.

Now Colby pointed a finger at Gilbert. "Stay away from my place, you hear me? You come back and this will be the least of it. I promise you do not want to test me. I won't tell you again. And if you go near my friend or his wife, you might as well cash in your chips. You understand what I'm saying?"

Gilbert didn't respond. His wrists and forearms were slick with blood, and it was dripping onto his shirt and jeans.

"You understand?" Colby said, more firmly this time.

Gilbert gave a very small nod.

Colby straightened up and looked at Dustin. "Everything I just said applies to you and your brother, too."

Dustin held his hands up. *No problem.*

Garza and Tatum withdrew from the immediate vicinity around the doorway to the coach's office, as Grady Beech had demanded. Better to comply. If the door opened and the first thing Beech saw was a uniform, he might panic.

"Okay," Garza called out. "All clear."

No response. Nothing happened for ten seconds. Was Beech having second thoughts?

Then Garza heard the deadbolt lock slide out of the door frame. The door swung open slowly and Kurt Milstead emerged, looking haggard and terrified, but otherwise unharmed. Tatum quickly frisked him—standard procedure—then directed him down the hallway, and Milstead scurried away as quickly as possible. There was a pair of deputies stationed at each exit door—preventing anyone from entering the building—and one of them would take Milstead directly to the sheriff's office for an interview, assuming he didn't request any sort of medical attention.

The door to the coach's office had already closed again, and Garza heard the deadbolt lock sliding back into place.

"Ten minutes," Grady Beech called out.

Garza was willing to give him that, and quite a bit more. Once a hostage is released and out of danger, there's far less reason to put pressure on someone who is holed up alone.

All was quiet. Garza heard nothing from the coach's office. He looked at Tatum, who shrugged. Twelve minutes later, Grady Beech said, "I'm coming out!"

"Wait a second, Grady," Garza said. "I need to give you some very specific instructions—for your own safety."

Grady Beech followed them to the letter.

CHAPTER 36

Dusk was settling in. Most of the vehicles passing by on Highway 281 now had their headlights on. No sign of the dog runners yet. But a lifetime of waiting in deer blinds had honed Red's patience to a fine edge.

Earlier, Red had kept watch while Billy Don had gone into the Super S for supplies. Now they were both gnawing on jerky and enjoying a cold Keystone Light. It wasn't unlike their normal hunting routine, except this time they were seeking a different kind of prey.

"Soon as it gets all the way dark," Billy Don said, talking with his mouth full, which was one of his bad habits, "they're likely to head out huntin'."

That was both encouraging and discouraging. On the one hand, if the dog runners were holed up in a motel room somewhere, nightfall would get them up and moving again. On the other hand, there were so many different places they might go hunting, the odds were slim that—

And that's when Red realized they'd been overlooking the most obvious way to track the redhead down. Maybe not a foolproof method, but Red figured it had better odds for success than staking out the highway. Hell, they could stake out the highway *while trying* this other method.

"Goddamn it," Red said.

"What?"

"Know what we should've done from the start?"

"What?"

"Instead of looking in motels and restaurants and bars,

we shoulda gone straight to the landowners. Them boys gotta be day-leasing a place, right? And how do you think they went about it? They're not from around here, so they probably called some of the phone numbers on all them little flyers posted all over town."

Billy Don stopped chewing. "You know what, Red? That's real smart of you. I never woulda thought of that."

Red was a sucker for a compliment, even from a source as dubious as Billy Don. "Run back over there to the Super S and pull a bunch of them flyers off the bulletin board."

Billy Don did as he was asked, and a few minutes later he was back with a fistful of flyers. He picked one at random and dialed the number on his cell phone. Red listened as Billy Don said, "This here's Billy Don Craddock. You got a big redheaded sumbitch hunting over there? I'm looking to kick his ass."

"Jesus," Red said, shaking his head.

Apparently the landowner said no, because Billy Don hung up.

Red said, "Think maybe you oughta be a little more subtle?"

"Like how?"

"You announce straight out why you're looking for the guy, nobody's gonna want any trouble like that. So make something up. Say he's your cousin, but you lost his cell phone number. You need to get in touch with him."

"Oh, that's good. You're on a roll tonight."

Billy Don dialed another number. Said exactly what Red had told him to say. No luck. Then he dialed another, and another, and another. He was on the phone for nearly twenty minutes, and now the sun had set fully.

On the twenty-third phone call, Billy Don hit pay dirt.

Marlin was making good time on Highway 281, anxious to get back to Johnson City. Bobby Garza had called a few minutes earlier to say that Grady had released Kurt Milstead unharmed, and a few minutes later, Grady had emerged from Milstead's office and allowed himself to be taken into custody. That was the latest. They still didn't know how Grady had learned that Milstead had given Sammy a cash payoff.

Garza had offered to hold off on questioning Milstead or Grady Beech until Marlin got back to Johnson City—which was a nice courtesy—but Marlin had told him to go ahead. Maybe everything would be wrapped up soon.

Now Marlin called Nicole to make sure everything was quiet around the house, and then he updated her on all that had happened, both in Dallas and at the high school.

When he was done, she said, "Wow. Milstead is a first-rate scumbag."

"Appears that way. Now I'm thinking about the things Milstead told me when I first talked to him. He said I needed to look outside Blanco County, and he fed me all that stuff about street agents and hostesses—trying to throw me off the trail."

"But even if he gave Sammy money, that doesn't mean he was the one chasing him. He might've wanted to throw you off solely because of the money he gave Sammy. That would've been enough to end his career, right?"

"Absolutely, but I also think it makes him the leading suspect in Sammy's death."

"Oh, I agree, but it sounds like you're gonna need more. Maybe a confession."

She was right, of course. Milstead had motive, but that

didn't mean he was guilty. Marlin said, "A confession or more evidence."

"Maybe Grady can fill in the holes," she said.

"I hope so. Pretty good chance he knows something we don't."

"Well, all this excitement explains why I haven't heard back from Bobby or Bill."

"About what?"

"Armando Salazar's memory is coming back. He says he's ready to see a photo line-up."

"Oh, that's great." Marlin always tried not to let his personal feelings influence his on-the-job attitudes, but he couldn't help being thrilled that Gilbert Weems might yet face justice.

"And he'll be getting out of the hospital tomorrow," Nicole added.

"Excellent."

He had the cruise control set at seventy-five. Traffic was sparse—there was no other vehicle within a hundred yards of him—but a deer or a pig could dart from the darkness into his path at any time. In his big Dodge truck, that wouldn't be a problem, as long as he didn't swerve.

"You be careful," she said, as if she'd known what had just crossed his mind.

"Will do."

"You're going straight to the sheriff's office?"

"Maybe. Depends on what happens between now and then. I'll call you when I get closer to home."

"Please do. Hey, wait a minute. How was she?"

"Who?"

"This Babikova woman. How did she look in person?"

Giving him a hard time. Teasing.

"Hideous," he said. "Sunken eyes. Couple of missing teeth. Had a unibrow. I think some of those pictures on the

Internet were Photoshopped."

"Yeah, right. That's why she can bend young men to her will so easily. Because she's an old hag."

"In all honesty, if the two of you were standing side by side, nine out of ten men wouldn't even notice she was there."

"Liar."

"Never. But I have to ask—why are we, as a society, so hung up on looks anyway? Can't we get past that?"

She laughed. "I'll see you later tonight."

"Yeah, he's hunting here," the landowner said. "Him and two other guys—twin brothers. Near as I can tell, they've been getting here around nine or ten every night. Stupid, driving in after dark like that, 'cause them pigs are liable to come to the feed right after sundown."

Now Red and Billy Don knew exactly where to find the redhead. The dog runners had leased a place on McCall Creek Road, not far from Grady Beech's place, and even closer to the Kringelheimer Ranch, where Red and Billy Don had seen that small brown-and-white pig—possibly the bounty pig—two days earlier.

Red started the engine and pulled out of the Super S parking lot.

"Only problem I can see," he said, "is that we'll be dealing with some brain-damaged half-wits who'll also be heavily armed. You figured out how you're gonna go about it?"

"Go about what?"

"What do you think? Kicking this dude's ass without either of us getting shot."

"Not really."

"Well, you'd better start coming up with a plan."

It was a curious situation, and Bobby Garza wasn't sure where to begin. Coach Kurt Milstead was both the victim of a crime and the suspect in another crime. Should he interview Milstead about the crime committed against him, or interrogate him about the crime he allegedly committed? That's what he'd been contemplating earlier—until Milstead took the decision out of his hands by refusing to talk about any of it.

Immediately after Grady Beech had freed him, Milstead had ridden with one of the deputies to the sheriff's office. But there he balked. Decided he didn't want to answer questions of any kind. In a bit of arm-twisting, the deputy warned Milstead that the possession and discharge of a gun on school grounds was a serious crime, and that until they determined exactly what had happened in that office, well, they couldn't rule out the possibility that Milstead was the one who'd fired the weapon. They could probably even get an arrest warrant for him. It would be better if Milstead would go on the record and state what had happened. But he wouldn't budge. He called his wife and had her pick him up. Garza could only imagine the story Milstead had told her.

That left Grady Beech.

He'd been Mirandized, and he hadn't asked for an attorney, which was a good sign. Garza had offered to hold off on questioning until Marlin returned, because Marlin had worked hard on this case and dug up some valuable information from Aleksandra Babikova. But Marlin had declined. Told him to go ahead and get started.

Would Grady Beech be willing to talk? He hadn't said a word on the ride over from the high school—but he'd had an odd grin on his face. A satisfied smirk. Garza wondered what that was about. It almost certainly had something to do with those few minutes when Beech was alone in Milstead's office, but what had he been doing?

It was time to find out, because Bill Tatum had just finished with the booking process—fingerprinting, mug shots, an inventory of Beech's personal property. Beech stayed silent through it all. Now he was waiting in the interview room.

Garza was just rising from his chair when Ernie Turpin, one of the deputies, appeared in the office doorway holding a small radio. "Bobby, you've gotta hear this. Friend of mine just called and told me about it."

Turpin turned up the volume and Garza heard what sounded like a couple of DJs hosting a sports talk show.

"...you missed it earlier, there's an absolutely incredible story coming into the newsroom from central Texas tonight, and it's already getting some coverage on ESPN. You might remember a football player out of Johnson City named Sammy Beech, who died in a motorcycle wreck a few months ago."

"Incredible halfback. You ever see his highlight reel?"

"I did, and I have no doubt he would've shattered all kinds of NCAA records. The kid was a phenom, no doubt about it. And then he died, and it was of course a tragic loss. Then we heard the strange twist just a few days ago that someone had actually been chasing this poor kid and firing a gun at him, or at least firing a gun to scare him, right before he wrecked his motorcycle."

"It was like something out of a movie, wasn't it? I mean, this stuff just doesn't happen in real life."

"*Apparently it does, and more, because we're not done with this story yet. Today, this boy's father—Grady Beech—he allegedly barged into the office of the football coach down there—*"

"*Kurt Milstead. Used to coach up in Richardson. Won a state championship at one of the 3A high schools up there.*"

"*Right. Anyway, the father barged in—*"

"*Allegedly.*"

"*—allegedly, right, he barged in with a gun and kept this coach, Milstead, hostage for a short period of time.*"

"*Incredible.*"

"*Why would he do that? Why? It all sounds fairly mysterious, until you hear the recording I'm going to play for you. Turns out the father recorded his little chat with this coach—*"

"*This is nuts.*"

"*See, he used his cell phone to record an audio clip—the entire conversation, and then, before he was arrested, he emailed that clip to various media outlets around the state.*"

"*And we've got that clip.*"

"*Of course we do. You might be able to guess why the father would go after the coach like that—but you'll never guess who else is implicated in this story.*"

"*Can we give them a hint?*"

"*Okay, just one hint.*"

"*The other person allegedly involved in this story won a very prestigious award.*"

"*That'll do it. I bet the listeners are going crazy by now, so we're going to play that recording—right after the break. I guarantee you won't want to miss this.*"

"*This story has everything—infidelity, violence, money...*"

"*Don't give it all away!*"

"*Sorry. My bad.*"

"*I will say this: It's going to shake up college football recruiting as we know it.*"

"*You are correct, sir.*"

"That is not hyperbole."

"No, sir."

"Back in three. Stay with us."

CHAPTER 37

"I'm gonna get that fucking asshole, mark my words," Gilbert Weems said from the darkness of the back seat, and this time Dustin could smile without being seen. Gilbert sounded funny, because his nostrils were packed with toilet paper. It was the only way they could make the bleeding stop. Gilbert had refused to see a doctor. Dustin was pretty sure Gilbert's nose was broken.

"I will break that son of a bitch in half."

He was already slurring, because he'd opened a bottle of whiskey thirty minutes earlier. They were sitting in Dustin's truck, parked amongst some cedar trees on the small ranch they'd leased right after coming to town. They had a perfect view of the deer feeder eighty yards away. They'd also thrown out a bunch of range cubes to bring the pigs in. There was plenty of moonlight tonight—almost like daylight, really—so if anything showed, they'd see it from the truck.

"The only question at this point," Gilbert said, "is how bad I'm gonna fuck him up."

"Man, Gilbert, it seems like it's time to let all this shit go," Dylan said.

"Oh, hell no! No damn way."

Dustin said, "Truth is, we're ready to head home. We decided to cut out in the morning."

There. He'd said it. Told Gilbert how it was going to be. Not asked or suggested. Told.

"You did, did you?" Gilbert said.

"Yep. Too much trouble around here, and besides, we figure that pig high-tailed it. Probably in another county by now."

"Well, shit, that's fine with me. Y'all go on. I don't care. I'll stay here and take care of business. No way I'm letting that son of a bitch off easy."

"How will you get home?"

"Who the hell cares, Dustin? I'll steal a fucking car. Ride a bus. Hitchhike. But I ain't leaving yet."

Dustin opened his mouth, but before he could reply, Dylan said, "Check it out."

A small pig had just appeared under the feeder. Dustin raised his binoculars. Looked like a brown-and-white one.

Gilbert raised his rifle.

"Dad!"

Ryan Crabtree hurried into his father's office, breathing hard, but Dexter was nowhere to be seen. Ryan needed to tell him what he'd just heard on the radio. Major shit going down. This was horrible.

"Dad!"

Ryan hustled past the desk and peeked into the adjoining bathroom. Empty.

"Dad?"

Ryan had been using the computer in the adjoining room, and his dad wouldn't have been able to leave the house without Ryan knowing. This was weird. But his dad had been acting downright bizarre lately. He'd gone from obnoxious and impatient to absentminded and maybe even delusional.

It was the Adderall. Ryan had seen the empty bottles in the trash plenty of times, so he knew what was what.

"Dad!"

The curtain behind the desk moved, then settled back into place. A breeze. He parted the curtain and saw that the window was open. Moonlight gave the front yard a warm glow.

His dad was sitting in the middle of the immaculately groomed lawn, with his legs crossed, like he was doing yoga, or perhaps meditating. He was nude.

Grady Beech remained seated when Bobby Garza entered the interview room.

"Sorry for the delay," Garza said, pulling out a chair. "I was busy listening to that recording you sent to all the TV and radio stations."

There it was again. That satisfied smirk on Beech's face. Garza couldn't blame him. He had nailed Kurt Milstead in the most humiliating way possible. And Leigh Anne, too.

"That's what you were doing in there?" Garza asked. "After you let Milstead go?"

"Had to give the email time to go out. Big file. Did they play the whole thing?"

"They did. Several times. I have to admit, Grady—I never heard anything like it. You went there to confront Milstead about his affair with Leigh Anne, but wow—you got so much more. Obviously, you hadn't suspected that he was the one who'd chased Sammy."

"That took me by surprise."

"And Dexter Crabtree? I hadn't heard that name in years."

"Me, neither."

"It was pretty remarkable. But I have some bad news. If you were hoping we could use that recording to nail

Milstead, well, there's almost no chance we'll be able to use it in court."

Now Beech looked a little more somber. "Why the hell not?"

"You were holding him at gunpoint. His confession was coerced."

"Yeah, but he blurted that out on his own."

Garza noticed that Beech did not object to the contention that he'd been holding Milstead at gunpoint. He probably figured it was futile. The assistant coach's testimony alone would probably be enough—plus the other evidence Garza and his team would be able to collect—even if Beech didn't confess.

"Doesn't matter," Garza said. "Any decent defense attorney will be able to get that tossed. I am sorry about that. Truly."

"So Milstead is going to get away with it?"

"Not necessarily." Earlier, Garza had debated whether he should tell Grady about Aleksandra Babikova, and he hadn't been able to think of any reason why he shouldn't—although he intended to keep her name out of it for now. "We have another witness," Garza said.

Grady perked up. "Really? Who? What sort of witness?"

"Someone who says Sammy made a statement about Milstead paying him cash to play ball at UMT."

"Who?" Grady repeated. "Another player?"

Garza shook his head. "Let's see how it pans out. For now, I need you to walk me through the incident at the school this evening. Obviously, you somehow learned that Leigh Anne and Milstead were seeing each other, and when you found out, you decided to confront him. So tell me how that got started."

That was another strange thing about this situation. Garza was sworn to uphold the law, but he didn't really want Grady to be punished too severely for what he'd done. The man had reacted emotionally and violently to a painful situation, and he needed to be held accountable—especially since he'd been stupid enough to carry a gun onto school grounds. That alone was a third-degree felony, to say nothing of holding Milstead at gunpoint. On the other hand, Grady Beech had been through a lot with the death of his son, and Garza knew that he was a decent man at heart.

Grady hadn't answered yet.

Garza said, "When you went over to Milstead's office with that gun, what was your plan? Why were you there?"

Unfortunately, any punishment Grady might receive would be out of Garza's hands. If he confessed, he might be looking at a prison term. On the other hand, if he played his cards right, he might be able to plead it down to probation.

"I don't think I'll answer that one, Bobby. No disrespect."

"You saying you didn't take a gun over there?"

"Not saying anything one way or the other."

"The gun we found in Milstead's office is registered to you, Grady. We'll match it to the slug in the wall. Your prints will be on it. Plus, Deputy Tatum is about to come in here and swab your hands for gunshot residue."

"Don't you need a warrant for that?"

"We do, and we have one."

"Well, it's not a problem anyway. I did some shooting at my place earlier today."

"Target shooting? Skeet?"

Grady was smart enough to mull that question over. If he'd shot at targets or skeet, then he'd have to explain why a search team couldn't find any used targets in the trash, or any shattered skeet in the fields.

"No, I shot at a couple of doves. Didn't hit any. It is dove season, you know."

"What time was this? Was anyone with you?"

Grady grinned. "You know, at this point, I think it would be best if I talked to my attorney."

Smart move, Grady, Garza thought.

"I've thought about it," Billy Don said.

"Good."

"But I don't got it all worked out just yet."

"Bad."

Earlier, Billy Don had opened the gate on the Kringelheimer Ranch and Red had backed the truck onto the property, thirty yards off the county road, hunkered in the trees. They'd have a perfect view of passing vehicles, without being seen themselves. Only two cars had passed by so far—one in either direction. The ranch where the dog runners were hunting was to the right, so they'd come from the left, on their way to the ranch.

"Here's what I've come up with," Billy Don said. "Ain't no way we can sneak up on 'em while they're hunting."

"Agreed."

"So we'll have to wait 'til they leave, which is a pain in the ass, 'cause we might have to sit here half the night, but there ain't no way around it."

"Makes sense."

Red could see the headlights of another vehicle, but it was coming from the right. Wrong direction.

"And when they finally do leave," Billy Don said, "we'll follow and see where they go."

"Okay. Then what?"

The vehicle was about to pass the Kringelheimer gate.

"See, that's what I don't have figured out yet. Might have to play it by ear. If they go—"

"Holy crap!"

"What?"

"That was them!"

CHAPTER 38

"Have you seen the internal locomotive machinery of a butterfly?" Dexter Crabtree asked.

They were in Ryan's car, on the way to the emergency room. Ryan had hastily dressed his dad, but he'd neglected shoes.

"It has crystalline properties that boggle the mind," Dexter added.

"Dad, how much did you take?"

"Chia pets are currently on back order."

"How much Adderall?"

"Adderall?"

"Yes, dad, how much Adderall?"

"I like to put Adderall up my butt."

Red gave Weems and his buddies a thirty-second head start, then he pulled onto McCall Creek Road and followed. The dog runners' big diesel had been moving along at a good pace, so Red pushed his truck pretty hard around the curves of the county road.

"Gotta pick it up," Billy Don said.

Red's tires were already squealing.

"If they reach 281…" Billy Don said, and he didn't need to finish the rest. If they reached 281 before Red caught up, he and Billy Don would have no way of knowing which direction they'd gone.

But that's what happened. Red reached the highway, and they still hadn't seen the diesel.

"Crap," Billy Don said.

"I say we go north. They're staying in Johnson City, so they'd go north. Agreed?"

"Agreed. Let's get moving."

Red punched it, and this time, his truck responded. He'd slapped some new spark plugs in this morning, and that had done the trick. Soon he was cruising at ninety with no problem. They barreled past the 281/290 intersection. No sign of the dog runners. They passed County Road 209. Still nothing, and Johnson City was coming up fast. They passed Odiorne Road, and Red finally saw taillights.

"Gotta be them," Billy Don said.

Red kept his speed up to 70, even though they were on the edge of town now, and the speed limit dropped to 50, then 45. The vehicle ahead was moving at least 60. Why were they in such a hurry?

Billy Don leaned forward. "Yep. That's them."

Red eased off the gas a bit now, about sixty yards behind the target vehicle. They passed the Super S, and then, sure enough, the dog runners slowed and pulled into the same convenience store where Weems had assaulted Armando.

"Go on past," Billy Don said.

"Huh?"

"Go on past. I have a plan."

Red did as instructed, passing A. Robinson Road, as Billy Don pivoted in his seat to keep an eye on the dog runners. "Pull over here," he said, indicating the parking lot of a gas station that had been shut down for quite some time.

Billy Don had the door open before Red even came to a stop. "You just watch from here. When you think the time is right, you drive over and get me."

Before Red could ask any questions, Billy Don had

sprung from the vehicle with surprising agility.

Despite everything that had happened—despite the fact that Gilbert had finally made it crystal-clear that he was a psychopath who deserved to be locked up—Dustin Bryant agreed that a celebration was in order. A big celebration. Maybe the biggest of their lives.

He whipped into the convenience store and parked on the north side—in the same spot where they'd parked two nights earlier.

Gilbert was in the passenger seat now, hooting and hollering, singing along with the radio, apparently no longer concerned about the man named Phil Colby. His anger had evaporated. Now he was a happy drunk. More whiskey was in order, but, once again, he needed something to mix it with.

Gilbert stepped out of the truck, turned around to say, "Y'all want anything?" and then Dustin heard somebody say, "Hey, buddy, turn around for a second."

Red had his truck in gear, and he eased over to the edge of the parking lot. The dog runners' truck was just across A. Robinson Road, no more than thirty yards away.

Billy Don had already crossed the road and Red watched as he approached the truck with no stealth at all—just lumbering forward at full speed. The big redheaded dude stepped from the truck, and now Red could see that he had some kind of bandage across his nose. Had he broken it? Regardless, at this point, he was still unaware that Billy Don was bearing down on him.

Red was grinning. This was going to be great—assuming nobody got shot.

The redhead turned to say something to the other guys inside the truck, and now Billy Don was just a few yards away. He must've said something, because the redhead turned in his direction, and Billy Don caught him square in the bandaged nose with a big, looping right-hand punch.

Even from across the street, Red could hear the howls of pain.

Billy Don wanted to punch him again, but the guy was already on his knees, screaming, and judging by the bandage that had been on his nose, Billy Don had only added to some sort of damage that had already been done. Blood was streaming down the guy's wrists and arms as he cradled his face.

Billy Don turned to check the guys in the truck—one driving, one in the backseat—to make sure one of them wasn't about to shoot him in the back. But they weren't budging—just watching with wide eyes.

So Billy Don figured everything was even-steven. He hadn't beaten the guy to a pulp, but this was good enough, and he figured Armando would be pleased. Without another word, Billy Don turned to leave, because he heard the rumble of Red's truck coming this way.

And then—oh, my God—he noticed the brown-and-white carcass in the bed of the dog runners' truck.

It was one of those rare moments when Billy Don wasn't confused or puzzled or under the influence of too much Keystone Light. He knew exactly what he was looking at. He saw the pig and he just knew. And he didn't hesitate. He grabbed the small pig by the tail and hoisted it easily out of the bed, just as Red swung up behind the big diesel. Billy Don jumped inside, still holding the pig, and shouted, "Go, go, go!"

Dustin watched as Gilbert staggered to his feet and yelled at the red Ford as it peeled out of the parking lot.

"You see what he did?" Dylan asked from the back seat.

Dustin knew his brother well enough to know he wasn't referring to the hellacious punch the big guy had delivered to Gilbert's nose.

"The pig?" Dustin said.

"Yep."

Meanwhile, Gilbert was outraged, trying to get back into the truck, but he was still too drunk to accomplish that simple task.

"Yeah, I saw," Dustin said. "And I'm having a hard time caring anymore." It had also occurred to Dustin that Gilbert would probably try to claim all of the bounty money himself, even though they'd agreed to split it three ways.

"Me, too," Dylan said.

Gilbert finally managed to plant himself into the passenger seat and close the door. "Let's go, goddammit!"

"Nope," Dustin said.

"They stole the pig!"

Dustin opened his door and got out. Dylan did the same. Then Dustin closed his door and spoke through the open window to Gilbert. "We're done, Gilbert. I'm not chasing them."

"What the fuck?"

"Also, you do not have permission to take my truck."

It was a scheme Dustin had concocted just then, on the fly. His remark naturally caused Gilbert to check the ignition, where the keys still hung.

"You hear that, Dylan?" Dustin said.

"He doesn't have permission to take your truck."

"Right."

"Fuck both of you," Gilbert said as he struggled over into the driver's seat and cranked the ignition. He backed out of the parking slot, slapped it into drive, then smoked the tires out of the parking lot.

Dustin calmly pulled his cell phone from his pocket and dialed 911.

Red hadn't really thought about which way to run. He'd simply taken a hard, screaming right on Highway 281 because turning left would have taken them past the sheriff's office. So, by default, he went north, on wide open highway, and it wasn't long before he had it up to 90 again.

Billy Don was looking backwards through the rear window. "Don't see 'em yet."

"Is that what I think it is?" Red asked, referring to the pig in Billy Don's lap, and wondering if there was really any chance that God would allow them to have such good fortune. He could hardly control his breathing he was so excited. It was a small brown-and-white pig, just like Armando had described. Just like the one they'd seen from the deer blind two nights ago.

"Don't know yet," Billy Don said.

"Check its ears!" Red shouted.

"Just wait a sec," Billy Don said, still watching through the rear window.

And right then Red saw a light appear in the rearview mirror.

"They're coming," Billy Don said.

The vehicle was several hundred yards back—so far back that the headlights looked like one light—but it had to be the dog runners, because the vehicle was going faster than Red's Ford. He mashed down on the gas pedal, but it was already floored.

"Can't outrun 'em," Red said.

"Shit."

Red rounded a curve and the headlights disappeared for a moment. Then he came to a straightaway and the headlights reappeared. It didn't look good—but Red had an idea.

"Billy Don, get ready to hang on."

"What? Why?"

"Just get ready to hang on, right after this curve."

"Don't do anything stupid."

There was an old trick that game wardens used. They'd run a line to a switch underneath the driver's seat, and when they'd flip that switch, it killed the power to the brake lights. That way they could sneak up on poachers without giving themselves away. Not long ago, Red had installed the same type of switch in his truck, so he could poach without giving himself away. He hadn't used the switch yet, but it was just about to get its first tryout.

Now the single light in the rearview mirror began to look like two lights. Not good. They were gaining.

Then Red rounded another curve and the lights disappeared again.

"Hang on!"

He flipped the switch under the seat, and then he stomped the brakes hard, and even harder, and harder still. The truck began to groan as it was forced to lose its momentum quickly.

And then Red saw what he was looking for: a small caliche driveway to the right, almost hidden by the thick cedar trees that covered the roadside. Red had snooped around in this area before. He knew the driveway led to a cabin set far off the highway. No gate blocking the way. No chain.

Red violently whipped the Ford to the right, careening into the driveway, and for a second or two, it felt like the truck was up on two wheels and it might tip over. But the moment finally passed, and Red goosed the gas hard, slinging gravel as he shot down the narrow driveway.

"Jesus H. Christ," Billy Don said. "You are a fucking lunatic."

Red reached out and killed the headlights, then hit the brakes, and the truck came to a stop, hidden in the cedar trees, with no lights revealing where they were.

"I thought we was dead men," Billy Don said.

Both men turned and looked behind them at the highway bathed in moonlight. Ten seconds passed. Then the dog runners' truck roared past.

CHAPTER 39

"Your father's heart rate, blood pressure, and body temperature are elevated. He has vomited twice, but the last time was well over an hour ago. Obviously, as you know, he isn't thinking clearly. A few minutes ago, he tried to convince me that he is the all-being master of time, space, and dimension. If memory serves, that's from an old Steve Martin routine. We're running some tests on his kidneys and his liver, and we'll have to see what those tell us, but I see no swelling in his lower extremities, no signs of fluid retention or abdominal pain, so we are cautiously optimistic. Based on my exam, it appears he has been abusing Adderall quite extensively, and for quite some time. Nevertheless, based on his condition at the moment, and assuming he is willing to address his addiction, I think there's a good chance he can make a complete recovery. Do you have any questions?"

"No."

"Is he currently taking any other prescription or over-the-counter medications?"

"No."

"Has he ever abused any other drugs?"

"No."

"Does he drink heavily?"

"No."

"Any history of heart disease?"

"No."

"Thyroid problems?"

"No."

"Hypertension?"

"No."

"Epilepsy or seizure disorder?"

"No."

"Any mental illness?"

"Yes. He's obsessed with college football."

Marlin was six miles south of Round Mountain, in northern Blanco County, when a vehicle shot past him at a speed he could only estimate at approximately one hundred miles per hour. He immediately hit the brakes, brought his own speed down, and made a U-turn. By the time he was turned around and northbound, the vehicle was no longer in sight.

Marlin grabbed the radio microphone. "Seventy-five-oh-eight to Blanco County."

"Go ahead, seventy-five-oh-eight," said Darrell Bridges, the dispatcher.

"Currently in pursuit of a vehicle traveling at a high rate of speed, northbound on 281. My current location—just passing Arrowhead Road. You might want to alert Burnet County."

"Ten-four. Do you have a description of the vehicle?"

"It appeared to be a blue truck, but I couldn't get the make or model."

"Seventy-five-oh-eight, be advised that we just received a 10-99 on a blue, dual-cab GMC truck that was last seen northbound on 281."

The radio code—10-99—meant the truck was stolen. But that wasn't the only part that caught Marlin's ear. A blue, dual-cab GMC? What were the odds?

"County, who called that complaint in?"

"The registered owner—last name of Bryant, first name of Dustin. Suspect is a Gilbert Weems."

Darrell had no way of knowing the significance of that information.

"County, do we know how many occupants are in the vehicle?"

Marlin wanted to know if Dylan Bryant was with Weems. It was doubtful, but he couldn't take anything for granted. Maybe there'd been a falling out between Dustin and Dylan, and Dylan had taken off with Weems.

"According to the complainant, it's occupied one time."

One person. Just Weems.

"County, please ask any available units to respond."

The moment of truth.

Billy Don grabbed a flashlight out of the glove box and turned it on. The small pig carcass was still resting in his lap, and warm blood—from the instantly fatal gunshot wound to the porker's neck—had seeped into the thighs of Billy Don's jeans. He didn't care. Wasn't the first time.

"Well, come on," Red said.

Billy Don tugged one of the pig's ears and illuminated the inside.

Nothing. No tattoo.

He turned the pig's head and illuminated the inside of the other ear.

"Yeeeeessss!" Red screamed, and he began pounding the steering wheel with excitement. "Hell, yeeeessss!"

The tattoo was there.

One mile short of Round Mountain, Gilbert Weems came to the conclusion that he'd been screwed. The pig thieves in the red Ford must've turned off somewhere. They had to be back behind him. Otherwise, he'd have caught up to them by now.

He stomped heavily on the brakes and then made a wide, looping U-turn.

Marlin saw headlights in the distance—at least half a mile away. But they were coming fast. Marlin's speed alone couldn't account for how quickly this vehicle was approaching.

Could it be Weems? Had he turned around?

Marlin played a hunch and took his foot off the gas. Then he switched off the red-and-blue lights mounted on the grill.

He began to apply the brake.

Now the oncoming vehicle was about a quarter-mile away, and there was no doubt that it was really moving. Marlin had to wonder why Weems would have turned around. And what caused the rift between Weems and the Bryant brothers? Why would Weems have stolen Dustin Bryant's truck? None of that mattered for the moment.

Marlin pulled to the shoulder and waited. The vehicle was eating up pavement quickly.

Two hundred yards.

One hundred yards.

Then it zipped past, and Marlin saw that it was a blue dual-cab truck. He cranked the wheel, made yet another U-turn, and gunned it, with the red-and-blues flashing again.

Weems recognized the green game warden truck—he'd seen plenty in his day—and he knew the warden would turn around and give chase. And he did.

Weems was flying at well over ninety—and the warden probably wouldn't be able to catch up—but staying on the highway was a no-win situation. It would take him right back to Johnson City, where deputies would be waiting.

That left one option.

"Seventy-five-oh-eight to County. Be advised that the blue GMC is now southbound on 281."

"Ten-four, seventy-five-oh-eight."

"Correction: he just turned westbound on County Road 307."

"Ten-four."

Marlin made the turn, but once again, the GMC had a big lead, and he didn't know if he'd be able to close the gap.

Red came back down to Earth and said, "Here's the deal. I don't blame you at all for grabbing the pig—I woulda done the same damn thing—but we need to settle down for a minute and think this through."

"What's there to think about?" Billy Don asked.

They were still parked in the driveway off 281.

"Well, I have no idea what the law says about a situation like this, but I'm betting those boys can say we stole the pig. Cops'd probably agree and give it right back to them."

"But they ain't got the pig and we do. Everybody knows repossession is nine-tenths of the law."

"I think that's an old wives' tale."

"So what are you saying?"

"I don't know yet. I guess I'm saying we shouldn't get too excited. Not until we see if they call the cops."

Every 10 or 15 seconds or so, Marlin would catch a glimpse of the GMC's taillights in the distance—and then they'd disappear around a curve. Marlin wasn't sure if he was losing any ground on the narrow county road, but he definitely wasn't gaining any. That's because Weems was driving like a man with a lot to lose. Marlin couldn't push his own truck any harder—not without losing control, and it wasn't worth it. If he couldn't catch Weems tonight, Weems would get caught eventually—tomorrow, the next day, or next week.

On the other hand, the chase wasn't over yet—and Marlin had one distinct advantage. He'd driven every back road in Blanco County, including this one, hundreds of times. He knew every inch of pavement, every cattle guard, every low-water crossing, every patched pothole.

And every unmarked ninety-degree left-hand turn.

Gilbert Weems couldn't help but grin. Every so often he'd sneak a peek in the rearview mirror, and he could see that the game warden couldn't keep up. What a wimp. Too chicken to push the limits. Didn't have the balls to—

Holy hell!

With no warning, the road took a sharp and sudden left, and Weems had no choice but to whip the wheel violently. And he knew immediately the truck couldn't hold the road.

The tires were squealing—screaming bloody murder as

the truck began to slide sideways—and then the tires went silent as they lost contact with the pavement.

Weems had a sickening feeling in his stomach as he realized the truck was beginning to roll.

Marlin saw it happen.

He was eighty yards back when Weems approached the hard curve much too fast, and then there was a wild jumble of lights twirling and tumbling. The GMC had left the road and was rolling several times.

Marlin applied the brakes and eased to a stop. Then he grabbed the microphone and told Darrell to send EMS as quickly as possible.

He jumped from his truck and jogged toward the dog runners' truck, which had come to a rest upside-down, its roof partially crumpled, all windows shattered.

As Marlin got within ten feet, he heard, "Son of a bitch!"

Weems was alive.

But Marlin could see an orange glow coming from the engine compartment. Flames. The wind carried the acrid scent of burning oil and rubber.

He bent to one knee beside the driver's door and peered inside with a flashlight. Weems was making a feeble effort to crawl out of the cab, but he was obviously disoriented—and possibly injured.

The fire was growing more intense, and now black smoke was swirling in the air. Time was short. Hell if Marlin was going to put himself at risk for long for this idiot.

He got down on all fours, then reached inside and grabbed Weems by the collar. He pulled, and out Weems came. The adrenaline was definitely flowing, because Weems felt no heavier than a fifty-pound bag of feed.

"Fuck. Ow. Let me go," Weems said, but he made no effort to stand. He obviously couldn't.

Marlin kept dragging him, across rocks and possibly cactus, and now flames were beginning to erupt from the engine compartment. The men were twenty yards from the truck, but that wasn't far enough.

Marlin dragged him some more.

"Goddammit! Asshole. Gonna kick your ass."

Finally, a good forty yards away, and with his arms beginning to ache, Marlin stopped. This would have to do. He quickly assessed Weems for injuries and saw nothing obvious—except for a bloody bandage across his nose. Looked like somebody had clocked him earlier. But Weems appeared to have survived the wreck unscathed. Lucky bastard.

Marlin glanced at the truck and saw that the fire had spread to the passenger compartment. It wouldn't be long before the entire vehicle was engulfed in flames.

Suddenly Marlin realized that Gilbert Weems was up on his feet. Swaying, but on his feet. Before Marlin could take a step backward, Weems threw a slow, lazy haymaker directed at the side of Marlin's head. Marlin ducked and Weems's fist swept the air above him.

Without even considering other options, Marlin responded by delivering a crisp overhand right to the bridge of Weems's injured nose.

Weems yelped in pain and dropped to his knees, cradling his face. He said something that sounded like, "Fuck! That hurts!"

Marlin pulled his handcuffs from the back of his belt, saying, "I can't tell you how much I'm going to enjoy this."

CHAPTER 40

Red woke at seven o'clock the next morning, still sitting in his recliner, and with a half-empty beer can still wedged in his crotch. Correction: It wasn't half empty, it was half full. Life was good. Damn good.

He and Billy Don had done some cautious celebrating last night. They'd sat on Red's porch, drinking beer and waiting for the deputies to show up. It would only be a matter of time, right? The redheaded hick from East Texas would report the theft of the pig, give the cops a description of the perpetrators, and the cops would know immediately who did it. And they'd investigate right away, before Red and Billy Don had a chance to hide the pig.

Except the hours passed, a case of beer slowly disappeared, and the cops never showed. Long about midnight, Billy Don said, "Think we're home free?"

Red said, "I hate to get our hopes up too much, but...it's starting to look that way. For sure I'd say if the cops don't come snooping around tomorrow, then it's a done deal. The pig is all ours."

"Ours?" Billy Don said. "I'm the one who grabbed it." Red swung his head around, surprised, and Billy Don said, "Joking. We'll split it right down the middle. I figure my getaway driver deserves half."

Not long after that, Billy Don had walked home—too drunk to drive, and not stupid enough to call Betty Jean at that hour—after they'd agreed they'd wait until five o'clock this afternoon to claim the bounty. "By then," Red had said, "we can be goddamn certain they ain't reportin' it."

Red could hardly allow himself to think it was coming true.

Twenty-five thousand dollars. He'd never had that much money to his name in his life. He'd be one-quarter of a hundred-thousandaire.

Then he thought: *What about taxes?* He figured the goddamn IRS would want a chunk for sure, because, well, when *didn't* they want a chunk? No way of dodging it, either, since the bounty had been so well publicized. He figured the winner would be, too. Probably some sort of write-up in the newspaper. Maybe some interviews on the Austin or San Antonio news.

Then he had a brainstorm. What if he and Billy Don could parlay this slim bit of upcoming fame into a larger career as some sort of pair of pig-hunting experts? Didn't really matter that they hadn't actually killed the pig, because who would know? Maybe they could get some sort of TV show. There was already one pig-hunting show on TV, and there was probably room for another. Viewers today loved watching shows about country people, like that one about that Louisiana family who made millions of dollars on duck calls.

It was exciting to think about it. Five o'clock couldn't come fast enough.

It was a beautiful morning: temperature in the mid-seventies, low humidity, a light southerly breeze, and not a cloud in the sky. Marlin rode in the passenger seat of Garza's cruiser with the windows down. Bill Tatum was in the back. All three men remained quiet, simply enjoying the silence.

Marlin had slept for less than three hours, but he'd found

upon waking that his lower back was tight. Not sore, but tight—from dragging Weems away from the burning truck. Weems had initially been charged with attempted assault of a peace officer, evading arrest, auto theft, and driving while intoxicated. Then, late last night, the Bryant brothers had surprised everyone by spilling their stories—about Weems shooting at Marlin, and then assaulting Armando Salazar— and now Weems was facing a veritable tidal wave of legal trouble. He was looking at multiple convictions on a range of charges, and if Salazar could identify Weems in a lineup, that would be the icing on the cake. Nicole said victims often gained some measure of closure by playing a direct role in sending the perpetrator to prison. It gave them a sense of control. Regardless, Marlin was thrilled that Weems wouldn't be walking the streets anytime soon.

Something else that had tickled Marlin to no end. Weems had told some wild tales once he arrived in cuffs at the station. First he said that Phil Colby had assaulted him in the parking lot of El Charro late yesterday afternoon. Said Colby punched him in the nose for no reason at all. Then Weems claimed he and the Bryant brothers had shot the bounty pig yesterday evening, and that two men—whose descriptions matched a couple of local rednecks named Red O'Brien and Billy Don Craddock—had assaulted Weems and stolen the pig from the bed of Bryant's GMC truck.

Funny thing is, the Bryant brothers denied that any of those events had taken place. Both of them said Weems was a pathological liar. Marlin sensed it was the Bryants who were lying in this case—probably simply because they had grown sick and tired of Weems. Good enough. Nobody would, or could, take Weems's word for any of it. Weems insisted that Marlin could find pig blood in the back of the GMC but, well, now it was nothing but a burned-up shell. If there had been any blood back there, it was long gone.

Garza took a right on a residential street, then another right, followed by a left, and now they could see Milstead's house, with the white truck parked out front—just as one of the reserve deputies had said it was when he'd driven past in his personal vehicle ten minutes earlier. Not surprising. Where was Milstead going to go? Probably too ashamed—or afraid—to show his face anywhere.

Deputy Ernie Turpin sat across the conference room table from Armando Salazar and Nicole Marlin. He had a manila folder in front of him.

Turpin said, "I'm going to show you a series of photographs, one after the other. If you see anyone you recognize, please tell me."

Salazar nodded.

Turpin opened the folder and removed a single photo of a redheaded man. Was it the suspect? Turpin himself didn't know, which prevented him from giving any unintentional nonverbal cues to Salazar. This was known as a sequential, double-blind lineup, which helped eliminate cases of mistaken identity.

Salazar studied the photo and shook his head. Turpin placed a second photo on the table.

"That's him," Salazar said immediately. "Without a doubt."

"Where do you recognize him from?"

"That's the man who assaulted me outside the convenience store."

When Kurt Milstead opened his front door, Bobby Garza said, "Coach, don't worry—we're not here to ask you any questions. You've already made it clear you don't want to talk. But we have a search warrant for your truck, and in about five minutes, a flatbed trailer is going to show up and haul it away. See, what nobody outside of my staff knows is that Sammy Beech used his phone to shoot video of the vehicle that chased him. It's not a great video—you can't make out the vehicle itself—but Sammy dropped his phone, and it captured the sound of the vehicle passing by. I'll be happy to show you that video if you're interested in seeing it. But here's the point. That audio—the sound of the vehicle passing by—is very useful to us. What we can do is make a similar recording of your vehicle passing by, then get an audio expert to compare the two clips. The software they have nowadays for audio pattern matching and signal analysis is incredible. It's just like matching two voice recordings to see if it's the same person. You see what I'm getting at?"

Garza finally paused. Milstead remained silent. His expression was a total blank, but Marlin noticed that the blood had drained from the coach's face.

Everything Garza had just told Milstead was a gamble. It was true that one audio recording of a passing vehicle might very well be matched to a second recording—if all the conditions were right. But the audio from Sammy's phone almost certainly wasn't good enough to allow any conclusive findings.

Now Garza said, "We also have a shell casing with a fingerprint on it that we can't identify. It came from a nine-millimeter handgun, and it turns out you qualified for your concealed-carry permit with a nine-millimeter. That's why we also have a search warrant for your home."

Milstead was visibly trembling, and Marlin almost felt

sorry for him.

Garza said, "Now, at this point, it wouldn't surprise me if we don't find that handgun in your house. But we don't need it, really. All we need is your fingerprints, and that will—"

"Stop," Milstead said.

Garza went quiet.

What the sheriff and Marlin and Tatum wanted—what they *needed*—was a confession. A good defense attorney could explain away a shell casing found on the side of a rural county road. Maybe it bounced out of the bed of the coach's truck. Maybe Milstead couldn't resist shooting at a speed-limit sign. There were all sorts of possibilities that could be offered up. And since the audio from Sammy's phone wasn't nearly as valuable as Garza made it out to be, and since Grady Beech's recording of Milstead's confession almost certainly wouldn't be admissible in court, that didn't leave much on which to build a case. Yes, Grady's recording had humiliated Milstead, and it would hound him for the rest of his life, but it wouldn't convict him.

Milstead was beginning to shake his head ever so slightly, but he didn't say anything. He needed one more nudge.

So Garza, in a soft voice, said, "Kurt, we understand you didn't intend for Sammy to get hurt. Everybody knows that. It was a tragedy. But you need to own up to what happened, or people will always wonder whether you have any remorse at all. Do the right thing. Your players are counting on you. Show them how a man handles adversity. It doesn't have to wreck your life forever. You can set things right."

A tear ran down Milstead's cheek. After a very long moment, he nodded. "I've been carrying this damn thing around inside me for two months. I can't do it anymore."

CHAPTER 41

Eight hours later, after a long nap, Marlin changed into civvies and took a drive out to the Double Eagle Vineyards. He found Grady Beech's Chevy Avalanche parked outside the visitors center, with a few vehicles parked near it. No BMW.

Marlin went inside and saw that Grady was conducting business as usual—pouring wine samples for two different couples. If friends or family members had stopped by to offer Grady their emotional support—he'd been through a lot in the past few days—they'd since departed.

Marlin gave Grady a wave and took a seat at a table. He had a few minutes to himself, and he realized it was enjoyable to simply sit quietly.

He thought about Kurt Milstead and the full confession he had given. Everything had happened exactly as he had told it to Grady. He'd lost his temper with Sammy and the chase had turned into a life-changing mistake. Milstead hadn't tried to rationalize or justify his own actions. He'd owned up, exactly as Bobby Garza had urged him to do.

Marlin thought about Aleksandra Babikova. Her testimony wouldn't be necessary, and at this point—assuming she'd seen the news about Milstead's confession and knew she wasn't needed as a witness—she'd probably refuse to tell anyone what she had told Marlin in her loft. Would she be hounded by NCAA investigators? Marlin didn't know and didn't care.

He thought about Gilbert Weems, and he wondered how

anyone could develop into such a sociopath. How do you change a man like that? And what about the Bryant brothers? What had made them decide to do the right thing?

His train of thought was broken as one couple left the visitors center, followed a few minutes later by the other couple.

Grady came to Marlin's table with two glasses and an opened bottle of wine. He sat down and let out a deep sigh. "Been a hell of a week."

Marlin laughed. "I'm glad you were able to post bond so quickly."

"I assume this is an unofficial visit?"

"It is. Just wanted to see how you're holding up."

"My lawyer would probably want me to ask you to leave. He'd say you're here to milk information out of me."

"You want me to leave?" Marlin wasn't going to share it, because it wasn't set in stone, but he'd heard from Garza that the county prosecutor was likely to offer a short probation term for Grady. A slap on the wrist, essentially, but Grady had to pay some penance for carrying a firearm onto school grounds. Grady would be wise to accept it and move on.

"Nah," Grady said. "I'll take my chances." He poured each glass half full with white wine from the bottle, then placed one glass in front of Marlin. "Another Viognier," he said. "You'll like it."

Marlin took a sip. "That's really good."

Grady drank from his own glass.

Marlin said, "I don't mean to pry, but I don't see Leigh Anne..."

Grady let out a sad laugh. "I haven't either. Doubt I will, and that's the way I want it."

Marlin left it at that.

Grady said, "Can I tell you something?"

"Sure."

"I need to get it off my chest. Everything else is out in the open now, so I need to share this with somebody, too."

Marlin waited. He hoped Grady wasn't about to say something stupid.

"I first started suspecting that Leigh Anne was having an affair about a year ago. She'd been acting distant, and, well, I just knew something was going on. Anyway, I came home one day—a Saturday—and she was out in the pool with Sammy. They were out there horsing around, splashing water at each other, and then they started to wrestle a little bit. It was innocent—they were just having fun—but that's not how I saw it at the time. I started to wonder if Leigh Anne was sleeping with my son. I realized pretty quickly that it was total nonsense, but what kind of father distrusts his son to that degree for even a minute?"

Marlin didn't know what to say.

"I feel so much guilt about that," Grady continued. "Especially now that I know the truth."

"Sammy was a good kid," Marlin said. "And you were a good father. He was lucky."

"I appreciate that, but I just don't know."

Marlin took another drink of his wine. Then he grabbed a paper napkin and pulled a pen from his pocket. He wrote Nicole's cell phone number down, then slid the napkin across the table to Grady, who looked at it and raised a questioning eyebrow.

"You should call her sometime," Marlin said. "Just to talk. She has a way of looking at things that can make you feel better about facing the world every morning."

Grady slipped the napkin into his shirt pocket. "I'll do it. That means a lot and—"

Grady was interrupted by the sound of somebody urgently honking a horn. The honking was from a distance, but it grew louder.

"Of course, you've all heard by now that Kurt Milstead, that football coach in Texas, has been charged with manslaughter in connection with the death of one of his players, Sammy Beech, two months ago."

"Tragic. That's the only word for it."

"And you've heard that Dexter Crabtree had some indirect involvement in the form of a very serious recruiting violation."

"He allegedly paid big bucks to Milstead to steer Beech toward UMT."

"There's also been a rumor that Crabtree was rushed to the emergency room yesterday evening as a result of some sort of drug overdose, although—"

"That is unconfirmed. The overdose part. We do know that he was in the hospital overnight."

"You can probably tell I'm laying the groundwork for the latest twist in this bizarre tale. Just minutes ago, an NCAA investigator, speaking on condition of anonymity, revealed that Crabtree is implicated in another recruiting violation—"

"Here we go."

"—and this one involves a player's parent. Allegedly, Crabtree approached the parent directly and offered cash for this player to commit to the University of Middle Texas, Crabtree's alma mater."

"And that, alone, is pretty stupid..."

"And the parent—oh, I love this—she immediately told investigators. Moments after he contacted her—in person—at her place of employment, she got in touch with the authorities. And what they did was have her play along, like she was eager to make a

deal, and Crabtree ended up sending her a box of cash by way of UPS."

"And that is monumentally stupid."

"We should repeat that all of this is alleged."

"Well, sure, alleged."

"We'll discuss this in detail after the break. Also, are today's basketball players too tall for the good of the sport?"

"Back in three. Stay with us."

Marlin and Grady Beech stepped outside the visitors pavilion and saw an old red Ford truck coming up the hill, the driver still honking the horn.

"Red O'Brien," Grady said.

Marlin knew what was about to happen, but he stayed quiet. As the truck got closer, he could see that Billy Don Craddock was in the passenger seat. O'Brien gave the horn one last blast as he entered the parking lot, then pulled at an angle into a parking spot. Both men immediately hopped out. It was obvious they were excited—or pretending to be.

"We got 'im!" O'Brien shouted. "We got the pig!"

"I'll be," said Grady quietly. He was smiling.

Billy Don Craddock was now standing beside the bed of the truck, and he hoisted a small pig carcass, as if to say, *Don't believe me? Here it is!*

Grady stepped forward and Marlin followed.

O'Brien, grinning, said, "I'll admit this is the first time I've ever been glad to see the game warden." He reached out to shake Marlin's hand. "This way everybody'll know it's on the up and up."

"Why would anyone think it's not on the up and up?" Marlin couldn't resist asking.

"Well, you know, I've been known to stretch a few game

laws on occasion."

Grady was standing beside the truck, looking at the pig carcass. He reached down and lifted the pig's right ear, to inspect the inside. "Yep. This is the pig. Congratulations, boys." Grady was plainly excited that his contest had reached a successful conclusion. Maybe Nicole had been right—that the contest had provided Grady with some sense of closure about Sammy's death.

O'Brien and Craddock both let out howls of celebration and gave each other a high five.

"Fifty grand, baby!" O'Brien shouted.

"I feel like we should have a news crew here," Grady said. "But I hadn't really planned that far ahead."

"We're happy to hang around for a press conference," O'Brien said. "If you want to set something up."

"That would be great," Grady said, and he pulled out his cell phone. "Let me make some calls." He moved a few yards away.

Marlin stepped closer and rested his forearms on the bed of the truck, looking down at the pig. He grabbed one leg and felt the stiffness. "Which one of y'all got him?" he asked Craddock.

It was almost comical the way the big redneck glanced quickly at O'Brien, revealing that they hadn't even discussed the answer to that question. Marlin waited.

"I got 'im," Craddock finally announced proudly. "'Bout an hour ago."

"Nice, clean shot," O'Brien added.

"Money sure will come in handy," Craddock said. "I'm getting married in a few months."

"And I'm his best man," O'Brien said.

Marlin could think of several questions worth asking.

You shot it an hour ago? Then why is it in rigor mortis? Why is the blood so coagulated? Sure you didn't steal it from the back of

Dustin Bryant's truck?

He had no doubt that he could separate them and pick their story apart. Make them reveal the truth. End up filing charges against them.

But he glanced over at Grady, who was apparently chatting with somebody at one of the Austin TV stations. Sounded like a camera crew would be on the way soon. Grady looked so genuinely happy.

Marlin couldn't do it.

He turned back to Craddock and O'Brien and said, "Congratulations to you both." Then, more quietly, he said, "Y'all might want to rehearse your answers before the reporters get here."

Craddock opened his mouth, but O'Brien elbowed him in the gut.

Marlin gave Grady a farewell wave and Grady waved back. Then Marlin climbed into his truck and cranked the engine.

ABOUT THE AUTHOR

Edgar Award-nominated author Ben Rehder's Blanco County comic mysteries have made best-of-the-year lists in *Publishers Weekly, Library Journal, Kirkus Reviews*, and *Field & Stream*.

For more information, visit
http:www.benrehder.com.

OTHER BOOKS BY BEN REHDER

Buck Fever

Bone Dry

Flat Crazy

Guilt Trip

Gun Shy

Holy Moly

The Chicken Hanger

The Driving Lesson

Gone The Next

Get Busy Dying

Stag Party

Made in the USA
Middletown, DE
17 November 2021